Keep It In The Dark

JUSTIN ARNOLD

For everyone who's been asked to stay in the dark, has been told they can't cry, has felt the need to hide, has been villainized for existing, or has been the only one like them in a crowded room.

And for those who helped bring me back when it drove me feral.

Keep It In The Dark

"When I looked around I saw and heard of none like me. Was I, then, a monster, a blot upon the earth from which all men fled and whom all men disowned?"

Mary Shelley, *Frankenstein*

CHAPTER ONE
ROWAN

Senior year starts with blood on my pillow. Then a scream.

Breathe in, I urge through pain. *Breathe out.* This is what I get for being careless while hanging the second fencing sword on the wall above my bed.

Daring a look at the cut, I hiss through clenched teeth. I cut my right index finger on the tip of the blade, deep. Blood stains my finger. I barely manage to hop off the bed before it drips onto the sheets.

"Are you dead?!" a voice calls from the doorway. I spin around to face Diego, my best friend. "Because if you're not, I'll kill you for scaring the crap out of me."

I show him my finger. "Cut myself."

"You got a Band-Aid in here?"

I nod to the cardboard box that sits on the brand-new futon I shoved where another student's bed would usually be. Diego wastes no time in digging through it.

"Are you supposed to have those swords in the dorms?" Diego asks. "They're weapons."

I shrug. "No, but I doubt the headmaster is going to write me up."

"Yeah, yeah, your dad's the headmaster; you're very special." Diego tosses the box of Band-Aids at me as hard as he can. It hits my stomach, and I double over as though he's truly wounded me. "Let's have five minutes before Golden Boy Rowan comes back to school."

"I have concerns." Reed, our third musketeer, swaggers in and hops atop the futon to perch on the backrest. He scrolls through his phone with an exaggerated shake of his head. "I'm looking at your guest list, and it's all over the place."

"How?" I fish a Band-Aid from the box. "I only invited the most elite seniors."

"Sophie Campbell isn't one of us," Reed says. "She's out-of-state and not going to add to the atmosphere."

"If we didn't invite a few randoms, it would just be half the dorm," I say.

Reed twitches his lips in thought. "Okay, that's fair. Also, why isn't Dakota on here?"

I set about applying the Band-Aid. "Uh, we haven't hung out in a while."

Diego and Reed gape at me.

"Dude," Diego says. "The hell did you *do*?"

"Nothing!" It's true: I did not do a thing. Besides, she's talking to the guy down the hall now. "Tell Quentin to bring her."

Reed types a text to whom I'm assuming is Quentin. Today is move-in day, and tonight is the night the three of us have been planning off and on since we were freshmen.

Tonight, we're throwing the party of the year right here in Club Rowan. Since Mr. Abadi, our house dad, keeps his apartment on the first floor, we won't be heard way up here on the fourth. We just have to keep the noise down. Even quiet, it's going to be wild, highly secretive, and only open to seniors who are the best of the best. We're going to do so much stupid stuff we'll never be able to run for office.

This is just the start. It's *my* year, and I've got it all planned out.

Homecoming king. Prom king. Captain of the fencing team. Quarterback. Oh, and model student, I guess. Then it's on to Cornell, where every man in my family has gone, then right back here to take over and be the headmaster so my dad can play golf to his heart's content.

No one's going to ruin this for me.

My phone buzzes in the pocket of my uniform chinos, and when I pull it out, I see a text from Dad.

Where are you?

"Uh-oh," I say. "It's half past seven. The usurper's almost here."

In the excitement of moving in and thinking about how to get the club vibe just right, I'd forgotten I have to use what little free time I've got to show around the new senior coming in. I don't get why—Mockingbird Preparatory gets new students every year, on all grade levels. Apparently, this one is important enough to warrant VIP treatment, which means he's probably richer than all of our families combined.

"You're not inviting him tonight, are you?" Reed asks.

"I might have to," I say.

"Don't do it." Reed shakes his head. "The whole family's sus. I spent all summer working at Dad's realty office. I met his mom and his aunt when they came in. Both hot, by the way. *Beautiful.* But weird. They didn't even want to see the house. They just bought it, insisting they knew what they were doing. Dad even had to get them investigated to make sure it wasn't some mafia thing. But everything came out legit."

That tracks. The boarded-up old manor house at the end of Main Street was empty for decades. One night, the lights turned on. No one's seen the whole family at once, but a series of electricians, cleaners, and carpenters have been going in and out at all hours— mostly at night. Rumors about it have been tossed around Mockingbird like footballs.

"Okay, it's suspicious." I nod. "Either way, I'm stuck with him for the afternoon. Now I'm *really* late. Thanks, Reed."

Diego perks up. "Can we watch while you polish his shoes with your tongue?"

I respond with my middle finger before pulling a royal blue blazer with the little red emblem featuring a mockingbird off its hook. "See you tonight."

They drift into a debate about music, and I rush down the stairs of my dorm. I check the time again. With the dorm being at the furthest back edge of campus, I've got quite a way to go. Dad will *not* be pleased.

I push my way out onto the tree-lined path that leads to the main campus and break into a full run. Across the athletic field, the main campus, with all its gothic buildings, looks like it ought to be somewhere in Europe, not upstate Vermont. Above it all, at the front gates, is the white-lit clock of Gorham Tower, the highest structure on campus.

That's my destination. When I finally reach it and zoom around to the front steps, I come face to face with the man who could be my double except for the three-piece suit, gray hair at his temples, and crow's feet.

"You're late," Dad says.

"Sorry." I show him my finger. "Had an accident."

He grabs my hand and inspects the cut. "You should've been more careful. I don't want you to get an infection."

"I'll be fine."

He opens his mouth to say something else but is cut off by the sound of an approaching car. "They're here," he says. "Look smart."

I do my best to stand exactly like Dad, pulling my shoulders back and clasping my left hand around my right wrist. A long black car pulls through the gate and lumbers along the horseshoe drive that winds around the statue of our mascot, Mocky, a monstrous, Sasquatch-like beast.

"Remember," Dad says, never taking his eyes off the car, "the Belamy family is *very* important."

"Got it."

The car parks yards from us. A gruff-looking man with a shock of white hair steps from the driver's seat, and for a moment, I think he'll never reach his full height. He could easily be a champion weightlifter or professional wrestler because he's *huge*. A black T-shirt pulls tight against his chest, with a light black jacket covering his probably terrifying biceps.

Also, he's the palest person I think I've ever seen.

He steps around the car and opens the back door. Another man steps out. He's tall, though not as tall as the first man, with wavy dark brown hair smoothed back in a style that reminds me of a hero from an old black-and-white movie. He wears a high-end black suit that would look at home on a red carpet. What's really impressive, though, is that he looks nowhere near old enough to have a son my age. This guy has to be early thirties maximum.

"That's Malcolm," Dad murmurs.

The man, Malcolm Belamy, smiles at my father with closed lips and reaches to the open car door. A delicate hand takes his, and a woman who I assume must be the mom steps out. She opens a small black umbrella and holds it over herself as the setting sun paints her white dress orange.

Camille, as Dad tells me, has thick dark hair that falls in curls down her back like you'd see on an antique porcelain doll. Reed was right: she's capital B *Beautiful* but odd. An umbrella? In dry weather?

And then . . . there he is.

"Casper Belamy."

"Casper," I whisper back to myself. All I can think of is a ghost, with his pale complexion offset by dark sunglasses protecting his eyes from the sunset. Like the others, his face is almost too perfect, with high cheekbones and lips so pink and full they'd pop if you put a needle to them. His hair is as black and glossy as licorice, thick with curls falling in perfect cascades, pushed back from his face.

He pulls back his broad shoulders that fit nicely under his black jacket, which pulls over a tight satin shirt and tucks into his tailored pants. He's tall as well, especially in the black boots he's wearing, accentuating the fact that his legs are long and his torso is short, and that's *not* fair.

Seriously, he's seventeen years old. So am I, and I have acne on my shoulders. The least he can do is have *one* flaw.

"Mr. Belamy." Dad extends his hand to the too-young father. "Welcome to Mockingbird Preparatory."

"Malcolm, if you please," he responds with a diplomatic tone that I've never heard my father attempt. "And this is . . .?"

"My son, Rowan." Dad pats me on the back before gripping my shoulder—the command button to turn on the charm.

I flash my best smile and offer a hand, but I can't stop staring at Casper, who has yet to look my way. When his dad takes my hand, the smile drops from my face. I fight the shiver that creeps up my spine. It has to be the unusually cool air because this man has the coldest skin I've ever felt.

Dad finishes welcoming Camille, so I shake her hand as well, and—okay, I was starting to worry they'd all be freezing, but her hand is warm. Actually, it feels *too* warm, like the world's worst fever rages through her.

I glance at Casper again, prepared to greet him. He pouts as he scans the administration building and the campus. I can't tell if he's upset or just thoroughly unenthused.

"Casper," Dad addresses him, and at first, he doesn't answer. Does he not realize my dad is talking to him? "Casper?"

Camille jabs his shoulder.

"Oh," he says, and that single syllable makes my knees shake. His voice is smooth, deep, and sure. I have to outdo him before he completely alpha-dogs me.

"I'm Mr. Young, headmaster of Mockingbird Preparatory Academy," Dad says. "I'm so glad you're completing your senior year with us."

Casper forces a half-smirk before looking away.

"Well," Dad says, his voice suddenly tight, "shall we step

inside?"

Casper's parents and the huge driver join Dad, making their way into the building and out of the sunlight, which is taking its sweet time hiding behind the horizon. But Casper seems unwilling to follow, opting instead to appraise his surroundings as though they're works of art he has no intention of buying. When his eyes fall on me—or I assume they do, considering his sunglasses— his perfectly bored face is disrupted by his nose wrinkling and his lips pursing.

Wow.

I clear my throat, puff out my chest, and make my way toward him so he has no choice but to speak to me. "Hello, Casper," I say, giving him the grin reserved for school pictures, Christmas cards, and students who need to watch their attitude. "I'm Rowan Young. Nice to meet you, man—"

He shuts me up by lowering his sunglasses and revealing the most ethereal, ungodly, and angry blue eyes. I feel so exposed and vulnerable and—

"Get that away," he snarls, rolling those blue eyes at my hand. He slides his sunglasses back up before pushing his way around me and disappearing inside, leaving me rejected.

CHAPTER TWO
CASPER

He. Smells. Delicious.

I can't get away from him fast enough, and there are several reasons why. First, his face. The arrogant smirk, the fraternity-brother gleam in his ivy-green eyes, and that well-rehearsed offer of a handshake, pretending like he wouldn't throw me to the wolves.

Second, he looks expensive, from his sand-colored hair, carefully maintained with every strand perfectly placed, to the remaining tan of whatever exotic location his parents whisked him away to this summer.

But the third and most important reason is that he. Smells. Delicious. Woodsy, with traces of vanilla and something so sweet and potent it makes my jaw lock up: the scent of pure, untasted blood, a flavor every vampire loves but seldom indulges in. He's a walking, smirking bottle of it. My tongue is watering, my lips twitching, and my fangs are begging to descend in my mouth for just one drop from the cut on his finger.

This is dangerous. Very dangerous.

"Come in." Mr. Young extends a welcoming arm over the threshold of his office. "We'll get Casper on track and allow him to get settled."

Oscar, my ever-stoic bodyguard, leads Malcolm and Camille to the door, but I hang back, flicking my eyes over the foyer for something to grab my attention before I drool at the memory of that boy's blood.

At least the school is antiquated, all polished oak and black-and-white tile, the walls lined with sconces that seem as though they could be the originals. Portraits of previous headmasters and important figures in the school's history line the walls, and a quick glance at the plaques reveals that most of them have the surname *Young*. A generational position, then.

"Casper?"

I stiffen as that forbidden sweet, cozy, woodsy smell slips into my nostrils. A weight shifts behind me. My fangs, hidden in my gums, descend as the urge to drink him returns, and subtly, I reach into my mouth and push them back up before I whirl around and his eyes snap to mine—but not fast enough for him to mask that he'd been eyeing me up and down.

He cocks his head toward the office, folding his arms.

Oscar, from his place next to the office door, coughs to get my attention. He would never dare to order me, but if I remember anything from my feral days, it's that I shouldn't test him unless I want to be tossed like a baseball. I meander to the office and almost gasp with relief as Rowan's scent fades behind me.

I'm so thirsty.

"Shall we?" Mr. Young asks as I enter a room that might as well be carved inside of a tree. Everything is oak: the desk, the chairs, the window trim, the shelves. Beneath my feet, a thick rug with a depiction of the school seal, a mockingbird alighted on a branch, peeks from beneath two large blue-and-silver Victorian-patterned sofas, upon one of which my "parents" have seated themselves, making sure to leave a gap for me. I sit between them as Oscar follows me in.

Mr. Young reaches for the door, but before he can close it, Rowan's expensive-looking face appears. Thankfully, his father whispers, "Wait out here," and shuts him out. Now *I'm* the one who gets to smirk.

Malcolm pulls my sunglasses off, dropping them in my lap. I squint. The sunset's last rays are shooting straight through the large, latticed window, and I fight the urge to hiss. They tell me my sensitivity to sunlight will fade with time, but right now, it's awful.

To help my eyes adjust, I focus on the wall ahead. A large oil painting, an old ship barely weathering a storm, hangs on the wall behind Mr. Young's desk. I tilt my head, trying to focus my eyes. The plaque on the bottom of the frame reads *Voyage of the Attercop— Artist Unknown.*

By the time I've memorized this, the muscles around my eyes have eased a bit, but I still have to squint as Mr. Young reaches across his desk for a file.

"Now then," he says, taking his seat on the opposite sofa. His eyes drift to the figure looming behind us, only just noticing that Oscar has joined us. "Oh. Hello."

"Evening." Oscar's voice is as emotive as a dial tone.

"This is Oscar." Camille gestures to him. "He's part of the family. We wanted to ensure Casper was settled safely."

Mr. Young raises an eyebrow, not understanding.

"He's my bodyguard," I offer. Malcolm and Camille stiffen, and I remember I wasn't supposed to explain that. No one's supposed to know we're *that* important.

Mr. Young nods. "Okay. I'll admit, I knew you were a very"— he tilts his head—"*special* student, but . . . Mr. Belamy, remind me, what is it you do?"

"Government," Malcolm says, and Camille half-snorts, which makes me want to laugh. *Monarchy* would've been the more accurate answer. "International relations, but we wanted Casper to complete his education stateside."

"You couldn't have chosen better than Mockingbird Preparatory Academy." Mr. Young grins, and I resist rolling my squinting eyes. When Camille showed me pictures of the school, a cluster of caste-like structures perched atop Mount Constant like a tiny medieval city, I was excited. I thought I'd be among brilliant, if mortal, peers. We would debate literature and the beauty of life and death while strolling through cobblestone alleys and dusty libraries. But that boy out in the hallway, if he's their best example, doesn't leave me much hope.

Mr. Young goes through my previous education, and I only half-nod while Camille confirms everything: how well I did at my last school, how my test scores are excellent. It's all fabricated. There is no Prince's American Academy in Belgium. I've never been out of the country, though that will change, hopefully sooner rather than later. Everything about Casper Belamy was invented in the three months since they found me feral in a New York subway tunnel.

I don't remember who I was before I was *this*.

Malcolm came up with Prince Academy because the Belamy clan is the royal vampiric family of the American East, which makes me, of course, the so-called prince.

That's the thing I really love about being a vampire: I choose who I get to be.

"I'm sure you'll have several questions as you continue to acclimate," Mr. Young says after speeding through my schedule. The only thing I really cared to know was that my dorm number is 410. I can't wait to get there and shut the world out. "You'll find everything in this folder, but for now, are there any questions?"

Camille doesn't waste a second. "How are students kept safe? What is security like? Cameras? Gates locked? Are the whereabouts of students known at all times?"

Mr. Young's expression tightens, no doubt because of the urgency in her voice. But he must be used to handling parents, because he paints on a smile and says, "Student safety is our top priority. That said, we take the phrase 'young adult' seriously, and we trust our students to keep on their best behavior."

"So he isn't surveilled every minute," Camille presses.

Mr. Young's expression darkens. "Not unless he breaks our

trust."

My shoulders relax. It was a trick. Camille wasn't concerned about how I'd be protected; she was ensuring I wouldn't be filmed feeding outside at night or caught brushing my fangs. Part of this whole scheme is for me to learn how to live undetected among mortals.

"Camille is a worrier," Malcolm says, trying to ease the tension. He claps me on the back. "But Casper has always been a model student, and I'm sure you'll agree once the semester has begun."

"Of course." Mr. Young nods. "I'm certain he'll make an impression. Well! I believe we have everything in order. If you like, Casper, I'll have Rowan show you the ropes."

My eyebrows knit together as I process what he said. Rowan. Will show *me* the ropes. As in I have to follow him around school? Alone?

"Christ." I pinch the space between my eyes.

"I'm sorry?" Mr. Young asks.

Camille grabs my shoulder and digs her fingers in so hard her nails pinch. "I think it's a lot for Casper," she says. "Might we have a private moment before he continues?"

"Oh." Mr. Young stands. "Of course. I was just about to step out."

When he does, leaving us with a soft thud and the echo of his son whispering a slew of questions outside, Camille turns to Oscar. "Shut the damned curtains."

"I'm so thirsty," I grumble.

Camille reaches into her purse and produces a silver flask. She thrusts it into my hand, and my fingers shake as I fumble to get the lid off. A second later, lukewarm blood is pouring down my throat. It's not sweet, flat from being in the flask too long. But it's all I have for now.

"The first rule of going undetected is not giving in to the irritability that comes with your thirst," Malcolm says.

I breathe in through my nostrils as the blood does its work. The veins in my temples relax, and my shoulders unclench. My hands stop trembling. The edge is gone, but it'll be back with a vengeance the minute I'm around that boy again.

"Don't leave me in this zoo for the overprivileged," I say.

"It's temporary," Malcolm says, pacing. "You are over your initial thirst, and you must hone it, along with your discretion. Every vampire across the East looks to us. It's up to you to show them you won't endanger us."

"Right," I say. "Let's rest the future of a vulnerable population on my eternally seventeen-year-old shoulders."

"Malcolm, perhaps he isn't ready," Camille muses, one arm draping around my shoulders while the other pulls me closer so my cheek rests against her collarbone. "He's still a newborn. What are we doing, throwing him to these cruel, pubescent wolves?"

"Very well," Malcolm says. "If Casper doesn't want to stay here, he doesn't have to."

My heart twitches with microscopic hope, but I sense a catch. Still, I ask, "Really?"

"Although you won't be allowed to go on the tour if you don't."

There it is. Malcolm and Camille's promise of sending me on a grand old-fashioned world tour—provided I don't murder anyone or expose our secret—has been dangled like a carrot in front of me since I could form a coherent sentence. The chance to get out of my attic room in Belamy Manor and see the world, to walk the same streets bohemians and revolutionaries once walked, where history was made and twisted. To see other vampires!

"That's unfair," is the best argument I have.

Camille runs her long fingernails over my cheek. "Your father has a point, and I agree with him. You have to complete the obstacle before the reward. But if you aren't ready, we will wait."

"But sooner or later," Malcolm adds, "you must do this. It's important to experience first-hand how our subjects get by. You might not always have the luxury of your casket, a bodyguard, and an endless supply of blood acquired for you. If you're going to mess up, it's better on this small playing field than in front of the entire world."

No choice; only do.

Camille and Malcolm must sense my resolve because they wrap me in a hug. I wince, unsure why I do whenever they show me affection. I make myself lean into it.

"You are our son now," Malcolm says. "We believe in you."

Though I'm not entirely sure how to think of them, they're all I remember knowing, and I'm about to be without them. Alone. The only one like me in the entire school.

I'm scared. And angry. And already tired of it.

My throat dries up, and my chest tightens. It would be a nice relief to cry a little in this moment. Even if it was only a break in my voice or a misting eye, it might make me feel a little less angry. But vampires don't have tears, so it all stays bottled in my heart.

The door swings open, and my nostrils flare with the smell of wood, vanilla, and horrible temptation. I pull from Malcolm and Camille's arms.

"Sorry," Rowan's irritating voice almost burns my ears off. "Didn't mean to interrupt."

The school year cannot end fast enough.

CHAPTER THREE
ROWAN

Casper hasn't blinked. It's like he's been in a trance, walking—no, *stalking* through the halls while I've shown him around. Luckily, no students have spotted us yet. All classrooms have been empty, and the dining hall was cleared out, everyone having drifted to either the common lounges or the dorms to settle in and catch up before the semester starts tomorrow. Now we're wrapping it up in the fine arts center, and he *still* hasn't blinked.

"What about painting?" I ask, flipping the art room light on and gesturing to the well-appointed easels and blank canvases awaiting the new year. "Ever do that?"

Casper half-shrugs. "Mmph."

I inhale sharply and bite the inside of my lips. I'd like to know exactly what his problem is. Does he not want to be here in general, or does he not want to be here with *me*?

Well, that's okay because I don't want to be here with him, either.

Quickening my steps, I head out of the building, not bothering to stop by the auditorium. The sooner we get this done, the sooner I can leave him to whoever his misfortunate roommate is and open

Club Rowan. Hopefully, I won't have to deal with him again.

A string of vibrations pulses in the inner pocket of my jacket. I pull out my phone to find a flood of texts from Diego, Reed, and a number of other classmates who want the lowdown on the mysterious new senior. I respond quickly to tell them they'd rather not meet him and drop the phone back into my pocket. When I look up, I startle. Casper has appeared right in front of me, blocking my path.

"Well!" I squeak. I could have sworn he was behind me only a second ago. "That's everything . . . Uh, shall we?"

I rush down the steps of the building and lead us into an alley. With the sun long gone, it's lit only by one security light, and the sound of Casper's lumbering steps behind me makes me want to bolt.

"We'll get you to your dorm," I say, as if to remind myself that he's *supposed* to be following me and this isn't a murder scene waiting to happen. "And then you can settle in—"

"What's in there?" Casper asks, and I stop, doing a double take. It's the first full sentence he's said to me since the tour started. His sharp gaze is transfixed on the building forming the right side of the alley.

It's the oldest structure on campus, and it shows. Where the gothic architecture of the other buildings has been painstakingly maintained over the years, this one has been left to rot. Slats between two-by-fours reveal slices of stained glass windows, while eroding gargoyles perch atop stone shelves, always following us students with their cruel eyes. But Casper is sizing up the oak double doors kept locked with rusting chains.

"That's the old chapel," I say. "It's off-limits."

Casper's eyes flick to me, and the back of my neck tenses under his unblinking stare. "But what's in there?"

I rub the prickling patch of skin that's growing around my throat. "Nothing," I say. "Storage, I guess. It's too old and tired to bother renovating."

Casper doesn't seem convinced, arching a straight black eyebrow and giving it all a last once-over before rejoining me. I zip from the alley as fast as I can without running, out to the lawn that separates the main campus from the athletic center and beyond that, the upper-class boys' dorm.

When we get across the lawn, I start up the narrow path that leads through a cluster of basswood trees to the dorms. It's another castle of a place, with a hundred latticed, yellow-lit windows and a red-and-blue school flag waving from the corner turret.

"Are you kidding?" Casper mutters. He's paused in front of the plaque at the stone column where a gate used to hang. I don't need to read it—I know too well what the dorm is officially named.

"Young House is named for my great-great-great-something uncle," I explain, "not *me*. This is where he and the family originally lived when the school was first built."

Casper insults me with another glare, so I spin on my heels and head up the front steps. "Let's find your roommate," I say as nicely as I can. What I really mean is *get the hell away from me*.

Entering the dorm is like a sigh of relief. It's warm, well-lit, and filled with my friends. Guys fall back onto the bean bag chairs strewn around the common room or shout over a foosball game. A few are gathered in a corner near the house library shelves, arguing over some philosophical idea, no doubt wrapping up a summer project.

I greet a handful of them with made-up handshakes and fist bumps. And maybe I make a point of being more overt about it than I usually would, but a big part of me wants to instill in Casper that he's in *my* house and his attitude won't get him far.

Everything changes when it's clear I have the new guy with me, and the fist bumps and the shouting die down to frenzied, curious whispers. Being new at Mock is like being new in any New England town—people are friendly, sure, but you earn the welcome. And at this school, you earn it with privilege.

That's probably not a good thing. Mom would have slapped the back of my head for saying it. But it's the truth, and I didn't make it that way.

Casper makes a point of not looking at anyone, opting to study the decor, just old group photos of nameless boys who lived here from the early 1900s up until the forties.

"Everyone, this is Casper," I say almost apologetically. I cock my head for him to follow before anyone gets the chance to approach him.

I lead him from the common areas to the stairs that wind up the four floors to the Senior rooms.

"I'm sure it's not as grand and magical as you're used to," I say, bounding up a few steps. "Where was the last school? Austria?"

"Belgium," he says, flatly and too fast, as though it's a preloaded phrase he's tired of saying.

"Yeah, that." I let the conversation die.

It's a long way up, and by the time we reach the fourth-floor landing, my breath is heavy. I wipe a bead of sweat from my forehead and ask, "Which room are you in?"

"Four-ten," he says, not out of breath at all.

My stomach lurches, and I shake my head, assuming I misheard him. "Sorry, what?"

"Four-ten," he says, his tone impatient. "It's what your dad said."

"Are you absolutely sure?" My voice is at a higher pitch than I thought I was capable of reaching.

"Yes," he says. "Can we please go?"

"There has to be a mistake," I say, studying his face for a hint that this is a poorly executed punchline. But his expression remains neutral, somewhat irritated. My eyes grow to twice their size. "That can't be right."

I push past him, bolting down the hall to Room 410. This is a huge error, a terrible, colossal misunderstanding. I push open the door for proof that I'm right. This isn't Casper's room. It can't be because—

My room, my *private* room, has been compromised. My bed has been pushed against the wall on the left-hand side. My futon, TV, and *Avengers* posters—which I hung so thoughtfully this morning—are piled around it.

Another bed, with a purple comforter, is pushed against the right-hand wall. Floating shelves have been drilled above the headboard. Crates and boxes are stacked around it, all marked with the red scrawl of a psychopath. They read *Casper's Stuff.*

"Those are my things," he says, and I jump. I didn't even hear him come up behind me. "As I said, I'm in 410."

I don't respond. My heart beats too loud in my chest, and I can't hear my own thoughts as I stumble into the room and try to process. Maybe *I'm* in the wrong room? Yes, that's it. I'm in Room 415, 412, *any other room.*

"This is all a mistake." I pull out my phone and text Dad with the speed of a cheetah. "You can't be in 410. *I* am in 410."

"You mean"—Casper's voice quivers, the only emotion I've heard from him—"we're sharing the room?"

"Absolutely not." My index finger slams against the SEND button, and I stare it down, waiting for the dots to appear. But the text remains unread.

"I thought I had my own room," Casper continues, staying at the threshold and folding his arms. "You mean I have to share a room?"

"I don't know what's going on." I kick my shoes off and crawl over the pile of my things to get onto the bed. All I wanted was to come back here and throw a rager. Now I have this creeper looming in the doorway, ruining my plans.

"Come in!" I half-shout. "You're making me nervous."

Casper rolls his eyes and crosses the threshold, his hand falling on the door handle.

"No, don't shut the door," I say, and I realize I've scooted up against the wall, the stone cold against my back. Casper glares at me. "Uh . . . I mean wait until I hear back from Dad."

My father still hasn't responded. Maybe he's already aware and is fixing it right now. He can't have put me with Casper. He knows how excited I was to have my own room this year. I've earned it. And I'm about to have, like, thirty people sneaking up here. With a groan, I lean back so I'm half-sitting on my pillow.

Bright, multicolored flashes of light fill the room. It takes me a second to figure out that someone's hidden little puck-sized DJ lights atop the wardrobe and around my trophies on the shelf above my bed. "What the—"

"Turn. Them. Off." Casper shields his eyes with one hand while fumbling in his pocket for those sunglasses with the other.

"Hey!"

Casper and I both jump at the loud voice. Diego leans against the doorframe, a remote for what I assume is the lights in one hand. He shoots me a lopsided grin. "You like my lighting design? I put them up when you left to get the new guy."

Reed pushes past Diego and looks around at my upturned stuff. "What's happened in here?"

"No idea. Diego, enough!" I say, and Diego stops pressing the strobe buttons on the remote.

"It wasn't like this when we left," Reed says.

"Who are *you*?" Casper demands. "You don't *all* live in here, do you?"

"That's Reed," I explain. "That's Diego."

Diego nods. "How's it hangin'?"

Casper doesn't respond, sliding his eyes to me again. I watch as the blues of his irises grow noticeably darker until they're almost navy.

"Hey, I'm talking to you." Diego swats his shoulder, but Casper doesn't break his stare, the navy dipping to a dusky black.

"Guys . . ." I say, unsure of what I'm seeing, "back off."

"Hey, dickhead." Reed leaps to his feet. "What are you staring at?"

Casper closes his eyes, and when they reopen . . . *his eyes are violet.*

When he speaks, his voice is unnaturally even. "You, at the moment."

"You found your room! Great!" a jovial voice chimes. Mr. Abadi peers at us from the doorway with a coy smile as he dips a teabag in and out of a steaming, oversized mug. "Now, boys, our new student has had a big afternoon. Shouldn't we let him get settled before we all campaign for his friendship?"

My phone buzzes, and I pull it out to check the message from Dad.

Sorry, son. It's the only available spot this semester.

Every cell in my body deflates. It's not a mistake. He knew Casper would be rooming here, and he didn't bother to tell me.

"Later, man," Diego huffs, and he nods to Reed. Before filing past Mr. Abadi, he adds a "See you around" to Casper, who glares back. The violet has disappeared from his eyes.

Mr. Abadi watches my friends go before flashing Casper a warm smile. "Hello, Casper. I'm Amir Abadi. I'm the live-in resident director here in Young House, which is a long way of saying house parent. I'm also Mockingbird Prep's librarian. I see you're already loaded up." He gestures to the floor, and for the first time, I notice the stacks of books tied with brown strings nestled against the boxes. "Be sure to come check us out when you get through those."

Casper gives him a smirk. (Okay, so he *can* smile.)

"You can call me Mr. Abadi," Mr. Abadi continues, "Or Mr. A during school hours. Here in the dorm, you can call me Mr. Amir. The Mr. is required. Basically, don't call me 'Hey, you'. Dig?"

Casper nods.

"Rules are simple. Study hours are for study, lights out is for the dark. Also, I know it's silly to expect a uniform bedtime for everyone—we've all got our own rhythm, and that's a-okay—but please, *please*"—he clasps his hand against the mug—"I *beg* of you, *don't* feel like you have to stay inside this pickle jar all night. I do not mind if you hang out in the common room so long as you're quiet. Just don't go wandering. Dig?"

"Dig," Casper responds.

"Oh, and one more thing." Mr. Abadi leans in conspiratorially. "No partying in the dorms." My heart drops as Mr. Abadi slices his gaze to me. How did he know? "Dig?"

I shrug, disappointedly glancing at one of Diego's lights on the wardrobe. "Dig."

"Okie-dokie, artichokie," Mr. Abadi says. "Labor Day's coming up, so I think I'm gonna go put up my holiday decor and leave you boys to it!"

And short of a smoke bomb to mark his exit, Mr. Abadi is gone.

"That is a strange man," Casper muses.

"Who told him?" I ask, mind on my foiled party. "I've been planning this for so long."

Casper sizes me up and then the room, as though suddenly aware that we're alone. He makes a beeline for the books and unties their strings. "Planning what?"

"It doesn't even matter." I crawl off the bed and set about gathering up Diego's lights. "Everyone's going to be pissed at me."

Casper must not realize I can hear him because he whispers, "They can join the club."

"What did you just say?"

He stiffens, somehow more than I've ever seen someone do before. For a second, he seems like a statue, then he slowly lifts a book to place on his shelf. "I said, 'Are you part of any clubs?'"

I give a threatening snort, but I'm already in danger of Abadi letting Dad know about my party plans, and for whatever reason, he trusted me with this prick. At least for one minute, I have to be nice.

"What are you reading at the moment?" I ask, watching him slide leather-bound volumes gilded with gold and silver onto the shelves.

"*Frankenstein*," Casper says, "*The Count of Monte Cristo, Crime and Punishment*"—he picks up a pink paperback and wedges it onto the shelf—"and *Red, White, and Royal Blue*."

"Maybe you can recommend something," I venture, mainly

because silence is more uncomfortable than small talk.

He tosses an old book at the foot of my bed, and I pick it up. "*A Tale of Two Cities?*"

"Obnoxious guy admits he's obnoxious and signs himself up for the guillotine. You might relate."

My grip on the book tightens, heat flushing my cheeks. "Was that necessary?"

He doesn't respond and continues to unpack his things, including a series of white wax candles, which we aren't allowed to have. He unfurls a yellowed map of the world, covered in red Xs, that he pins to the wall. He smirks hungrily at it, brushing his thumb over the Atlantic as if he's mapping the route from Vermont to Europe.

"By the way," I say, standing up from the bed, "I know they can be annoying, but those were my friends in here, and they're going to be around a lot. So—"

"This is my room as well." Casper narrows his eyes at me.

"Up until this moment, it was *mine*."

Casper takes a step toward me, and I notice for the first time that he's nearly a head taller than me. I swallow.

"It's not just *yours* anymore," he says.

I stomp my foot on the floor and drag an invisible line between us. "There. That's your space, and this is mine. And I'll have *my* friends on *my* side whenever *I* want."

His nostrils flare, exactly as they did when I tried to shake his hand. He pulls in deep, sharp breaths. His hands curl into shaking fists, and for a split second, I think he's going to punch me.

But with a gasp, he flees.

I stand alone in the room, finally rid of him, at least for now. But I'm too worked up to relax. I have to talk to Dad and make him fix this.

My body shakes, as though I'm trying to rid myself of his poisonous energy tainting my room, my entire senior year. Move-in day is ruined. My party is ruined. He has to go. My gut knows, though it's hard for me to verbalize just what, that something is seriously off about him.

CHAPTER FOUR
CASPER

I don't return to the room until I can safely assume Rowan is asleep. I've stayed crouched in a shower stall of the fourth-floor bathroom, holding the curtain shut with one hand and scrolling through an e-book of *Northanger Abbey* on my phone with the other. It's been nauseating. A handful of guys came in smelling of musk and sweet, nourishing blood and left smelling of soap and—unfortunately, still—sweet, nourishing blood.

This is part of the challenge: to keep myself fed without drinking from a classmate. But I'm trapped in a buffet of blood types. The longer I hide, the more nervous I become. The more nervous I get, the more blood I need.

Nothing could prepare me for the agonizingly wonderful burst of scent when I open the door to Room 410 as silently as I can and slip inside. The woods, vanilla, and that intangible aroma of untasted blood instantly makes me dizzy.

Living at Mockingbird Prep is bad enough without having to share a room with *him*—him who lies there innocently, filling me up with his dangerous smell and soft murmuring. When he's asleep, Rowan appears almost kind. Awake, he's smarmy and infuriating.

Unplugged, he reminds me of a puppy in a calendar, and that only infuriates me more.

I can't stay here with him while I'm thirsty. Find blood. Find a place to hide from sunrise. Don't get caught. I can do this.

I slip back into the corridor. The slow heartbeats of a hundred dreaming boys fills my ears, and my stomach tightens, my own immortally slow heart skipping a beat. A voice deep in my brain screams, *Just one drop!*

I make for the stairwell with silent steps before temptation can overtake me.

On the ground floor, I peek through open archways into silent, moonlit rooms. The abandoned foosball table and the bean bag chairs, still dented from the boys lounging on them, are drenched with the lingering smell of life, youth, and bad ideas.

Find blood. Now.

A rodent would do. But when I cock my ear for the sound of scratching and squeaking between the walls, all I hear are the sighs of my soon-to-be-classmates above. This isn't good. If I don't feed soon, I'll go feral and massacre the entire dorm, and then every vampire in the region will call for my head.

But there is nothing nearby. No birds alight on the windowsills; no squirrels climb the trees beyond the common room window. I rub my temples. All I can picture is Rowan, looking up at me with that cocky smirk, and me wiping it off his face by biting his neck so hard that practically nothing remains of it.

A silent scream of agony rips from every cell in my brain. *We're losing control,* I think as my hands shake violently and a string of drool oozes over my lips. My fangs descend, nearly stabbing my tongue.

This is it! My hands tremble as they rub over my mouth, my temples, up into my hair. *We're starving. We're going to lose it.*

I should call Malcolm. He'll come and help before I kill anyone. But then I'll have failed before I started. Either way, this is bad. But I. Need. *Blood.*

Soil and creek water and—fur. I sniff, my nose leading me to the window of the common room as I identify the distinctive smell of woodland animal blood. A stag, its antlers knocking against twigs as it emerges from the thicket of trees behind the dorm.

It grazes, unaware of the vampire licking his lips behind the windowpane. I bolt from the room, tearing open the door to Young House, and run out into the dark, whipping around the building.

The stag stops grazing, its ears perking. Barefoot in the wet grass, I tilt my head and focus in on it. My core tightens, and my jaw loosens, my fangs glinting in the moonlight.

With a growl, I speed full-force at it. Arms spread, I catch it right when it thinks to run. Its body crashes down on me, and we roll until I'm able to swing my leg over and straddle the great mass of its neck. Its body struggles to be free of me, bucking its hooves, but I won't be moved. My jaw practically unhinges as I throw my head back.

Ready, and—

A sickening robotic shriek fills my ears and snaps my attention to the dorm, my grip loosening for a second. The stag leaps up, sending me rolling over the grass as he charges for the trees. The shrieking plays on and on.

Wait. It's not a shriek. It's the alarm. I've run out here, and now the alarm is going off, and—dammit! Every light is coming on across the dorm, dark windows flashing to bright yellow.

My thirst and the fear of getting caught combine into the decision to run. Pushing to my feet, I rush after the stag, the dormitory fading behind me as I dart around tree trunks, leaping over exposed roots in the soft, muddy earth.

Shouts call out behind me, guys scared half to death from their sudden and rude awakening. I skid to a stop, the mud piling up before me from the sheer force of my speed. I inhale, but the smell of the stag is gone. It's escaped, leaving me alone with the trees and the sound of the alarm, a building of guys who will more than likely form a mob and stone me for waking them up. But I am *so* thirsty.

Another shift. The smell of oil and wind. A wing flaps around me as an owl escapes a shallow hole in a tree. But it isn't fast enough. I snatch it by its wing.

No, I don't enjoy feeding on living animals. It feels wrong and cruel. But not every vampire has the luxury of a *cask*, a willing mortal to serve them, like my family members do. Being able to drink from a fresh IV bag that's been collected especially for me is a privilege.

I have to do what I have to do. And god, do I feel so much better.

A shout grows louder behind me. I drop the poor, lifeless owl and lick a drop of blood from the back of my hand. Someone is coming. I retreat backward, deeper into the shadows of the woods. One unsure step after another, and—

My heels hit a low-lying branch, and I tumble down a hill that seemed to come from nowhere. Mid-roll, I somehow manage to push against the ground and stand, only for my legs to catch against a boulder. I spin and fall, and—

A pale face stares back at me, their eyes inches from mine. I shout and jump up, stumbling back. Doubling over, I try to calm myself as I see the face isn't a living person. Not a dead person, either. I'm staring at the statue of a woman lying with her arms folded peacefully atop an aboveground burial vault. A bouquet of granite flowers rests beneath her hands. Upon further inspection, I note that they aren't flowers—she's holding twigs dotted with berries. On the front of the vault is a name: *ELIZABETH GORHAM*.

I take a step back from it, unnerved. Why is this woman buried on campus, and with such an ornate resting place? I scan over the rest of the clearing and find she isn't alone. A meadow of moss-covered tombs and headstones springs from the earth like toadstools. As far as I can make out, all of them seem to feature the same stone twigs—one as a wreath on a cross, another wrapping around the eyes of a bust. I take a closer look at the years engraved on them. Mockingbird Prep was here before these graves appeared.

Why would a school need a cemetery?

Twigs snap behind me. Another animal to feed on? Whirling, I leap onto the figure as it emerges from the brush, and we topple to the ground.

Wood and infuriating sweetness.

Oh no. No-no-no-no. This is no animal; it's a golden retriever.

"What. The. *Hell?*!" Rowan shouts from beneath me.

CHAPTER FIVE
ROWAN

No, seriously—what the hell? Why is Casper all the way out here?

He crab walks off me and leaps to his feet. I shine my phone's flashlight at him, and his hand shoots up to shield his eyes.

"Sorry," he says. "I didn't know it was you."

"What are you *doing?*" I move the flashlight from him to—are those *graves?* "What is this?"

"I don't know."

I step toward the nearest grave, an aboveground one. A sculpted woman with a fractured face lies in peace. The back of my neck prickles. I'm unsure where or when, but I feel like I've seen those twigs in her hands before, someplace.

"Do you have any idea?" Casper asks, and I jump. He's somehow appeared next to me. How does he keep doing that?

"No. Why would I come this deep into the woods except to follow *you?*"

"You were following me?" Casper's eyes darken. I gesture to the space between us as though to say *clearly.* "How did you even know I was here?"

"You weren't in the room when the fire alarm gave me a heart attack," I say. "I noticed the movement in the trees during headcount, and I ran after you. Anyways, *why are you out here?* And why did you have to pull the fire alarm?"

"Fire alarm? I thought I'd set off a security alarm when I came outside. I was only going for a walk."

"You were going for a walk in the woods barefoot?"

Casper looks at his feet, which are covered in mud and dead leaves. His lips twist. He's clearly not a good liar, and I can't help but smile. It's kind of fun to watch him squirm. "Everyone does that in Belgium."

"Yeah, sure." I raise an eyebrow. "We should get back to the dorm before Abadi calls our parents."

I make my way to the slope that leads from the cemetery and back toward Young House before Casper has a chance to respond. I quicken my step before an oddly-shaped form in my peripheral vision catches my attention.

"I can tell you're waiting for some convoluted explanation," Casper says. "I don't have anything beyond stepping outside."

I've only half heard him. The shape isn't just an odd root or a weird boulder; it's a dead owl, dropped carelessly at the foot of a tree.

A cold chill shoots up my spine, and I slide my eyes to Casper, who's kept his gaze fixed ahead. I glance at his fingers, and for the first time, I notice faint, wet streaks of red running down the back of his hands.

"What?" He snaps his attention to me.

I shake my head. "Nothing."

I'm sharing my room with a psychopath.

A psychopath who's lying rigid on his bed with his hands clasped on his ribcage. He's so still I'd almost swear he was a corpse and not a very-much-alive guy.

An alive guy who goes for night walks without shoes and . . . kills owls with his bare hands?

I didn't see it happen. A fox could have gotten that owl. And it *was* dark. I could've imagined the blood on his hands. When we got back to the room, I made a point to look. Nothing was there. It wasn't on his clothing, either, so he couldn't have wiped it off considering he was right behind me the whole time. It had to have been a trick of the moonlight.

My gut, however, won't accept this explanation. He was still out there barefoot. He was still in the woods. And him, or someone, pulled that fire alarm.

I'll figure it out one way or another. He's not going to drag me into trouble and ruin my senior year. It's *mine*.

I nestle my head deeper into my pillow, but an odd shape sticks out beneath me, and I hear something like paper crinkling.

Slowly, I push my fingers beneath the pillow, and they graze against . . . an envelope, I see as I pull it out, with my name scrawled on it in a barely-legible hand. Whoever wrote it didn't have much time.

I open it with trembling hands and fish out the contents. A pendant on a silver chain drops onto the mattress.

Lifting the chain to inspect the pendant, the air leaves my lungs. I'm looking at a miniature ring of berry-covered twigs, the same kind the woman on that grave was holding. Glancing back at Casper to ensure he's still asleep, I lean over the side of my bed and push the pendant beneath my mattress and roll back over, squeezing my eyes tight.

Could it all be Casper? It's all so eerie. This new guy shows up, takes over my room, happens to find a forgotten cemetery, and then a pendant with the same symbol from said cemetery magically appears under my pillow? It's beyond "off".

Why did he come here, anyway? What would make his parents decide to move here randomly and drop a lot of money on the creepiest house they could find and enroll him?

Casper—not Casper—*someone* knows things about Mockingbird Prep that I don't. And clearly, they want me to find out.

CHAPTER SIX
CASPER

Gray light tempts me awake, and I shift my legs, which are stiff from being pulled to my chest for the last few hours. A wardrobe isn't ideal for sleeping, but it's the best I could do without my casket.

A strange smell wakes me fully up. Mortal breakfast cooking? Coffee dripping? No. It's worse. It's . . . *smoke*.

I look down at my bare chest to see a small patch of my flesh has burned away to ashes thanks to the morning light sneaking through the crack in the doors.

"Hell!" I shout and scramble to yank down a navy-blue jacket to throw over myself.

"Exactly!" The doors swing open. Rowan stands right over me while I manage to get beneath the jacket. "What the hell?"

This is bad. I was supposed to get out of here and into the bathroom before sunrise so Rowan wouldn't notice I was sleeping in my wardrobe.

"Don't," I grunt, flicking the ashes away with my left index finger, holding the jacket tightly over my head with the other.

The burn will be alright; I just have to get past the initial sting. My skin will be rejuvenated by lunch hour if I keep it covered.

Besides, I had worse burns before the Belamys found me and taught me how to protect myself during sunrise, when the rays are guaranteed to burn us.

"Don't what?" Rowan keeps shouting. "Don't wonder why the hell you're sleeping here?"

"Why are you even opening my wardrobe? You have your own."

"Some of my things are still in this one. I wasn't expecting a roommate, remember?"

"Sorry." I risk reaching out to pry the wardrobe door shut, but Rowan keeps his grip on it, and I remain half-naked and stuck beneath the jacket with this prick leering at me. "I couldn't sleep with the sound of your snoring."

"I don't snore."

"How would you know?"

He slams the door shut, leaving me in pitch darkness.

"Go left here," Rowan spits through clenched teeth and makes a sharp turn down the next corridor.

I focus on the black-and-white tiles and pull at the hem of my itchy blazer as I follow him. My ears are filled with the heartbeats of my soon-to-be-classmates, and my nose is stuffed with a hundred blood types. Chocolate, honey, and a slew of other scents all mixed together in a vampire smoothie.

"Sup, Young?" says a boy with a voice he's undoubtedly forced down an octave.

Others call out, but I keep my eyes down. Everyone's happy to see Rowan, which I can't fathom. No one tries to talk to me, which is just as well because my forehead is pulsing so violently my head could fall off. The owl was enough to keep me from losing control, but not enough to erase the need for more.

"Sorry the party got busted last night, man," the boy with the forced baritone says. "When I find out who told, I'll torture them for you."

"Everything for a reason, I guess," Rowan responds.

I lift my eyes to the sea of faces peering back at me, the lanky, pale, dead-faced new senior who may or may not have pulled the fire alarm and woken every upper-class boy up last night. The uneven blotches and bumps of mortality are clear to me beneath their veneers of lotions and makeup. I imagine skincare products and haircuts don't come cheap in their houses. The look of everyone screams *money*. I dig my hands in my pockets and hunch my shoulders.

"Young," a girl with a gap between her front two teeth whispers to Rowan, though not quietly enough to keep me from hearing, which I think is what she wants. "Who's the outlander?"

I side-eye Rowan, who's pursed his lips to keep from smirking.

"This is Casper." He volunteers my information, but I pretend that I don't hear him. "Don't mind him."

Thankfully, he doesn't force me to talk to the girl. He continues along the corridor, catching up with or saying hi to almost everyone he passes, a prince returning to his kingdom after a long quest at sea.

Finally, Rowan stops at the open door of a classroom and hitches his thumb without looking my way, his face dropping the half-cocked smile he used for everyone else. "You're there."

Where's the nice-making golden boy who was talking to everyone else mere seconds ago?

"Thanks," I say, though I don't mean it. Rowan taps his foot while he scrolls on his phone. "Uh, see you around?"

He's still not looking at me, his feet pointing as far away from me as possible.

"Okay," I say. "Have a good day, sweetie. Try to learn something."

Now he looks at me, with a glare that could kill. Satisfied, I make my way into the classroom. I risk looking back over my shoulder and relish the sight of him storming off. But I bump into a huge oak desk, folders piled haphazardly on top as well as an abstract sculpture of what I think is a percentage sign.

A woman with gray hair and even grayer skin peers up at me through an exaggerated frown. "Are you quite alright?"

No, I'm not quite alright. I need blood. Now. And it looks like you don't have any in those veins, so if you'll excuse me—

"Tripped."

"Easy does it," she says, a taunting tilt of her lips replacing the frown. She glances at a roster. "Belamy?"

"Uh-huh."

"Grab a seat."

Snickers and stifled laughter flurry across the room, and a guy whispers angrily, "He's the one who pulled the alarm."

I spot an empty desk in the back corner and beeline for it. A few of my tired-looking male classmates acknowledge me with a scowl. One of them, the one who whispered about me, scoots his desk three inches away and locks hands with a girl seated next to me.

He doesn't know he's safe—the amount of body spray he's doused himself with would likely poison me.

Thirteen blood types is far less than the hundred outside of the classroom, but I still feel like my head could explode. Body spray or no, I'd devour half the room if I thought I could get away with it. My right foot taps against my will, so forcefully and violently it earns me a few more glares. As a distraction, I keep a laser focus on my desk, studying the carvings some other student did. *EK ♥ s DC.* I get busy thinking up who they must be, how many kids they might have, whether or not they're paranormal like me, and get so lost in my imagination that I almost forget I'm surrounded by fresh, forbidden blood.

Sweet, incredible blood. Blood that will dull this ache. Refresh my skin and heal the burn on my chest. That will keep me alive forever . . . nice . . . nourishing . . .

I. Need. Blood.

Every syllable this teacher utters at the front brings me closer to the edge. My jaw twitches right and left; my head bobs back and forth. My fangs are desperate to come out. I may as well have not drunk the owl because I need more, more, more.

I gasp when the school bell brings an end to class and everyone jumps up to race for the next, taking their scents with them. All of them survived me. I sigh with relief and a little sense of accomplishment. Now I just have to manage through the rest of the day. Perhaps the worst is over, and today won't be so bad.

This day is horrendous.

Rowan didn't meet me after Calculus, so I had to find my own way to my classes. In English Literature, which I was actually looking forward to, I found out the summer reading was *Flowers for Algernon*. I mean, really, are we twelve? *Flowers for Algernon*?!

To add insult to injury, I then had to go to the Fine Arts Center for Drama, which I had fought hard against taking. Malcolm argued that it will give me more formal training in acting like a human and help me with public speaking. He's right, of course, but the last thing I want to do is perform for anyone. *Plus*, the entire class was about some musical called *Pippin* and how we're devoting most of the year to it. I almost dropped out and plotted my route back to NYC when the teacher Mrs. Spencer made it clear that auditioning was a requirement to pass.

It won't be any use trying to persuade Malcolm to let me drop— the vampire king loves musical theater.

With that fresh on my mind, I now have to follow the hoard of sweet-smelling mortals to the dining hall, which is so cruelly ironic that I'm seriously considering opting for another year in the attic. Europe isn't worth this.

Housed in the same building as the admin offices, the dining hall looks more like the inside of a cathedral, with vaulted ceilings and huge latticed windows that let in way too much sunlight for my comfort. The clatter of silverware and the yelps of students with far too much energy drown out my thoughts. The smell of mortal food covers the smell of blood, and I feel instantly nauseous.

A few feet away, in the line for food, a girl listens to her friend zip through a string of Halloween costume ideas. When she spots me, she yanks the girl toward her. The commotion causes other people in line to take notice, and before I can even process what's happening, they're all taking a step back from me and looking away like they're trying to unsee me.

"That's the weird one I told you about," a girl with a yellow braid whispers nearby.

My shoulders hunch, and I look to the ground. I could hiss at everyone, or I could smile and wave; nothing would make it better. It's five hundred against one in here. There's no other like me, and anything I take on here, I take on alone.

"Getting in line?"

I flinch at the smell I've come to loathe and spin around to find Rowan and his goons right behind me. He must be aware of people watching because he's got that alpha-dog smile painted on.

"I mean, you must be starving," he says, "after running around all night."

I shuffle around him and dart for the door before the smell of vanilla and pure hatred ruins everything.

"You have to come get me, or I'm going to chug a douchebag."

Scarlett's laugh on the other end of the line makes me cringe, and I bang my forehead against the door of the second stall of the Fine Arts Center's boys' room.

"I'm going to let what you just said pass on by, Baby Sheik," she says. "Don't pay that jar of applesauce any mind."

"You know I don't understand you when you use 1920s slang," I say pointedly, rubbing a hand over the now-unburned skin on my chest. "Keep to the present, please."

"Don't worry about douchebags." I can almost hear the eyeroll in her voice, and the clink of her pearls, too, as she runs her long fingernails over them. Scarlett must be feeling her speakeasy days— or her glory days, as Malcolm sarcastically refers to them. "Eyes down and focus on the reward."

How can I focus on anything with Rowan Young around?

I reach inside my mouth and force my fangs back up before pushing open the stall door. "I miss you. I miss the quiet. And I miss having one decent thought that isn't about that prick."

"Listen, I'd love nothing more than to have you here to tease. But if I get you, Camille will punish me for all of eternity. You should've heard her in the supermarket this morning when we went to 'normal it'. Everyone, including the meth head in the parking lot, learned her baby boy is attending Mockingbird Prep."

"We're in a town with an astronomical cost of living. *Most* kids attend Mockingbird Prep."

"*Point is*"—a hard edge enters Scarlett's tone; she must be getting thirsty—"she's proud. All of us are. Even Oscar smiled when it came up, and I thought he was gonna shatter his granite face."

This one gets a genuine chuckle from me.

"It's a test, Baby Sheik. We all have to prove our control at some point. When you're thousands of miles away, around other vampires, seeing that side of this big universe, this one year is going to feel as simple and short as a trip to the barber."

She's right, of course. I *do* still want the tour, more than anything. Scarlett has told me about the vampires where I'm going—their glamour, their wild, unadulterated, bohemian ways. I want that. I want to be a bloody freak and somehow still be the least-weird person around.

"Besides," she continues, "before you know it, it'll be Halloween. Remember what happens then?"

How could I ever forget? Halloween is the most important holiday to my family. It's when they host their annual Feeding Ball. Almost every vampire and cask in the region flocks to their home for a night of bloodthirsty revelry. Not only will this year be my first, but it will also mark the first time I'll drink directly from a human.

I want to get my thirst under control so I can pull that off.

"Fine," I say with a groan. "But you have no idea what I'm putting up with."

"You don't need your contemporaries—they'll be your elders in a matter of months. Now, get to the barber and keep it simple. I gotta go feed, or *I* might be the one chugging a douchebag."

After a couple more goodbyes, I let Scarlett off the phone. Once again, I'm all alone.

My chest tightens, and my throat dries out. I have to go to even *more* classes and be around *more* people who wouldn't understand what I am?

I squint, wishing for a teardrop or two to fall and make me feel a little bit better, but they don't. I'm able to see things mortals can't. One day, I'll be able to levitate. I can feel every emotion, every strand of fabric, every subtle shift in the breeze multiplied by one thousand. But simple tears? Out of the question.

I consider calling Scarlett again to ask when this will end, but she's probably in her cask pantry by now, so I eject myself from the stall and head into the corridor. I don't know how to get to my next class, and I was so borderline feral that I don't remember which way I came from.

Eventually, I come upon increasingly narrow hallways, marking the shift in the building from renovated wings to the original structure, built when people were a lot smaller. Oil paintings dot the walls, works from prodigal students of the past.

I pause before one of a man in a gray robe, looking rather stern and holding a branch. The plaque reads CONSTANT YOUNG

FOUNDS MOCKINGBIRD, 1756. ARTIST SIMEON CRESS (b. 1739).

Constant must be Rowan's great-great-whoever. That explains the douchiness.

Turning back the way I came, I take a few steps and then stop again at a four-way connecting two halls. The building falls into silence—

Except for a single footstep.

Perhaps it was an echo? I take two more steps, stop. Two more footsteps behind me.

I look over my shoulder—as a shadow retreats around a corner.

"Hello?" I dare a few steps toward it, ready to come across a student or a teacher who's running late. But when I make it to the corner and peer around, the corridor is empty. "Hello?"

Nothing there. No more sounds.

I head back to the four-way, but a door back around the corner swings open and slams against the wall as whoever it is runs.

Someone is messing with me.

Not today, foolish mortal.

I dart after them, picking up speed, following the faint sound of a speeding heartbeat. I'm getting closer. And closer. I'm zooming toward a set of double doors. I skid to a stop.

My nostrils fill with the smell of aging paper, autumn spice, and the dust of book spines. I push the doors open. Dark oak shelf upon dark oak shelf, lousy with books, span before me, in stacks so tall they require ladders on wheeled tracks. Study tables with little desk lights that have wine-colored shades and thick, shaggy carpets fill out the room. At the far end, a large, circular window looks out over the quad.

Whoever I was following must have staked me through the heart. I must be dead, and heaven is a library.

"I don't think," a voice says behind one of the stacks, "I've seen *anyone* enter a library with such gusto."

I jump, spotting Mr. Abadi's face smiling at me through a gap between the books.

"Sup, buddy?"

"Uh . . . hi," I say. "I was lost."

"And now you're found?" He comes out of the stack pushing a roller cart of books. "Or here to study? Wait—did you already get through that massive collection of your own?"

"No, I really did get lost," I say. "Did someone else come in here?"

"Not that I'm aware of." Mr. Abadi lifts a book from the cart and slides it into its rightful place. "Time for bed, Mr. Dickens, until you're chosen again—probably for English III next semester. Who's next?" He checks the spine of the next book. "Salinger, you old bastard. I thought they'd banned you again. Well, let's get you home." He nudges the cart, glancing back at me. "Am I being weird? I tell myself not to be weird, but it never lasts long."

"Do you talk to all the books?" I look at the stacks as we make our way to the *S* section of the Fiction shelves. "Like they're people?"

"They *are* people," Mr. Abadi says. "Their ideas, anyways. When you think about it, someone's book is kind of like an urn. But it doesn't hold the ashes of their body. It's their thoughts."

Yeah, he definitely doesn't have a lot of people to talk to. Which I understand.

Something prickles the back of my neck, and I whirl around, but no one is there. I stare at a bare study table.

"When you consume a book," he says, "you're consuming the person who wrote it."

I swallow the urge to let my fangs descend at the thought of consuming a person and whirl back to him, my already slow heartbeat skipping. "Where are you going with this?"

"Absolutely nowhere. I'm just enjoying the stroll."

"Ooo-*kay*." I cringe. But his mention of an urn reminds me of last night and gives me an idea. "I can appreciate waxing morbid. Speaking of which, do you have anything on cemeteries?"

Mr. Abadi blinks. "Inspired by my analogy?"

"*Local* cemeteries. Like maps, trails. Some people are into cemetery tours. So, do we have anything like that?"

"I don't believe so." He looks at me with a raised eyebrow, sliding Salinger into place.

"Goodnight, Salinger," I say, and he gives me a pleased smile. "Maybe that's the wrong question. What about stuff on the school? Maybe a yearbook or local history?"

Mr. Abadi tilts his head with narrowed eyes. "I'll need to check. They might be restricted."

Oh, there are definitely books on that, but for whatever reason, he doesn't want me to find them. I may need to use Google for the time being.

"Don't worry about it." I turn to leave. "Just curious, being new in town. Thank you anyways!"

"My library is your library," Mr. Abadi says, and he adds something else, but I don't hear him because I'm focused on the twig sitting on the study table that was vacant moments before.

I lift and inspect it, half expecting to find another clue etched into its bark. But it is only a twig. Except for Abadi, the library is completely deserted. But it can't be. Whoever left this is still watching.

Is Rowan the one messing with me? This looks eerily similar to the branches carved on those headstones. Come to think of it, wasn't Constant Young holding one in that painting out in the corridor?

"What about trees?" I call to Abadi.

After about thirty minutes of browsing, Mr. Abadi checks out a stack of nature books for me, and I've stowed my little present away in my book bag. I could look up what kind of tree it came from online, but I feel bad not checking anything out—he seems to get such a kick out of putting them away again.

When he reaches the final book, one I grabbed while he was curating the nature ones, he pauses.

"Where'd you find this?" He holds it up—*Dracula* by Bram Stoker.

"The *S*'s?" I knit my eyebrows together.

Mr. Abdi considers it, then shrugs before trying to scan it. A note pops up on the catalogue screen.

"Yeah, that's what I thought. This isn't in circulation."

"Hm?"

"It's not a book in this library."

"It has a sticker." I point to the evidence that it does, in fact, belong in this library.

"I'll have to ask someone higher up." He drags the book along the desk until it drops behind it, out of sight. "I'm sorry."

CHAPTER SEVEN
ROWAN

"What's going on?"

I snap my attention to Dad when he asks the question. Moments ago, he was checking in on me. It's something we do every week when school's in session since it's just him in our big house, and the pictures of Mom on his nightstand.

But the gentle way he asks after I've given him the usual "good" and "fine" tells me he can see right through me, and that all the "fines" and "goods" in the world won't get him off my trail.

"Nothing," I say. "Why?"

"Coach Bones says you're distracted at practice."

I shift in my chair, loosen my tie, and focus on the painting of the *Attercop*, the ship that carried over the original settlers of Mockingbird, behind him.

"I'm not trying to guilt you about it," Dad tilts his head. "I think you hung the stars; you know that. But this isn't like you. It worries me."

"You don't have to worry," I say too quickly. "I'm okay."

"It's not girl trouble, is it?"

"*Dad.*"

"I'm not ignorant," he says, his mouth pulling into a smile. "I was seventeen once. But believe me, it's not worth letting everything else slip."

"There's no girl," I say, silently reminding myself to watch my tone. *There might never be a girl.* "I'm fine."

Dad stares me down, likely trying to discern whether it's possible that there is, in fact, a girl and I'm lying to him. For someone who's never been in a relationship, you'd think I was quite the player the way he assumes I get around.

He doesn't know, of course, that I might not be into girls. That maybe I'm more attracted to guys. And I'm not calling it "gay". Naming it makes it feel so . . . settled, and I'm not sure that word is accurate yet.

"You'd tell me if something was wrong, right?" he asks, his gaze softening to one of pure concern. "You wouldn't keep something major from me?"

You mean like when Mom had a plan to leave us and never dropped a hint?

The truth is, Dad never checked in like this when she was here. The details of my life were kept to three questions: What is my GPA? How am I doing at sports? Have I gotten anyone pregnant? Those were asked to my mother, not me. Then she made her escape, having decided that two years in the lake house wasn't enough of a separation. I don't think he actually cares what's going on in my life so long as I'm not planning to abandon him like she did.

I take a deep breath. "You know I would."

Dad nods, and for a moment, I'm foolish enough to think the subject is closed. But he surprises me by asking, "How are things going with Casper?"

It's been three weeks since he arrived in his fancy-ass hearse of a car, and I still can't figure him out. That night in the woods or the morning when he was inside the wardrobe were strange enough, but he's continued to sneak out every other night.

When he's not doing that, he's in our room, flying through book after book, and I don't believe he's actually reading them. He claimed to read *Les Misérables* in two days, and that's flat-out impossible.

If *that* isn't enough, he's messy. He leaves these books all over the place. Piled on his bed, hanging off his shelves, stacked on the floor.

"Rowan?" Dad brings me back to the present. My face prickles with heat, ashamed of how long I've been thinking about him. "How's Casper?"

"He's . . . well, he's . . . he's the roommate from hell!"

Dad's eyes round as I spring from my chair, lean over his desk, and go over every single reason I can't stand living with him.

"And he's weird!" I say once I've blown through how messy and rude he is. "I tried to be nice the other night and asked if he wanted to go to the dining hall, and he refused. Not only eating with me— eating *at all*. He won't get to know anyone."

"I know Casper is different," Dad says, "not the usual sort who attends this school. But the world is full of different types of people. We have no choice but to accept that."

"But he's—"

"Weird." Dad shrugs. "He hasn't done anything that would require me to step in. If he gets up early to go for runs or nature walks, okay. Maybe you should join him. You might come to understand his little quirks if you get to know him better."

Go into the woods with Casper? Where no one can hear my screams? He can't be serious, but there's no point arguing. I'm his son—a representative, an ambassador. I don't get to refuse my dad when we're here.

"Fine," I sigh.

"Good man. Either way, we're almost to fall break, and then you'll get a breather from him."

"Morning, man!" I roll over and prop myself on my elbow.

Casper spins around to face me, his hand remaining on the doorknob. His eyes are so bright and blue I can make them out even in the dark. "Why are you up?"

"Coach wants my legs stronger," I lie, switching on the lamp. Casper winces at the sudden brightness. "I thought maybe I could join you."

"Join me for *what?*" His tone darkens, and he stands even taller.

"For a run," I say, flashing my most charming smile, the one that says, *Let's be buds!* "Or hike, jog, whatever this Belgian wood walk thing is that you do."

"Sure!"

I blink. "Wait, really?"

"Abso-*lute*-ly," he says. "We'll watch the sunrise over the mountains as we weave crowns of wildflowers, then sing a rousing chorus of 'Getting to Know You'."

"We don't have to take it *that* far."

"I'm not naive, Rowan." Casper pulls the bedroom door open. "I know you're just trying to spy on me."

"I'm not trying to spy on you."

"I believe that less than I believe that you're a nice person. Go back to sleep, Rowan."

"I'm a nice person!" I shout, but he's gone before my forcefully tossed pillow reaches the back of his head.

"What are you reading tonight?"

Casper's eyes slide from the page to me. I sit perched on the corner of my bed, holding a book of my own with a hapless expression that I hope says, *I'm genuinely curious.*

Casper rolls his eyes. "You wouldn't like it."

"Why wouldn't I like it?"

"It's mostly two men kissing. You might want to leave in case it's catching."

My ears burn. He's assumed I'm a homophobe, but right now, I'm curious about the book. How much kissing are we talking about? More than kissing?

"I don't care about two men kissing," I say. "What's it called?"

"What are you doing?" Casper snaps the book shut. I resist the urge to throw my own book at him. He deserves it, lounging so smugly on a bed he doesn't seem to sleep in, looking so effortlessly cool and uncaring. Like a cat. Or a young David Bowie.

"Also reading," I say, showing my book off. "You see, I'm trying this new thing: civility. Did they have that over at your Belgian-American millionaire school?"

"I'm fairly certain your family is almost as wealthy as mine," Casper says. "Perhaps not as powerful."

"I don't have power envy," I say. "I have a book. That I'm reading. I do that too."

"You read books upside down?"

"Of course I don't—" Casper's laugh drowns out my cursing when I see I've been holding the book the wrong way this whole time. "Dude, I'm only trying to get to know you better. I know I pissed you off the first day of class, but that was a month ago!"

"Only a month?" Casper rolls over and faces the wall, flipping the page in his book. "I thought surely we were nearing graduation by now with how it's dragged."

I resist the urge to grab his shoulders and shake him.

Showering is the only alone time I get anymore. Squeezing my eyes shut, I hiccup as a small sob escapes my chest.

I don't want to cry. I *don't* cry. But goddamn it, this semester has sucked. This is supposed to be *my* year. Get awesome grades. Lead the football team to victory. Kill it at fencing. Get into Cornell. Be prom king. My year isn't supposed to revolve around convincing a cold-hearted prick to give me the time of day.

I wipe my eyes with the back of my hand and take a deep breath. That's enough for now. No need to let it all out. No need to worry or think I'm doing a bad job. I'm okay. Today is the last day before fall break, and I'll get to go home for a week and get a break from it all. One more day.

But I'm still not free of a certain someone, and my mind shifts to the one person I don't want to think about. Casper, with his pretty, arrogant face and his unfairly long legs with muscular thighs that make zero sense for a nerd like him, holding up a heavy book while his pink lips pucker.

I shake my head and decide to condition my hair again, like it'll wash the thoughts out.

Let's get one thing straight: I do not find Casper attractive in that way—or any guy. Except maybe David Bowie, or Prince, or Harry Styles. Everyone finds them attractive; I don't care who you are. We've all seen Bowie in those Goblin King pants.

Now I'm picturing Casper dressed in Bowie's Goblin King pants. I drop the loofah, realizing exactly where I'd been holding it. Casper Belamy is *no* David Bowie.

I shut off the shower and dry myself quickly. Towel wrapped around my waist, I leave the stall and rush to the sinks to inspect myself.

Still not nearly as ripped as I want to be, and I'm worried I'll always have skinny biceps. There's barely any hair on my chest, and that pisses me off. After deciding I'm okay-looking but not excellent, I rush back to the stall to get dressed, but I can't.

My clothes, left folded on the bench in front of the stalls, are gone. I look around, trying to spot where I absentmindedly must've put them, but they're nowhere. Someone came in here and took my clothes.

And I have a strong suspicion who.

Tightening my grip on my towel, I make a quick break out of the bathroom and down the hall, slipping into the dorm before anyone spots me. Casper sits crisscross on the floor, his lap hidden by a glossy contemporary paperback. He glances up at me, doing a double take when he sees I'm in nothing but a wet towel.

"Where are they?" I demand, slamming the door behind me.

"Who? The colonists of Roanoke?"

"You know what I'm talking about." I stomp to my wardrobe.

"I assure you, I don't," Casper says.

"My clothes!" I whirl around, and Casper's eyes flick up to mine. Was . . . was he checking me out? "I need my clothes!"

"Try your wardrobe." Casper snaps the book shut. "Or your laundry hamper. I'm not the keeper of your outfits."

"I know you took them while I was in the shower. Give them back."

A smile breaks across Casper's face, although he tries to hide it by pursing them. Finally, he asks, "Why would I want your clothes?"

"I don't know," I say, and before I can stop myself, I add, "Maybe you want to see me naked."

Casper's eyes double in size and grow a shade darker (how does he do that?!). He stands. "Are you kidding? Because I'm gay, right? I must be trying to ogle you?"

"No! I . . . Never mind. Unless . . . I don't know, did you want to see me naked?"

"You're repulsive!" Casper snatches his book from the floor and wags it at me. "Or what? Are you *hoping* I'd want to see that?"

"What? No!" My heart hammers. "And get that out of my face!"

I reach up to knock his book away and—I used the wrong hand. The towel slips down my hips. I scream and grab for it as Casper gasps and spins around.

Now I *am* naked, and there's a guy who's arguably attractive enough to defy sexuality standing three feet away.

"Oh my god," I rasp, wrapping the towel back around me as quickly as I can. "Oh my god oh my god."

"I didn't see anything," Casper is quick to say.

"Shut up!" I shout as I reach for the wardrobe. "Don't look! I'm getting dressed."

All is silent except my pounding heart as I pull out a pair of boxer briefs, sweatpants, and a T-shirt. When I'm pulling the shirt over my head, I hear a cackle. Shirt on, I find Casper doubled over, clutching his stomach, wheezing between laughs.

"What?" I snap.

"I'm . . . I'm sorry," he says. "It's . . . your face!"

"It's not funny!"

He sucks in air over and over, shaking his head violently. "Yes, it is."

Maybe it's because he's laughing so hard, or maybe it's because him laughing at all is a weird sight and that makes it funnier, but I can't help but let out a small laugh myself. Then it grows, and before I know it, we're both laughing really hard, and I'm falling back on my bed, holding my stomach because my abs hurt so badly.

"Okay," I say when I can finally catch a breath, "yeah, it was sort of funny."

"You were like—" Casper imitates my face, and then he's wheezing again, dropping to his knees as he doubles over in another fit of laughter.

"Stop!" I throw my pillow at him, but that makes it worse and leads to another laughing fit from me.

"I'm . . . I'm sorry—" Casper keeps trying and failing to catch his breath. "I . . . can't . . . can't breathe."

"Stop laughing at me!" I spring from the bed, play-punching him. It's something I'd do to Diego or to Reed, something they'd do to me.

I never thought I'd horse around like this with Casper of all guys, but it's kind of a relief after the tension we've been having. He jabs me back with his elbows as I grab him, and soon, my fingers are on his stomach, and he's flipping around, and I tickle him.

"Stop!" he wheezes. "Stop!"

I'm cackling with my legs straddling his waist, and he's struggling, and for one split second, I catch myself thinking one forbidden, dangerous word: *Cute!*

"Enough!" I snap, the laughter leaving me in an instant. Casper stares back at me, unblinking, his lips twisting. "No more of that."

I stomp over to my towel and retrieve it, hanging it around my neck. Casper sits up, leaning his elbows against his knees. I reach for the doorknob. But when I open it, there they are, in a heaped pile in the hallway. "What the . . ."

I peer both ways down the hall. Whoever left my clothes is long gone. I step out to grab the pile and quickly close the door.

"They're home from their journey," Casper notes, retrieving his book. "I hope that lays suspicion of me to rest—"

He's cut off by a shout as something sharp stabs my finger. I drop the clothes onto my bed.

"Are you okay?" asks Casper.

I shake the clothes until something heavy drops out of them and onto the bed. A wooden stake, the kind you'd use to drive a tent into the ground. Except it's different—larger and sharper. I drop the clothes on top of it before Casper can see. Whoever gave me the branch must have added this to the mix.

They must think Casper is dangerous too. But why a tent stake? Was that the best weapon they could find for me?

Behind me, Casper inhales sharply, loudly. He's put his sunglasses on. His face is so still I'd think he was a wax figure if I didn't know better.

"What?" I ask him.

When he doesn't respond, only quivers his lips, my face flushes with angry heat. "What are staring at?!"

His pinkie finger half-lifts, pointing at my right hand. The nearly healed cut on my index finger has been stabbed open, leaving it once again covered in blood. Now that I've seen it, it feels like I've sliced it open with a chef's knife.

"*Ow!*" I hold the wrist with my free hand and inspect the cut, jumping when Casper's hand wraps around mine.

He's even colder than his father, so cold he almost burns to touch.

"Be still," he says, so strained I can hardly hear him. His voice is somehow different—tight and rich and so smooth I think his vocal chords must be lined with satin. "You're making it worse."

He's so close I can smell him: warm, cozy, like a pecan pie scented candle you'd find around Halloween, but also like soil—he's earthy—and an autumn bonfire. Now *I'm* the one wrinkling my nose and not him because he. Smells. Amazing.

He grabs my towel and wraps it tightly around my hand, pressing it against my finger. "Press this against it; it'll stop the bleeding."

He doesn't let go. The towel is the only thing keeping our hands from touching. His fingers clamp more tightly around mine, almost too tightly, and a hundred butterflies take flight in my stomach, and heat sears my cheeks. Am I . . . am I blushing? Or am I embarrassed at him coddling me?

Casper's chest heaves. He's been holding his breath. My eyes drift to his, but I can't see anything beyond the sunglasses. "Are you okay?"

"Don't move," he snaps and pulls himself back. "Just . . . stay there."

He flees the room, so fast I blinked and missed him. Whatever that moment was, it's over as quickly as it started, and I'm left wondering what even happened.

What exactly is his problem? For a moment, we were actually getting along. Then the second I got hurt, he changed. Does he have a phobia of blood, and this made him ill?

I think about the owl that first night, about him sneaking into the woods so many nights since, the grip he had on me moments ago. Maybe he's not afraid of blood. Maybe . . . it's the exact opposite.

Enough guessing. Tonight, when he sneaks out, I'm going to be awake, and I'm going to find out what he's hiding.

Casper crawls from his bed at two in the morning. Not a moment too soon because I've almost fallen asleep several times, lying perfectly still with my eyes closed, willing myself to pass for unconscious.

I make a point to keep my breath slow as he pauses beside my bed. Opening one eye, I stare at the wall and watch his shadow in the dim, blue-hazed room as he makes for the door and, as silently as undisturbed air, slips into the hallway.

After giving him a head start, I push off the covers, grab my sneakers, and creep out of the room. I tiptoe to the stairwell and look down just in time to catch Casper's shadow slip from view.

I follow as quietly as I can, pausing every few steps to ensure he hasn't heard me. The front door clicks behind him as I reach the second-to-last flight. Alone now, I check over my shoulder. What if whoever has been sending me things is also watching, waiting? My spine quivers, but I shake it off.

Twisting the doorknob as gently as I can, I slip through the front door and bolt down the steps, pulling on one sneaker after the other.

Low fog breaks around my ankles as I run around the building. I catch a flash of white as Casper ducks through the brush and into the woods, and I race after him, pulling my phone from my pocket and, with a swipe, open the camera.

I skid to a stop once I pass through the trees and listen. He should be somewhere ahead, but everything is quiet, still. *Too* still. And dark, the moon blocked by the trees. I can barely see anything, but if I use my flashlight, it's going to give me away. So I lean against a tree and listen with my arms wrapped around myself to brace from the cold.

All I hear is my breath, coming out in short bursts of fog.

Until—

It starts low, this strange gravelly noise, like the rattle of a snake. But as it grows louder, I realize what I'm hearing is a growl.

A *human* growl.

I turn toward the noise of a large something slamming against the ground, followed by a high-pitched whimper.

I wander closer, my camera ready for anything. The fog at my ankles flows down the slope that marks the same clearing from the last time I was out here the night before classes—that random cemetery.

Headstones rise from the white mist, the moonlight casting it in a sky-blue glow that makes me feel like I'm on the set of a horror movie.

I spot him, and my bones feel suddenly chilled. Now that I'm seeing this . . . maybe I *am* in a horror movie.

Casper balances atop a large, furry, writhing shape. A hooved foot kicks, barely grazing one of the headstones. I spot a large white branch—no, not a branch, an antler.

He's wrestling a stag.

I hold my phone up, ready to tap RECORD, when Casper tosses his head back, and his jaw drops down, down, down, like it's unhinged. I squint. What are those in his mouth? Are those his *teeth*?

Casper lowers his head, and his unbelievably large, sharp teeth stab the stag's neck. He's biting it. He's trying to eat it alive; he's—

My knees shake and my shoulders twitch at the sound of gurgling. He is *drinking its blood*.

"Holy shit," I gasp, and my knees buckle. "Holy shit!"

My leg knocks against an unearthed root, and I stumble, breaking the fall with my elbow, but it doesn't stop me from rolling down the slope, losing my phone in the process. I land on my stomach, and Casper lifts his head to glare at me with violet eyes that glow in the dark—and a chin dripping scarlet. He's on me in an instant, holding me down with his ice-cold hands.

"Be quiet!" he yells, his voice rocky and thick. "Calm down."

But I keep screaming, rocking my head back and forth at the sight of his enlarged mouth and his two very large, very pointy, red-stained teeth. The blood on his chin drips onto my shirt, and I think I'm going to vomit.

"Get off!" I shout. "Get offa me!"

He covers my mouth, and I have no choice but to look at him. His mouth is closed and, from what I can tell, back to its normal size. His eyes are blue again. His black curls fall over his forehead, tousled in the struggle. He would look almost angelic if not for the blood coating his chin.

"I'm not going to hurt you, Rowan," he says, his voice so calm I almost believe it, "though the rules where I'm from say I'm supposed to." My bulging eyes must give away my confusion because he laughs softly. "I told you to drop it. But you didn't; now here we are."

He shakes his head, cringes, and lifts his hand from my mouth. I waste no time wriggling from beneath him and crab walk halfway up the small hill.

"What did you *do*?" I stare at the dead deer.

"I had to feed," he says, as casually as telling me he made a lasagna. "I've been after him since night one."

I stare at Casper, looking for some sort of answer. The blood covering his mouth and pajamas. The pale skin and color-changing eyes. The beautiful, statuesque face that's been messing with my mind.

Blood. Pale. Won't eat. Adverse to sunlight. *Wooden stake in my dorm room.*

"You're a vampire?!" I feel so ridiculous saying it out loud.

Casper tilts his head, and I wince under his gaze. "No one is supposed to know."

A cackle rips itself from my belly against my will, and before I know it, I'm laughing maniacally. It's been a long time coming, but I think I might have cracked. "This is payback, isn't it?"

"Pardon?"

"The deer, the fog, the blood." I slap my knees. "You're in Drama! This is fake! It's a production. You're getting back at me for snooping around and giving you a hard time."

"You think this is a hoax?" Casper narrows his eyes.

"I mean, come on, a *vampire*?" I strut over to the deer. How did they make such a realistic prop? "'Ooh! Bleh! I shall suck zee blood from zee deeeeeer!' Did you honestly think I'd be scared of a—"

My fingers touch the stag, expecting to feel papier-mâché and wig hair. But what I feel is a very real dead deer. I gag as blood spurts out of its neck beneath my fingertips.

"You were saying?" Casper says behind me, making me jump.

"No!" I take a step back. "You can't stay here!" I flash back to earlier when the stake pierced my finger. The way he acted. How he'd touched me. "Oh my god! You want to suck my blood!"

"*What?*"

"You heard me." I stumble back. "You want to suck my blood! Make me a member of the undead army or whatever! Have you . . . have you been drinking it in my sleep?! Without my knowledge?!"

I yelp when he appears before me suddenly, his face inches from mine. "That's vampist, Rowan, and an attack on my character."

"Get back!" I shove his chest, forcing him to give me space. "Don't come near me!"

"I don't want to hurt you," Casper says slowly. "I'm only here to prove that I can be trusted among mortals."

"Go home!" I scream, bolting up the slope. "Go back to whatever pit of hell you came out of, you . . . you fucking demon!"

I bolt through the trees, expecting that any moment, the monster from my dorm room will catch up and snap my neck. But Casper never follows, even when I'm back in the dorm, curled up on my bed with all the lights on. I sit for hours, staring at the door, trying to process, to accept what I've seen and heard.

Casper a vampire? It's impossible. People don't drink blood and live forever. That's folklore. A Halloween costume. Anything but real.

Leaning over the edge of my bed, I reach beneath the mattress and pull out the stake. Someone knew I'd need this to protect myself. They've known for a while. So . . . as impossible as it is, there must be something to it. It must be true.

Somehow, beyond all reason, vampires are real. And Casper Belamy is one of them.

CHAPTER EIGHT
CASPER

He knows. He knows. He knows.

It's one of two thoughts haunting me, even three days after coming home for fall break a night early. Three days of jumping every time a car rolls past the house. Of cocking my ear toward each sound of the night birds swooping past the attic window. Of waiting for Rowan to show up with an angry mob. Because *he knows.*

And . . .

He called me a demon.

A fucking demon, that's what he said. Something from hell. Without a soul, or a heart, or feelings. *And* he accused me of feeding on him in his sleep.

I turn over in my casket, my cheek sliding against the smooth red satin pillow, but the movement doesn't change my thought patterns like it sometimes does. I keep hearing him calling me that.

Suddenly, my coffin lid opens, and I scream as a grinning face appears above me and shouts, "Hiya, Baby Sheik!"

I punch the side of the coffin, suck in a deep breath, and cover my eyes. Scarlett laughs. I run my hands down my face and squint at her as she tousles her flaming red hair back into perfect tresses.

"I told Oscar not to let anyone in."

"I outrank you." Scarlett grabs my left elbow and hoists me up.

"In what world does a duchess outrank a prince?" I ask.

She side-eyes the melting candles I've surrounded my casket with, and the phonograph that's playing one of Malcolm's records: a somber aria sung by a long-dead baritone. "Are you going to tell me why you're brooding more than usual?"

"I'm going back to bed." I reach for my casket lid, but Scarlett is on me in a fraction of a second, slamming it back with strength that proves why she outranks me.

"First, it's eight in the evening. Second . . ." She's adopted the snobbish voice of an aged dowager. "You've been requested in the dining room."

Another thing I learned quickly is that "being requested" means I'd better show up unless I want Oscar to throw me down the stairs. With another groan, I step out of the casket and adjust my gray cable-knit sweater while Scarlett sweeps my curls out of my face.

"They're worried about you," she says. "I am too. If someone hurt you, I'd take care of them for you."

I smirk. "I thought the point was to *not* kill any students."

"I don't always kill when I take revenge," she argues as we make our way down the creaking, cobweb-covered steps of the attic and out into the corridors of the top floor. "Sometimes I use slow, agonizing torture."

"You're the reason people assume we're awful," I say, glancing over oil-based portraits of my new vampiric parents and distant "cousins" from around the world that dot the green Victorian wallpaper.

"No." Scarlett's voice is as cold as snow. "I'm the reason they fear us."

A warm, fuzzy feeling fills my stomach as I follow her, and I hope that someday, I'll be as dangerous and uncaring of other people's opinions as her. I really have missed her, even if my parents think she's a bad influence.

A few minutes later, we've made our way to the first floor, where vampires in black soldier uniforms and coke bottle sunglasses stand guard around the main hall and outside the dining room, politely nodding to us as we pass.

"Little Bat has entered the hall," one of them says into an earpiece.

I roll my eyes. *Little Bat.* I'm taller than he is. I make a point to smile at each of them, mostly because I'm still not used to having a legion of the undead for protection.

When we cross beneath the columned arch that leads into the oversized dining room, lit only by the candles flickering atop the crystal chandelier, I do a double take. Multicolored streamers have been strung across the ceiling, confetti tossed along the antique table and over Styrofoam skulls that have been slapped with glitter.

Malcolm blows a noise maker, pink paper rolling out and inflating as a squeak sounds my arrival, and Camille tosses another cloud of confetti before donning a glossy cone-shaped party hat.

"Welcome home!" she singsongs.

"I've *been* home," I say.

"Don't think we haven't noticed how gloomy you've been," Malcolm says. "Do you think we're the sort to leave you sad and dejected?"

"It's a family game night," Camille announces. "Isn't that what mortal families do? It was between this and a movie night, but that revolves around snacks, and it wouldn't be ethical to exhaust our casks for the sake of familial bonding."

Scarlett, who's taken a seat in a high-backed Gothic-era chair, perches her chin on the back of her hand and smiles. "*My* casks certainly don't complain."

Camille tosses a party hat at her. "The baby is present."

I close my eyes and shake my head. Scarlett's pantry, as she calls it, is well-known in the vampire world for what it is—a harem. It's not taboo or shocking for us, and the casks are willing and *want* to be where they are. I'm hardly too young to handle the facts.

But I don't want to argue over it. After a month of being around people who think I'm weird and having to hide who I am, it's nice to have people I can be open around, even if I'm still learning to think of them as family.

"Isn't this nice?" Malcolm says as he takes a seat. "Much better than the attic, eh?"

"You really ought to move out of it," Camille says as she passes out Uno cards. "We prepared a lovely room for you when you came out of your thirst. I don't know why you insist on being around dusty objects."

"I *am* a dusty object," I counter.

"That reminds me, Scarlett, have you confirmed with the tailor for tomorrow?"

I tense. In all the stress of Rowan finding out, I'd blocked out that most of break would be spent preparing for the Feeding Ball. My attire has been handmade just for me. After the fitting, a vampiric dentist from NYC will be here to clean and examine my fangs. *Then* Malcolm has to go over contenders for which mortal will be given the honor of letting me drink their blood in front of everyone.

And to think Mockingbird Prep is abuzz with talk of the homecoming dance.

"Uno," a deep voice utters, and we all turn to Oscar. I hadn't even noticed him entering, but there he is at the end of a table, proudly holding a wild card and flexing his biceps. I'm glad he's been asked to play. Even if he *can* kick the stuffing out of me, I trust him, and he's actually really nice, considering he was a German headsman centuries ago.

Scarlett snatches the wild card. "You yell 'Uno' when you only have one card left."

"And it's my turn," Camille says as she lays down a green four.

"You can't play that." Scarlett points at the cards. "Malcolm played a wild. He said blue."

"When?"

"When Scarlett was explaining to Oscar," says Malcolm.

"I want it to be green," says Camille.

"It's not your wild card," says Scarlett.

Camille bats her eyelashes at Malcolm. "Darling, could we bury her in the backyard?"

My phone buzzes in my jeans pocket. That's odd. No one ever texts me. I sneak a glance but quickly shove it back when I see the strange number—and the text preview starting with who it is.

Why is Rowan texting me? I don't remember giving him my number.

"Wild card!" Scarlett announces. "Hmm . . . yellow. And it says draw four, Oscar. Sorry."

Buzz. I lay down a yellow card and sneak another look.

It will only take a minute.

What will only take a minute? Him and his cronies impaling me on a post in the town square? The citizens of Mockingbird burning Belamy Manor to the ground and staking all of us through the heart?

"Draw four," Malcolm says to Camille. "But I worship you, my queen."

"I'm going to bury *you* in the yard tonight," Camille responds. "But you may still worship me."

Buzz. Buzz. Buzz.

"When did you get friends?" Scarlett snaps. I lean back in my chair, shrinking under her red-glinting stare.

"I don't know," I say, my voice small.

"That's a risk," Scarlett reminds me.

"Getting along with mortals is necessary," Malcolm says wisely. "Take the call, son."

I grimace, trying to make it clear that I'd rather not. But when they don't resume the game and continue to look at me expectantly, I pull the phone from my pocket with a huff and dart from the dining room, ducking into the conservatory on the other end of the first floor.

"Yes?" I answer, making my tone as annoyed as possible.

"Oh!" Rowan's voice cracks on the other end. "Hi, Casper!"

"*Hi.*"

"What's up?"

I roll my eyes to the transparent glass ceiling. "*You* called *me.*"

"Right," he mutters. "Yeah . . . uh, sorry. I texted but . . . did you get my texts?"

"I didn't read them," I say, trying not to crush the phone in my grip.

"Okay," he sighs. "I only want to talk for a second. I was hoping you'd read the text. Uh . . . could you come to your porch?"

"Why?"

"Just come to the door!" he says, his voice shaking.

I grunt but stay on the call as I stomp out into the hall, making my way to the huge front door complete with panels of stained glass depicting a murder of crows. I pull it open, and—

Wood. Vanilla. Innocence.

Rowan whirls around, jumping at the sudden squeak of the door hinges, and almost drops the phone from his ear. Rowan Young is at my house. And under his jacket, he's wearing a *turtleneck*. My teeth grind in my sealed mouth.

He cracks a grin. "Hi."

Whack. I slam the door in his face and head toward the dining room, but when he doesn't knock and my phone doesn't buzz, I stop and consider. Glancing at the guards, I try to discern what they're thinking, but they only stare ahead.

I return to the door and crack it only enough to peer out. Rowan is still standing there, his shoulders slouched and his hands shoved in the pockets of his jeans, tracing his right foot along the black-and-silver welcome mat.

When he senses the door has reopened, he looks up, his eyes round and glossy, like a puppy who's urinated on the living room rug.

"What do you want?" I whisper, not wanting my family to hear.

He points a thumb over his shoulder down the hill of the front yard to the road, where his blue car is parked at the curb. "Do you want ice cream?" he asks, too loudly.

"Shh!" I wave my palm, and he flinches. "Do I *what*?"

"Sorry." He drops his voice. "Do you want to get ice cream?"

I point to my vampiric eyes. "Do you *think* I want ice cream?"

He cringes. "Oh. Right."

"What in the ninth circle of hell do you *want*?"

He rubs the back of his neck. "I've been processing everything."

I tilt my head, but he doesn't continue. It's a strange thing to see him like this, with his proverbial tail between his legs.

"How did you know where I live," I ask, "and how did you get my number?"

"Well, Dad has your number in his file," Rowan explains, "so I got that from him. As for your house, Mockingbird is small, and it's a really old historic house. It was kind of a thing when your parents bought it."

"Okay." But another question remains. "If you're out here, why didn't you ring the doorbell?"

His eyes widen into perfect circles. "Oh. I don't know."

I smirk. "You were afraid to, weren't you?"

"What? No!" He forces a laugh, dry and hollow in his throat. "What would I be afraid of?"

"COMPANY!" I shout as loudly as I can, pulling the door wide open and stepping back as Rowan's face goes from the light pink of embarrassment to the pale white of fear. The guards file out before they're seen.

"Company?" Camille singsongs as she tiptoes into the foyer, peering over my shoulder as she removes her party hat. "Who do we have here?"

Rowan looks as though he's about to shrink completely into his shoes. "Uh, hi . . . hi! I'm Rowan. Remember?"

"Of course; come in!" Camille takes him by the wrist and yanks him over the threshold.

This was a bad idea. Now Rowan is going to spill the truth, and then what? They'll have him killed for knowing too much?

Brushing past me, Rowan shoots me a look that practically spells out *SOS*, and this should be my moment to catch my mistake, but . . . okay, it's really satisfying to watch him be the odd man out for a change. I fold my arms and stick my tongue in my cheek.

"A boy!" Scarlett breathes from her new perch on the banister as she files her long nails. "We seem to collect those, don't we?"

"Down, girl," says Camille. "This is Casper's dorm mate, and he's far too young for you."

Camille links her arm around Rowan's, and he pales even more at the sight of her tiny hand wrapped around his bicep. Gently, he puts his free hand on hers and pries her off as subtly as he can. "I didn't mean to interrupt anything; I was passing by—"

He stumbles back—right into Oscar, who lets out a growl deep from his chest.

Rowan whirls and looks up at him.

"Uno. I achieved it." Oscar scowls at him.

Malcolm passes into the foyer and pats Oscar on the shoulder. "Easy, friend; you won."

Camille gestures to my roommate. "Everyone, this is Rowan, the headmaster's son!"

"Welcome to Belamy Manor, Rowan!" Malcolm says, thrusting his hand out. Rowan takes it absently. "Good shake! I noted that the first time we met."

"Thanks," says Rowan, and I don't think I've ever heard his voice hit that octave. "Uh. Nice house."

"It's Second Empire," Camille says. "We *adore* old houses."

"Good for dust," Scarlett adds, hopping off the banister and fixing Rowan with her narrowed gaze. "Are you aware that dust is made from tiny bits of people?"

"*Scarlett!*" Camille shoots her a warning look. "Ignore her. She has all the time in eternity to think up the most horrible things to say."

My shoulders tense. Ordinarily, I love that—sneaking eternal life in, hiding us in plain sight. But Rowan knows the truth, and Camille unknowingly left the door open for him to admit that. I shoot him a glare. He must sense me staring because he looks over at me, and I shake my head, hoping against hope he understands.

Rowan blinks at me, then them, taking each one in, and I worry that with each blink, he's going to faint. "Uh-huh. Well . . . um, I was grabbing ice cream and was passing by and-thought-I'd-see-what-my-buddy-Casper-was-doing-but-I'll-just-go-goodbye."

"Aw!" Camille coos. "It's sweet of you to invite him! I'm sure he'd love to go."

This is where I'm supposed to argue, but all I can do is gawk at Camille with angry eyes. I forced Rowan inside for my own sick amusement, not to be roped into spending one-on-one time with him. Besides, what if this is a trap? What if he just wants to lure me away so he and his goons can murder me?

"But," I stammer, "we're having *family night*."

"You should make time for your friends," Malcolm says with raised eyebrows and a pointed tone. He's made this a part of the test. Will Casper get through fake-eating ice cream with a jock who knows too much, or will he go to vampire prison without ever seeing a homecoming dance?

"Yes, absolutely," says Camille with a knowing grin. "Go ahead, honey."

"You heard your mother." Malcolm lunges and practically pushes me through the front door as Rowan uses the opportunity to hop over the threshold and escape. I hear a papery rustle as Malcolm pulls up the hem of my sweater and shoves money in my pocket, whispering, "You'll do fine."

"You don't get it," I mutter to him, "I don't like him."

"Fine. But he can't hang around here," Malcolm responds. "And he clearly wants to make nice, so make nice and show that people like us are safe."

And with that, he pushes me through the door and closes it behind me.

Rowan stands with one foot on the porch and one on the steps. His knees are trembling. "See?" he chokes. "Not afraid."

I fold my arms and size him up. "Tell me what you need to tell me, please."

With a deep breath, Rowan declares, "I'm an asshole."

"I'd heard rumors."

Rowan grunts and stomps back onto the porch. "No, really! I've been an asshole to you. And I'm . . ." The next words sound like the hardest thing he's ever had to say. "I'm sorry."

He tilts his head down but keeps his eyes on me, and I straighten up involuntarily, fiddling with the hem of my sweater, suddenly feeling very exposed. "Why?"

"Well." The word leaves his mouth like a sigh. "I thought you were weird and mean. But now I know why, and . . . I freaked out, and I didn't understand, but I've been rooting around online and kinda fell down a rabbit hole, a lot of theories about, you know . . . and processed a lot, and . . . like, I'm not totally completely there yet, but I can tell you aren't lying when you say you're a . . . you know."

"A vampire," I say.

"That," Rowan says, and I'll admit, it stings a little that he avoids saying it. "But, I don't know, I figured if you were going to drink my blood, you would have by now."

A silence hangs between us, waiting for forgiveness. Finally, Rowan takes another step back down the porch and says, "Like I said, I'm going to get ice cream. I know you don't eat it, but I want to know more about how all this works. Do you want to come and talk?"

I can tell he's trying, which is the best scenario I could have hoped for. But this is Rowan Young. The one who spied on and badgered me since I set foot on campus. The guy who called me a demon and assumed I'd assault him with my fangs.

I look him square in the eyes. "I'd rather be buried alive."

Rowan raises his eyebrows. "That's dramatic. But okay."

He spins and makes his way down the winding porch steps,

toward the road. I watch him make his way, then look back to the house. Something clicks. Malcolm said it: show that people like me are safe. That we *don't* bite the unwilling or pose a threat to mankind. That we aren't demons.

Rowan knows what I am, and for whatever reason, he's trying to understand. Shouldn't I allow that? Isn't that for the better?

"Wait!" I call out, and Rowan looks back with hopeful surprise. "Let me grab my house key."

CHAPTER NINE
ROWAN

It was a lie—that I'm not afraid, I mean. How could I not be? I went to a house full of vampires (which, I'm still processing, somehow exist), and proceeded to drive away with one in my passenger seat. The same one who recently killed a huge deer right in front of me— by biting it in the jugular with his *fangs!*

Inches away from me, Casper is as still as a gargoyle, watching Main Street roll by, its storefronts draped in garlands of autumn leaves and guarded by scarecrows with jack-o'-lanterns for heads. When we pause at a light, he turns fully to get a look inside a coffee shop, an open mic night advertised in chalk on the clapboard outside. Inside, the room is crowded with poets and indie guitarists.

Is he deciding which artist to make a human latte out of? I wrestle against a shiver as this fact bubbles up once again— vampires are real, and Casper is one. That's what I came to learn about, not constantly wonder how murderous he is. Perhaps he's just people-watching, like all of us do.

It's been silent save the voice of Hamish Hawk piping through the car speakers. When I realize the song is "Think of Us Kissing", I grip the wheel so hard my knuckles turn white.

The light changes, and I drive on, picking up speed until we come to the stone bridge that ends Main Street and leads into the woods between downtown and the outskirts. I urge myself to say something, but teeth and death are the only topics I can think of, and that's not a safe start. I'm not even fully sure of what exactly I wanted to talk about. I just knew somewhere in my core that I needed to see Casper. To let him explain, if he wants to, and then maybe, somehow, everything with him and the branch and the stake will make sense.

"Where are you going?" Casper ends the silence, one hand gripping the passenger door handle.

"Driving," I say too loudly. "Why?"

"No way is there an ice cream place out here. This is a trick, isn't it?"

I pull around a curve. "No. I don't know where I'm going; I just want to talk."

"Okay." Casper doesn't let go of the handle. "Go ahead."

I force myself to ask the first thing that comes to mind. "Are you actually a super old man?"

A closed-mouthed grunt is Casper's first response. "No. Not all vampires are centuries old. I really am seventeen. I was turned recently."

"Turned?" I slow to a stop as a train rolls past. "You mean got bit?"

"By another vampire, yes."

"So, it was a choice?" I ask. "To be what you are?"

Casper's eyes widen, and he slowly looks to me, head tilted. I feel practically naked when he does. "Are you talking about the vampirism or . . .?"

"Yes!" I answer as quickly as I can, and my cheeks flush with heat. "I know being gay isn't a choice. Why would I ask that?"

"I don't know where you're going with this or what you want," says Casper, and I'm unable to respond. Why would I show up at his house to find out about being gay?

I'm here to learn about vampires, not . . . whatever it is Casper does with other guys.

"There isn't a tried-and-true process for getting to know a . . . a . . ."

"A vampire," Casper finishes for me. "You can say it. Train's gone; you can drive."

I ease the car over the tracks. "A vampire. There. I guess my big question is what are you doing in boarding school if you're a vampire? Like, what's the end game?"

"I have to prove that I can be around mortals and not bite them. Or be discovered. You ruined that last part."

"So we're test dummies?" I let out a cackle, though it's anything but funny. "Mock is just an obstacle course to you?"

"More or less." Casper shrugs, ignoring my second cackle. "Malcolm and Camille are . . . really important in our world. It's necessary for any vampire to learn to live with mortals, but it's extra important for me. If I go rabid and kill people, others could follow. But most vampires don't do that. We're trying to live our eternal lives in peace."

Before stopping myself, I say, "You're not exactly doing a bang-up job."

"What does that mean?"

My foot leans on the gas as I take another curve, the dark, tree-lined road illuminated only by the car's headlights. "You've been kind of a prick, no offense. And you act suspicious. People might not notice so much if you'd dial it down."

Casper flips the music off. When he speaks, his voice is so quiet I can barely stand the murmur in my ears. "I should dial. It. Down?"

"I just meant—"

"Do you think I want to be the only vampire at school?" Each syllable rises in volume, and my hands wring the steering wheel, tensing, expecting the worst. "Don't you think I wanted to blend in? Don't you think I would be much happier if I *weren't* different?!"

"This is exactly what I mean!"

"Look out!"

The headlights cut across an opossum panicking in the road. I jerk the steering wheel and swerve, slamming the break. We skid to a halt. My arm reaches over on instinct, slamming Casper against his seat. He's so cold it burns even through his sweater. My arm drops from Casper's chest to his thigh.

"Watch it." He shoos my hand off, and I squirm, stammering. I don't even know why I did that.

But I don't have time to explain. I unbuckle my seatbelt and swing the door open, marching around the hood to inspect the front. The bumper grazed against a guardrail, leaving a horrible gray streak.

"It's brand new!" I half-shout, my heart hammering. Dad bought it straight from the factory for my birthday back in March. He's going to kill me.

Kill . . . kill . . . where's the opossum? I blink, looking around, until my eyes fall on Casper.

He's standing in the middle of the road, his breath heaving. A low growl quivers from his throat. He's staring straight down at the half-dead opossum squirming and shrieking between his feet. Blood is gushing from its side.

My stomach feels nauseous. I did that. I've never hit an animal before.

But Casper's fingers are twitching, and his eyes are glowing that poisonous, radioactive violet. His jaw lengthens.

"No!" I rush forward, pushing my hand against his bicep. "Leave it alone!"

He pushes me back with a force I should have expected but didn't. I fall against the trunk of the car and stare, spellbound, as he opens his mouth and lifts his right index finger to his left fang. He bites with a pronounced wince, and a trickle of his own blood, so dark red it's almost black, runs down his hand.

Lowering his finger, he kneels, scoops the opossum up into his arms as though it's an infant. "Shh," he whispers. "Deep breath."

I cover my mouth with the back of my hand as I watch him

plunge his finger maybe two inches into the creature's side.

"We function like mortals," Casper says softly, over the quieting cries of the opossum. "Our hearts beat, so we have blood that pumps through our veins. We have cells. Blood of the living is what rejuvenates us and allows us to live forever. But we heal like mortals. Albeit at a faster rate."

The opossum is silent now as Casper pulls his finger gently from the wound, but he leaves it pressed against the creature's body. It . . . I can't believe it. It's sleeping in Casper's arms, it's side completely closed. If not for the blood congealing in its fur, it would look as though the collision never happened.

"So it only makes sense that our blood can help others." His eyes, Siberian-husky-blue, flick to me. "Repair injuries, pass on a little youth. But only if we act fast, and if the circumstances are right. If you hadn't have hit him just right, he'd be gone."

I stare down at the opossum as Casper gently lays it on the ground. It leaps to its paws and scurries away, not asleep after all. "I thought you were going to finish it off."

"Don't think I didn't want to," Casper says, rising to his full height and slipping his hands into his pockets. He looks sheepish at this confession. "I'd have gotten to him faster if I wasn't fighting against the thirst."

"Fighting against . . ." I shake my head. "So, it's like a choice thing? Don't make that face. You know what I mean."

Casper sighs. "Yes. I can control it. But I'm new to it, so I don't always succeed. And, as my family says, I'm a growing vampire. I require more right now, hence the whole stag."

It's a lot to take in. A few nights ago, I found out that the reason Casper is such an asshole is because he's a bona fide creature of the night. Who might kill me in my sleep. Or my friends. Now I'm finding out he mends wounds and will pause to help the most despised woodland animal in the country?

"So, you're like . . . a nice vampire?" I say, fighting a cringe.

The smirk becomes a toothy smile. His mouth is back to normal, the fangs gone. Maybe it's the way the moonlight falls on him, or the intensity of everything, but my eyes linger on his lips—those pink, full lips that shouldn't exist—and on the slight mischievous dimple in his right cheek.

I'll admit it this once . . . he's pretty. For a guy.

"Well," I say slowly, smoothing a hand through my hair. What am I even *doing*? "I'm sure you're ready to get away from me now that I've grilled you."

Casper looks to the car, his lips twisting in thought. He smirks again, and I try not to notice (but *definitely* notice) the dimple of mischief appear again. "What, I save an animal's life and don't even get an ice cream?"

"It tastes like how a stable smells." Casper spits the ice cream into a napkin, and I snort. "I don't know how mortals eat this stuff."

"Because it's delicious!" I hold up the clear plastic cup. "Cookie dough ice cream is the greatest gift mankind ever received. I mean, it's cookies *and* ice cream! And you get to eat dough *raw!*" I take another spoonful and kick my legs like a child from my perch on the picnic table to emphasize my delight.

Casper rolls his eyes. "It's fifty degrees. How can you even eat it right now?"

"Hot-blooded," I say. "People gather around me when it's cold. I'm basically a baked potato. Speaking of hot blood"—Casper's eyes widen—"you said you have to drink blood, but why?"

"Why do you need clean water?" Casper retorts, and I shrug. "If I don't drink blood for a while, I get weird—rude, mean. Then come the headaches. Eventually, I start shaking. If it goes on long enough, I'll lose my mind. A lot of vampires have lost their humanity by being starved. We call them ferals."

"So, to keep your humanity, you have to consume humanity," I say. "That's . . . messed up."

"Well, it's vampirism," Casper says. "You're given eternal youth and beauty, but there's a price. Luckily, we can get by on animals, or casks."

"What's that?"

"It's kind of scandalous to mortals."

I lean in, intrigued.

"A cask," he explains, "is a mortal who seeks out vampires. They want us to feed on them. Not to drain them, though. They want to live with us. As our pets, I guess. Or like living bottles of wine."

My mouth hangs open, and I blink. "That's a *thing*? Do they, you know . . . with vampires?"

"Yes, in most cases," says Casper with a matter-of-fact tone, but I'm floored. "It's common in our world. Some vampires have a whole group of them. Scarlett, my aunt, has ten. It's called a pantry."

"Ten men who want her to drink from them?" I can't believe what I'm hearing, and I can't stop listening.

"Not just men. She's an equal-opportunity vampire." Casper smiles.

"Wow," I say. "I saw people who wanted to be bit when I fell into my Discord rabbit hole, but I didn't know the extent."

"You can't find this stuff online," explains Casper.

"Okay, what about crosses?"

"Not true," Casper says, and I take another bite of ice cream. "Neither is holy water."

"Garlic?"

"It smells pretty damned strong"—Casper shrugs—"but it's not going to kill me."

"Do you have a reflection?"

"Unfortunately," he says. "I'd be okay with never looking at my malnourished-scarecrow self again."

"Dude, you're hot," I say before I catch myself. Casper blinks at me. "What? I can tell if another guy is attractive. It's not fair how hot you are."

Casper rolls his eyes. "It's the vampire glow. I assure you, I'm ugly."

My feelings hurt *for* him. How could a guy who looks like him ever think of himself as ugly? I assumed he knew how hot he was, which was half the problem. If I keep insisting, however, it's going to come across as weird, so I drop it.

"So, as long as you feed and don't get chopped into bits or burned alive, you live forever?" I ask.

"Yes."

I take one more bite of the melting ice cream. When I look at Casper, it's different now. I don't see an incredibly pale, moody, unfairly attractive guy. The eased tension between us has made him different. Lighter. He's almost glowing. He looks *mortal*.

"You have a drip on your chin," Casper points out. I barely hear him; I'm still studying his face. "Rowan?"

"Oh." I lift my hand mechanically and wipe my chin. For a split second, I thought he was going to reach out and do it for me. Did I *want* him to? "Thanks."

Sleep has eluded me after hanging out with Casper and somehow ending up glad that I did. Now, lying awake, he's all I can think about. That's not new. What's new is the *way* I've been thinking about him. Even when Dad pressed me for information about where I went and who with, all I could think of was his fingers against my goosebumped skin.

Something moves at the foot of my bed.

I prop myself up on my elbows and stare wide-eyed into the dark, unable to speak, as a form takes shape before me. It's dark, and yet I can see everything because there's a fire in the large Gothic fireplace, the mantle carved of gargoyles and bats. Since when was there a fireplace in my dorm room?

Two ice-blue eyes shadowed by dark eyebrows appear at the foot of the bed.

Casper Belamy crawls onto the bed, his white satin shirt unbuttoned, revealing his long, veiny neck and pale, smooth chest. His hands brush along my legs, up over my knees. When did I lose my blanket? He appears sullen, with dark circles under his incredible Technicolor eyes. His lips pout in a melancholic expression.

He's going to kiss me. Casper is going to kiss me, and I need him to do it now, before I turn feral and lose my humanity.

His long fingers run up my cheek and through my hair as he pushes my head to the side.

Sharp pain shoots through my neck, and all I see is blood, blood, and more blood.

All I feel is pain and teeth and warm, wet blood. And I want more. But the dream fades, and soon I'm awake, for real this time, panting and hugging myself in my room at home, afraid of what this dream could mean. Afraid that I want to dream it again.

CHAPTER TEN
CASPER

It's been five days since we returned to Mockingbird Prep, and I'm already desperate for it to be winter break.

After my and Rowan's ice cream excursion, I'd thought perhaps things had turned around a little, that maybe we had started some kind of friendship. But that's not the case. If he's in the room when I get back from classes, he suddenly has plans with his friends. If I accidentally wake him up when I'm leaving to feed, he remembers an assignment due date and scurries to one of the common rooms.

He doesn't pick fights or give me a hard time anymore, but I almost preferred that to being ignored and avoided.

I've come to appreciate the hours spent in class. Now that I've figured out how to feed well and keep the cravings to a minimum, I can actually concentrate around my classmates. And learning gives me something to focus on that *isn't* Rowan, when I'm invested enough.

The caveat is drama. I still regret signing up for this class. In here, I can't just focus on the lesson and let everything else fade. Here, I have to participate, whether it's doing improv with a group (which I loathe) or being constantly told by Mrs. Spencer to "make bold choices" (whatever that means).

Today, however, she's once again ranting about auditions for *Pippin* and reminding me of the biggest reason why I shouldn't have enrolled.

"Remember, it's mandatory," she pauses while passing out scripts, her free hand clamping shut the book I'm reading as she gives me a sidelong glance. "You can't pass this course without auditioning."

No one else seems to mind, but it makes my insides turn to ash.

"Since you were wise enough to take this course, you have a leg up," she continues. "Chemistry is incredibly important in this particular libretto, so today, we'll work on being good scene partners. Pair up and read through it multiple times, and *really* listen to each other. React accordingly. We'll present at the end of the hour."

I swallow a groan. It's already difficult being a pariah, but "pair up" means that someone who doesn't act fast enough will get stuck with me, and it will be awkward. "Pair up" transforms a whole class of drama students into Rowan clones.

Except there's a hand on my shoulder. I turn around and find myself face to face with a girl with dark skin and glasses. "Would you like to be partners?"

I clutch my book to my chest. What's the catch? No one picks me first. Surely, there's a joke in here, and I'm about to be the punchline. But if I say no and avoid it, then I'm the jackass. So I nod. "Okay."

She snatches the book and inspects it. "I love *The Starless Sea*! You're at a good part. How are you just now reading this?"

"I've read it twice, actually," I say, gently pulling it back. "I read so fast that I run out of material."

"Me too," she says. "I only read queer fic, though. Not much of that to find around here. Sophie Campbell." She tips an invisible hat in a gentlemanly nod. "Bookworm, burgeoning star, and professional pain in the ass. You're Casper."

"Belamy . . . uh, bookworm. Undead royalty. Perpetually unimpressed."

Sophie snorts, squeezing her eyes tight. Her laugh and smile seem genuine, and I'm suddenly glad we're doing partner work. "Not bad on the fly."

If only she knew I wasn't joking.

"Uh-oh, here comes trouble," Sophie groans with a humorous air as two other people make their way toward us. "They're definitely going to annoy us."

"It's okay," I say.

"We're adopting Casper," Sophie nods to me, presenting me to a girl. A boy slides to her side and crooks his finger under the back hem of her sweater. Must be the boyfriend. "Don't scare him away, please."

I note that Sophie doesn't bother to properly introduce me, and I can't help but feel a little guilty. I've expertly avoided learning any of their names until now. I suppose I'm lucky they're even bothering this far into the year. I smile a little bigger and hope that I appear friendly and not ravenous for blood.

"Hi!" the girl says, dropping into the seat of the nearest desk and smoothing out her skirt. Her blonde hair is curled, and I note the hint of a pink streak hiding beneath a curl she's pulled back. "Dakota Gibbs."

"Theater girl, horse girl," Sophie says, "indelicate narcissist."

"You can sleep in the hall tonight," Dakota says.

"She's also my roommate, so I'm allowed to call her out."

The boy is looking at Dakota like he's watching the most delicious cupcake being pulled fresh from the oven. Finally, he pulls his eyes to me.

"Quentin Knoll," he says, extending his hand.

"Casper Belamy." I extend my hand, though I don't want to, and instantly find myself in a contest to see whose grip is tighter.

"Quentin's a chronic mama's boy," Sophie says. "Effervescent. Layered as mille-feuille."

He shoots Sophie a dark glare, and she snorts.

Dakota rolls her eyes. "Sophie, stop trying to boil people down to three things. And don't compare my boyfriend to a dessert."

Sophie looks to Quentin for confirmation. "Am I wrong?"

"I don't know what mille-fwee-fwee is," Quentin shrugs. "But I accept it."

"That's why I'm okay with you," Sophie says and then looks to me. "You must understand, Casper, that Quentin here seems to think he's heterosexual. It's a phase, Quentin."

"It better not be," Dakota giggles.

Quentin grunts as he sits next to her, making sure he protectively puts his arm around her shoulder.

"Dude, you gonna help me out?" he asks me, smiling.

"I don't know you," I say, watching his face drop. Oh. Was he trying to bond? "But . . . no, I don't think it's just a phase. Quentin's effervescent, as you say."

"Thanks," he says, but then narrows his eyes. "You came from abroad? Germany or something?"

"Belgium," I say. "I uh . . . it was okay. But I don't want to talk about it, if that's alright."

Sophie's eyebrows lift with an air of conspiracy. "Leave boy trouble behind?"

That can work. "Yeah."

"I feel you," she nods, dropping to sit crisscross, leaving me no choice but to join. "Me and my girlfriend broke up over the summer. I couldn't wait to come back here . . . What?"

I look away. To my knowledge, I haven't met anyone else at school who's out. "Nothing," I say, "just glad you get it."

"Ahem," a voice above us snags our attention. Mrs. Spencer taps her watch. "It's theatre time, not gossip time."

She moves along, and Dakota shoots Sophie a wide eye.

Sophie hands me a script with another toothy smile. "See? Us theatre kids aren't as feral as everyone thinks."

Perhaps I feel a little more at home with her, or perhaps it's just that I sense she can be as creepy as I can, because I say with total honesty, "I *was* feral once. I tried to filet a mailman."

She snorts. "Yeah. Puberty's a bitch."

It took a month or so, but I might have made a mortal friend. Scarlett would tell me that it's too dangerous, but Malcolm would applaud me. I'm not sure who I agree with, but it *is* sort of nice to have someone who isn't Rowan speak to me.

After drama, I opted to head to the library in lieu of pretending to eat in the dining hall. Sophie hasn't left my side, chatting on and on about her background. How she's from Louisville but her parents send her here. She has two older brothers and one niece who's five. She's been in and out of love since she can remember but has no recollections of finding it in the right place. I sense she's wanting me to reciprocate, but I can't tell her much without giving it away.

"What role are you hoping for in *Pippin*?" she asks as I push through the double doors leading into the library.

"Stagehand number four," I say.

"Booshwash, kiddo." A voice comes around one of the stacks, and Mr. Abadi appears. "You got moxie! We're gonna make ya a star!"

"One that burned out a millennium ago," I say.

"Not even close," he tsks, and Sophie shoots me an expression that says, *See?* "The minute you do the audition, you've already succeeded more than others. Some are too afraid to even try."

"Thanks."

"You're welcome," he says, then presses a finger to his lips as he makes his way to the desk. "Now *shh*! This is a library!"

"God, I love him," I admit.

"Me too. I feel bad for him," Sophie's eyes darken. "He deserves to be happy."

"What do you mean?"

"He was widowed recently," Sophie says. "Anyways, let's get to browsing. I need my fic fix."

My lips form an O shape. I never would have guessed by Abadi's upbeat demeanor that he was grieving. I feel bad for him. I've never been in love, but I can't imagine losing that person and having to live in a dorm with a bunch of obnoxious teenagers. No wonder he talks to books.

But my empathy is erased by an all-too-familiar laugh. Rowan struts into the library, heading for the tables with his book bag slung over his shoulder and his goons in tow.

Must he *strut* in his school trousers and button down? He just wants everyone to check him out because he knows how good he looks. And knowing how good he looks makes me even angrier.

"I'm going to nonfiction," I say, but Sophie flashes me a suspicious look as I go, as though she's wondering whether I'm browsing the books or my dorm mate.

I quicken my step to avoid the path of you-know-who, but it was the wrong choice. Rowan has entered this stack, too, and I'm forced to acknowledge him.

"Hi," I half-whisper.

Rowan raises his eyebrows at me as though he's offended that I'm talking to him, then turns back to the books. "I can't talk right now," he whispers back.

Seriously, what did I *do* to him? Answer every question he asked me? Get along with him for a minute?

"Ooo-*kay*," I whisper.

I just need to grab a book, any book, and get out of here. But as I reach for one, another hand appears. Our skin brushes, palm grazes knuckles, and Rowan's hand is suddenly right on top of mine.

He jerks away, stumbling back. "Sorry," he says. "Bad timing."

His scent envelopes my brain, and my eyes involuntarily roll back. The feeling of his hand on mine is still there, and my stomach and chest feel like they're on fire.

Blood. Now. His. Please.

"It's fine," I gasp. "It's . . . bye."

I dart out of the stack and out of the library, not stopping when Sophie calls after me. I don't need any of this: friends, a school play, whatever *this* is with my dorm mate.

CHAPTER ELEVEN
ROWAN

"What was that about?" Diego looks up when I return to our table with a random book I grabbed but don't actually need clutched to my chest. "What was going on with Casper?"

I sense Sophie behind me. She followed me the instant Casper left, also wondering why I freaked out and he fled.

"Nothing," I say, tightening my grip on the book. "At all."

Reed, in the middle of drawing a python on his homework, drops his pen. "I thought you two hated each other."

"I don't *hate* him," I say, but I need to be careful. I haven't told them about hanging out with Casper over break. I don't know how to without also clueing them in to the fact that he's a vampire. Or that I've been dreaming about him. Almost every night. And that it makes being around him even more difficult. "We just don't get along very well."

"Hmm." Diego's eyes scan over me.

"What?" I ask, dropping the book on the table as casually as I can.

"Nothing," says Diego. "Just a 'hmm'."

I need to get myself together before I confirm anything with my actions. Last thing I need on top of everything is for Diego and Reed to figure out I find Casper physically attractive, and that while I'll admit to myself that I've found other guys attractive before, this feels . . . different.

I jump at a loud squeak, but it's only Abadi, rolling his cart in and out of the stacks, whispering to himself as he returns each book to its shelf. I need to calm down.

I take my seat. Then I look down and finally see what book I grabbed. *You're So Gay: A Guide To Your Sexuality*. I yelp and slide the book onto my lap. Diego and Reed jump, half-standing with concern. Two tables away, Dakota and Sophie look up from their phones.

I force a laugh. "Thought I saw a centipede. They freak me out. You know what? I don't need this book; I'm going to put it back."

Reed squints at the book as I stand and try to shove it under my arm. "Is that—"

"About cars?" I ask, beelining from the table. "Dude, *yes*. Engines, oil, and grease. Macho-macho-macho."

That was stupid. We have never discussed cars. I don't even think I could tell the difference between models. But there's no backtracking now. I rush into the stacks where I grabbed the book.

But the gap I took it from isn't empty. Someone has left behind a folded sheet of paper, a silver twig sticking from its folds. I reach for it.

A note is scrawled in chicken scratch with purple ink.

Mr. Young,

By now you will be wondering who we are and what we want with you.

Your presence is required at midnight in the alley outside the old chapel. You will have received your pendant and a branch. These are our identifiers. Please have the pendant around your neck and hold the branch where it can clearly be seen. When asked, provide the password 'Attercopp'. Do not reveal your identity to the others. Only I shall know you.

Your discretion is key to all our safety, especially where your roommate is concerned. Your attendance is vital to our success.

Even before I was a student at Mock, I was always here. Running around the quad and the side yards, eavesdropping, waiting for Dad to finish work. I've never heard a whisper of a secret society.

I've reread the note over and over, trying to spot some clue or something that might give away who may have written it.

Sophie followed me to the tables the minute Casper left. Diego and Reed were at the tables, right? The only other person in the library was Abadi, but if the librarian is the sponsor, wouldn't it be too obvious to give me the note there?

Whoever my "sponsor" is, they're good at coming and going unseen.

I spent the rest of the evening in my room, trying not to let on as Casper scrolled through an online script for *Pippin*. He's so worried about this audition thing that he didn't notice as I continued to examine the letter. Or when the time came and I nestled the twig in the inner pocket of my jacket and explained I was going to play video games with Diego and Reed in their room.

I tried not to notice how cute he looked, lying on his stomach, poring over his script and sheet music, his feet twitching to songs I couldn't hear. I'm glad *someone* is able to focus around here.

Now I'm making my way to the old chapel, putting the chain around my neck and fumbling with the pendant. I haven't been able to figure out what kind of branch it is, or what the tiny wooden berries indicate. Between school and football and this whole "your arguably hot roommate is undead and drinks the blood of the living" thing, I haven't had the time to fall down botanical rabbit holes.

There was *one* hint in the letter: Attercopp. Also known as the ship that brought the first settlers to what became Mockingbird. Considering my family lineage and our connection to the ship, I wonder if the society is some sort of local history thing—some rich kid's club dedicated to making ourselves feel high and mighty.

Other than that, I have no answers. But that's about to change. I head down the alley, the stone steps leading to the chained double doors of the old chapel.

A breeze cuts down the alley, bringing with it a flurry of dried autumn leaves, and I shiver, pulling my jacket tighter around me. Leaning against a framed poster for a previous school production of *Beauty and the Beast,* I look up and down the alley for whoever my "sponsor" must be, but there is no movement. No noise, either, beyond the leaves scraping against the pavement as they roll past.

Could it have been Casper all along? Is this a test to see if I'll tell anyone about him?

Or did he want an excuse to meet me?

I shake my head and groan, turning to eye my reflection in the glass that protects the poster from the elements, and I stare myself down, my face like a ghost across an illustration of a dying rose. "No," I tell myself.

In the reflection, an extra pair of eyes appear behind me, seemingly from nowhere.

A hand presses between my shoulder blades and shoves me against the poster. The air is knocked out of me, and my hands rise instinctively, like I'm under arrest. "Oh my god," I wheeze.

"Password," they demand. The voice is unrecognizable, warped, deep, filtered through some sort of voice changer hidden within their mask.

"A-Attercop," I spit out, my voice higher than I thought it could ever go.

The person doesn't respond. They lift their free hand, and I'm about to make a break for it when everything goes dark as a scratchy sack is pulled over my head.

I smell must. And mildew. Old wood.

"Watch your step," the voice says, mechanical and static as they guide me, stumbling, over a stone floor.

The air temperature drops; my jacket does little to keep me warm. Suddenly, more low, mechanical voices whisper all around me.

Sweat drips from my hair down my forehead, the sack and the adrenaline suffocating me. I fear I'm being led to my execution. When my kidnapper takes my wrists, ties them behind my back, and then spins me around, I worry that fear is correct.

"Sit slowly," they order, and I obey. The back of my legs brush against a wooden stool.

"The Order shall now turn," the voice says, and I hear the scuffing of feet. A moment later, the sack is yanked off my head.

I gasp, my cheeks suddenly freezing. Moonlight streaming through the lattice and stained-glass windows helps my eyes adjust, and I take in a circle of white pillars that climb to the chipped and faded ceiling, painted with a fresco of angels dispatching demons with long swords.

Someone moves, and I finally get a good look at my kidnapper. A black robe hides their body, and a glossy black mask covers their face, a number twelve painted on the forehead in what seems like it could be bright red blood. I can't see their eyes. Two white irises have been painted on either side of the mask, with tiny pinpricks for them to see through.

They lift something metal—a real sword. I stand to run, but they reach out and push me back down. When I'm seated again, they pull something else from within their robe.

A black mask, exactly like theirs, except instead of a number twelve, there's a number thirteen on the forehead. After they give me a chance to see it, they slip it over my face, and my cheeks are back to broiling with the heat of adrenaline.

Then they remove their robe, only to reveal another beneath it. The discarded one is pulled around me.

"The Order will turn again," the kidnapper says.

Fabric and shoes swish and shuffle as a circle of robes turn and step forward. One, two, three, seven, ten—I quickly count twelve of them, including the kidnapper, all in black masks with different red numbers on the foreheads, the only thing differentiating them.

"The Thirteenth Son will remain silent," the kidnapper says, and I shudder. That must be me. "The Order shall now sit."

I didn't notice the chairs, high-backed and ornate with more of those branches carved out of wood, until everyone takes a seat and places their gloved hands on their thighs. They sit so still it's like I'm staring at twelve robed statues.

The kidnapper lifts the sword, and I wince, but they tilt it to the side, holding the blade delicately with one hand and the handle with the other.

"The First Son will now call us to order," they say.

The one with a number one painted on their forehead springs to life, standing and stepping forward with heavy booted footfalls. Number Twelve bows, presenting the sword to them. They take it, and Number Twelve slinks away to their own chair.

The First Son's mask isn't black and smooth like the others— it's rough and brown like tree bark, with splatters of red running down it, so real that for a second, I almost think they're dripping.

"This meeting of the Order of the Blackthorns is called to order," the First Son says, their voice deep and warped. *Blackthorn.* That must be what the branches are. "The Thirteenth Son will not speak and will only indicate his answers by a shake or a nod of his head. Does the Thirteenth Son understand?"

I'm trembling, but I nod.

They swing the sword toward my neck, making me jump. But I sigh when they place it gently on my shoulder, as though to knight me.

"If you lie at any point during my questioning, you will feel the blade," they promise. "It has come to my attention that you are aware of the existence of an undead, demonic presence on campus. Is this true?"

Demonic presence? Do they mean Casper? I nod, feeling queasy.

"Do you believe in the existence of the demon known as vampire?"

I nod.

"The Sponsor of the Thirteenth Son will come forward to give their recommendation," the First Son says; it's the one with the number twelve, my kidnapper, who stands.

"The Thirteenth Son has kept an eye upon the demon since its arrival the evening before the first day of term," the Sponsor explains. "His suspicion demonstrated the presence of the sixth sense of the hunter which runs through each of our veins. The Sponsor is well aware of the identity of the Thirteenth Son, and the Sponsor verifies the Thirteenth Son's lineage, which can be traced to a prominent passenger of the *Attercop*.

"The Thirteenth Son became aware of the identity of the demon the night before commencement of our autumn break," the Sponsor continues, "As witnessed by myself during my evening watch. This in hand with his lineage leads to my recommendation of his appointment. Furthermore, the Sponsor notes that the Thirteenth Son is from an upstanding and influential family of Mockingbird. The family has shown they are dedicated to upholding the ideals and traditions of our history, and the Sponsor believes that the Thirteenth Son will be committed to fighting back against the indoctrinating forces of the demon. Thank you."

Each member claps their gloved hands three times in sync.

What did that even mean, my family upholds the traditions and all that? Indoctrinating forces? Casper isn't trying to make anyone a vampire that I'm aware of. He's hiding what he is, so . . . I don't know, but I don't like the way this sits.

The First Son stands as the Sponsor takes their seat. "The Order of the Blackthorns will now vote. All in favor of the Thirteenth Son's appointment shall stand."

All of them stand. If only they weren't wearing robes, I would be able to notice *something* to put together later.

"It has been a unanimous vote. The Thirteenth Son shall be appointed to the Order."

They clap three times, and the First Son sweeps the sword's blade from my shoulder to just below my chin.

"Does the Thirteenth Son vow to protect our town and our way of life from the forces of evil invading our school?"

When I don't answer, they press the sword harder beneath my chin. I don't have a choice but to agree, do I? Slowly, I nod.

"Does the Thirteenth Son vow allegiance to the Blackthorns, to ward off the evil that will corrupt us all?"

I nod.

"The Thirteenth Son"—they lower the sword to my shoulder— "you are appointed to the Order of the Blackthorns. You, along with your brothers, are tasked with protecting Mockingbird Preparatory Academy and Mockingbird Town from the presence of undead demons. You will henceforth hold the title of Page, until such time we deem you worthy of advancement, when you will then come to know our identities. You will continue to be observed by your Sponsor, who will continue to ensure that you repeat nothing of tonight, the Order, or the existence of the demon. Your silence is paramount to the safety of your friends and yourself."

They press the sword against my neck, and I fight to keep from wincing. "The Sponsor will return the Thirteenth Son to the alley. The Thirteenth Son shall then return to their dorm and await further instruction. This meeting of the Blackthorns is adjourned."

CHAPTER TWELVE
CASPER

"Rowan?" I shake the side of his mattress with my hand, afraid that he'll blow up if I nudge his shoulder. "*Rowan?*"

With a soft cry, Rowan lifts his head and looks around, his eyes wide and confused. He blinks at me, and for a moment, I notice the hint of a smirk before its replaced with a dark scowl. "What?" he asks, his tone a threat.

"I think you were having a nightmare," I say. "You were crying out and pleading."

He doesn't respond at first, looking at the space just beyond my left ear. Finally, he sits up and spots his covers that have fallen to the floor. "I'm good," he says, though he doesn't sound good. He sounds pissed off. "Thanks."

"Sure," I say, unsure what to do now. He looks like a mad scientist, his bed head causing his hair to sit straight up and stick out every which way. Plus, he's pale, and not just because his summer tan has faded. As far as I can tell, the blood has left his face. My eyes drift down his body against their will, and—

Rowan Young is incredibly stiff.

"Here." I kick the covers up with my foot and toss them over

Rowan. "Try to relax."

He glares at me, and the paleness is suddenly gone, replaced with the light pink of a blush. Does he realize I just saw how hard he was?

"I'm going out," I say. "Um . . . goodnight?"

"Mmph," is all he manages.

When I'm out in the hallway, I pause with my hand on the doorknob, processing. The murmurs, the cries, the pleas, and the . . . Rowan was *not* having a nightmare, and I absolutely just woke him during one of *those* dreams.

I should be mortified. I *am* mortified, but . . . I cover my mouth as a huge, open-mouthed grin betrays me. Poor mortal Rowan. I'm sure the last thing he needed was for me to stand over him and notice his whole being betray him. I head to the staircase and start thinking about what creature I'd like to drink from tonight, but all I can think about is Rowan's blushing face.

I reach the first landing on my way down the stairs and pause. A pang is tightening my chest. My stomach is flipping like it's home to a Cirque du Soleil troop. Is this . . . is this what a crush feels like?

I don't have a crush on Rowan. I can't. He's so . . . so *normal*. And sunny. And so *typical*. I would rather sit on a Caribbean beach and slowly burn to death than . . .

Than admit that I'm lying through my fangs.

Dammit, Casper. I force myself to resume my flight down the stairs. None of this matters. So what if I admit to myself that he's actually really sweet and not so bad when it's just us and a container of ice cream? So what if he smells amazing and has a laugh with a timbre that would make an Italian opera tenor cut his voice box out with a spork in a jealous rage?

He's infuriating, a golden retriever who pees on rugs. And I'm leaving the country and never looking back at Mockingbird Prep ever again. This is a blink in my eternity. *He* is a blink in my eternity. That is all.

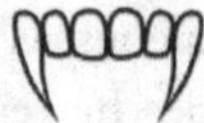

The blink in my eternity is now a blemish on the present, and I need to stop caring. But I can't. Something is off with Rowan. During the homecoming game, he stumbles around the field as though he's going for a Sunday stroll, not as if a marching band is blaring their horns and a stand of sports fans are screaming.

I don't have to understand football to see that the Mockingbird Beasts are losing and that a certain player keeps fumbling the ball.

"He looks like he's going to panic," I half-whisper, more to myself than Sophie, who's preoccupied dipping her chip into nacho cheese.

I'm worried about Rowan. His behavior has been growing more disturbing since I woke him from that dream. It's happened every night since then too, the crying and the pleading. I'm starting to think some of them *have* been nightmares.

Not to mention he just seems out of it, always staring into space, deep in his thoughts. I left my copy of *Call Me By Your Name* open on his bed yesterday, and he didn't get mad or throw it to my side of the room; he sat and stared at it. I think he actually *read* a page.

"Hell-*ooo*." Sophie snaps her fingers in front of my face, and I turn back to her, pulling my eyes off Rowan, who's slapping the side of his helmet. "I asked what's wrong? Oh . . . oh no . . . you're not . . . are you into one of the players?"

"No?!" I take one of her chips and dip it in the fake cheese, though I can't even eat it. "I've never been to an American football game before. Belgium, remember?"

"Mmhmm." Sophie narrows her eyes. "Okay."

"Well, that was depressing," Sophie notes as we make our way past the field and toward the dorms.

It was a dismal game, and I wouldn't be surprised if some diehard football fans have sworn off the sport forever. We lost *hard*, and I hate to admit that a lot of it came down to Rowan messing up. If he wasn't throwing the ball to the wrong player, he was zoning out, watching everything but his teammates. Short of scoring for the other team, he was a complete disaster.

"It's up to our wicked dance moves to save the night," Sophie says.

"Up to *you*, you mean," I say. "I don't dance."

Sophie starts her pep talk about how awesome I am. Usually, I would appreciate it, but I'm worried about Rowan. I slow my pace as we pass the field house.

"Casper?" She nudges me. "You in there?"

"Huh?" I fade into the present. "Yeah! I'll meet you at the dance. I want to freshen up."

"You don't have to tell me," she says, "but if you *do* have a straight boy crush, I strongly encourage you to keep walking. I've been there and done that with the girls at my last school."

If only she knew exactly how complicated this situation was—that I'm not wondering what kissing Rowan would be like; I'm thinking about drinking his blood. But she can't know. Ever. I feel a little guilt, hiding such big pieces of me. But if Malcolm and Camille were here, I know what they would say.

"It's all a test, I guess," I say. "School and straight-boy crushes."

"Pass it," she says, walking a few steps backward. "Pass. It."

When she's rounded the corner in the direction of the girls' dorms, I jog to the field house. I'll catch Rowan when he comes out and check in on him whether he wants me to or not. Even if he *does* want to avoid me, he shouldn't be left alone to spiral. But I stop when I'm about to round the corner. Someone is shouting.

"We're getting our asses beat, and you're out there sniffing flowers like Ferdinand the goddamned bull!" Coach Bones screams, and I jump when I hear something crack and bounce against the asphalt.

"I'm sorry," a voice murmurs. It's Rowan. I think I hear a sniffle, but it could be my imagination.

"Good thing it's your last year," Coach Bones continues, and I can practically hear the spit as he shouts, "'cause your ass'd be off my team pronto."

I'm about to reveal my presence and teach the coach what happens when you talk to kids like that in the presence of a vampire when a calmer, colder, voice takes over.

"Hold on," Mr. Young's tone snakes around the building. "I'd like a word with my son, please."

A string of four-lettered grumbles fades as Coach Bones disappears inside the field house, and I inch forward, perking my ears.

"Everyone has an off night," he says, but I don't think I believe him. There's something else to his voice, like he suspects the worst of his son. And perhaps doesn't care.

"Yes sir," Rowan says. He doesn't sound like himself, doesn't sound human, like he's made of gears and computers. A robot son.

"Do you have anything you need to tell me?" Mr. Young asks.

"Like what?" Rowan says, sounding confused.

"I've heard how out of it you've been. We've talked about this before. Now, is there someone? Something? Are you . . . listen, are you having sex or something?"

"NO!" Something clatters on the ground.

"Pick up that helmet!" his dad orders. After a moment of silence, he says, "I'm trying to talk to you and find out what's wrong, so you can drop the attitude."

"Will you stop?" Rowan snaps. My shoulders clench. "If there was anything I wanted to talk to you about, I would have. Stop freakin' smothering me."

"I'm worried about you—you're my son; I can't stop," Mr. Young says, but he still hasn't softened. Actually, his voice has only grown angrier. "Rowan, what is wrong with you? Why are you . . . are you . . . are you serious right now? Stop that . . . Rowan, man up . . . Fine, get to your dorm—right now. You can go to the dance when you've cleaned yourself up and remembered you're a man and not a little girl. Go!"

Cleats stomp against the asphalt, and I back away, but not quickly enough before Rowan comes storming around the corner, his helmet swinging in his hand, almost knocking into me. He stops and glares at me. His eyes are red, and his cheeks blotchy, but beneath that is a massive hurricane about to erupt.

"Hey," I say, quietly. "Are you okay?"

He storms on, leaving me there as though I didn't hear everything. But after about ten steps, he stops and looks back at me over his shoulder. "Get the fuck away from here."

I don't hesitate.

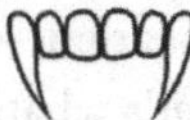

Multicolored lights flash, casting everyone in reds, greens, and blues as they hop around the sweaty gym, not entirely on beat. I wish I'd brought my sunglasses. Music blares so loud it vibrates in my bones. Squinting, I scan the crowd from our spot on the third bleacher, but I haven't spotted Rowan yet. He's probably in our room, spiraling without anyone to stop him. But hey, I tried. And he told me to get away.

If he doesn't want my help, then he isn't going to get it.

But I'm still worried about him.

"We should do a group costume!" Sophie shouts over the music. She and Dakota have been debating Halloween plans while Quentin pets Dakota's arm lovingly.

"Oh," I interject, "I have to be home on Halloween."

Sophie looks like she's catching me in a lie. "Nope! You're not getting out of it."

"Really. It's like Christmas to my family."

It's more than that: It's also my First Feed—my first time drinking directly from a cask. It's a rite of passage.

"Let's dance!" Sophie grabs my hand, but I pull it away.

"You dance!" I shake my head. "I don't."

"You're rejecting me on Halloween! You owe me this!"

I wouldn't call it *rejecting* her, but I let her win, and she takes my hand again with demented glee and pulls me to the middle of the dance floor, through a sea of bopping, overheated bodies, and I suddenly wish I'd fed a little before coming.

Sophie jumps up and down, spinning and dipping like an inflatable wind catcher in a car lot.

I decide to enjoy the moment. This is a new experience and gives me good practice for the inevitable club hopping abroad. I mimic her moves, doing my best to ignore everyone around me, but it's difficult when you feel hundreds of eyeballs taking note of you.

I try to remember what Scarlett says about this sort of thing. *"You're automatically better."* That's what she said when I was worried about coming to school. *"When they're dried up and past their prime, you'll still be young and beautiful. If that doesn't make you feel better, you also have the capacity to kill."*

That last bit earned a scowl from Camille, but it helps me as I close my eyes and feel the music, trying a little spin and throwing my hands over my head. After a few minutes, I feel *great*. What do I care what anyone here thinks? I'm going to live forever, go wherever. I have an eternity to fit in. Right now, I want to be weird.

I spin again and open my eyes.

There he is. Rowan, in a suit, pretending to be enjoying the music about five feet from me. His eyes aren't red anymore, and he seems more put together. But also like he's acting. His eyes are dead as they scan the crowd. He's probably thinking about how everyone blames him for the game, worried they're going to form an angry mob and rip him apart. He reminds me of . . . well, of *me*.

"I'm sweating!" I lie to Sophie. "Be right back!"

Before she can respond, I push my way from the dance floor and to the doors that lead outside.

October leaves sprinkle the big white stone steps. I take them two at a time and sit on the final one, unbuttoning the top of my black shirt and loosening the red tie threatening to strangle me.

The doors swing open behind me, and my nostrils fill with the last scent I wanted to smell. I stand and whirl to face Rowan, who's loosening his own tie and discarding his jacket.

"What now?" I ask, looking up at him. "Was I in your usual dancing spot? Is this your step I'm sitting on?"

"No?" Rowan's eyebrows knit together. "I only came out for some air."

"I don't believe you. I did something wrong, so what is it?"

"You didn't do anything wrong." He pinches the bridge of his nose. "Why do you think you did?"

"You were rude again when autumn break ended," I start. "You keep following me and glaring at me like you're . . . well, like you're profiling me or something. And earlier . . . well, you were upset. But you told me to get the fuck away. Remember?"

I think I see a lightbulb in Rowan's mind illuminate as he tilts his head, letting out a breath. "Oh. No, I didn't mean get away from *me*. I meant *here*." He gestures to the campus spreading out before us. "This place. I was upset. I'm sorry."

"Why are you out here, Rowan?" I put my fists on my hips. "You didn't come out for air the precise moment I did."

He smirks. I could bite those lips right off him for smirking right now. "Hoping I'd followed you?"

"You're obnoxious."

"You came out here alone," he says, rubbing the back of his neck and focusing on an orange leaf that's landed between us. "It can be dangerous."

"I can handle myself, hero."

"I know you can. I don't know, Casper, I felt like I should—" There's the smirk again. "Did you just call me a hero?"

"Sarcastically." I roll my eyes and take my seat again with a huff.

"Well. We're both out here. May I sit?"

I twist my lips, considering. He's been so back and forth; I don't know if I want to be chatty again only to have him change his mind by sunrise. Knowing Rowan and him knowing about me is like being strapped into the Scrambler, only any second my lap bar is going to spring open and send me crashing—crashing right into the tar pit that is being attracted to a straight guy.

But I'm still worried about him and not sure that he should be alone. So I gesture to the step, and with a grateful sigh, he plops down, sprawling his legs out before him.

"I hate dances," he says. "It's loud and hot, and everyone's so sweaty. And you can't even talk to anyone."

"I'd have thought this was your scene."

"No," he half-laughs, shaking his head. "I'm here only to save face after that catastrophe out there. I think everyone hates me right now."

"No one hates you," I say. "You can do no wrong in a lot of eyes . . . Are you . . . okay? I'm not trying to pry—"

"Dad just gets worried about me." Rowan shrugs it off. "And we argue about it. He's fine."

I note that he doesn't say that he, Rowan, is fine. We fall into silence, but I'm not sure if it's comfortable or not. There's an unspoken tension sitting between us.

Sweeping his hand behind him, Rowan reaches for a cluster of leaves. I watch as he arranges them into a small, dead bouquet. My stomach flips when he holds it out to me, but thankfully, I'm able to maintain an expressionless face.

"What is that?"

He shrugs, "An olive branch. Well, actually, it's dead leaves. Olives aren't in season; you understand."

I snort and take them, trying not to read into it or think of it as though he just gave flowers. Like this is any sort of romantic gesture.

"Why did you follow me out here, Rowan?" I look at him, but

he won't return my gaze, keeping his eyes on the sky. His ears flush pink. "Really?"

He bites the inside of his lips and blinks, thinking up some BS excuse, no doubt. But he surprises me when he shakes his head. "I don't know, man. Just wanted to meet up, I guess."

My stomach flips. He doesn't mean what I'm starting to think he means. And I don't even *want* him to mean that . . . do I?

"Meet up?"

"I thought it would be better if we kept our distance," he admits, his eyes lowering to the trees and windows of the buildings around us. "I didn't want anyone to notice we were suddenly getting along and think . . . think you're a vampire."

I snort. "You being friends with the likes of me would out my vampirism?"

He hesitates, and I sense there's something he wants to tell me. My mind races through a dozen options. He accidentally told someone. Or his dad is onto me. Or . . . or he wanted more than ice cream.

"How did you know you were . . . " Rowan picks up another leaf and rolls it between his right thumb and index finger. "How did you know you were a vampire?"

"Are you kidding me?" I ask. "I can't even answer that. You just *know*. Wait . . . do you mean vampire literally?"

Rowan doesn't respond. I know I shouldn't stare at him, but I can't help it. I watch as his eyes blink and his lip twitches. He's asking me something else. Something he doesn't want to mention.

"I think I know what you're asking me," I say. "Why are you wondering how I knew I'm gay?"

He shakes his head. "No reason. At all. Just being a friend, I guess."

"I don't need a friend for that; I'm well past the personal epiphany trauma," I say. "Are you . . . I mean, are *you* thinking you might be gay?"

He glares at me, and I scoot an inch away from him. "*No*," he says. "Forget I asked. I don't even know why I did."

"And we're back to being pissy." I stand. "This is why we can't be around each other. We argue and get too personal."

"I know," he says, softening his expression. He takes a deep breath. "Sorry. I want to be friends with you, I do. But that's so dangerous."

The words fall in my brain like a match into a puddle of gasoline.

"Yeah, okay," I say, making my way up the stairs. "No worries."

"Where are you going?" he calls out. "Casper! Come back, I didn't mean that as an insult."

"How else could you mean it? You seem to think you can say anything and then explain it away. If you have a soul, so do I. I have feelings. I'm not going to bite you, Rowan. All I want is to get through this year, prove that I'm over my thirst, and then I'm going away, far away."

"And that day can't come fast enough." His lip twitches, and I hear his heartbeat quicken.

Reed cuts off my entry into the gym, running out and patting my shoulder as he goes. I resist hissing at him. "There you are!" he says when he spots Rowan. "Get in here!"

"Not in the mood," says Rowan.

"Then I'm taking your crown."

Rowan looks up from his hands. "My what?"

Inside the gym, someone calls over a mic, "Rowan Young? Rowan Young! Where is our homecoming king?"

"Wow," I say, and Rowan looks at me with confusion. "Congrats, your majesty. Looks like you really can do no wrong."

CHAPTER THIRTEEN
ROWAN

Looks like you really can do no wrong.

That sentence has looped through my head since the night of the homecoming dance. It shouldn't bother me so much, and maybe if anyone else had said it, I'd let it go. But it was Casper. The one whom I've been dreaming about every night since we hung out over fall break. The one whose presence is completely shattering the glass I've spun around myself. Whose mere existence is forcing me to admit to myself that I'm attracted to guys, and that scares the hell out of me.

None of this was part of the plan. It's not who Rowan Young was meant to be. I *can* do wrong.

I lean against the frame of the open window and stare down at the path leading from Young House, at some of the guys as they smash pumpkins a day early, smearing the ground with orange and yellow guts. I should be down there leading the charge. Yet I'm here, hiding. Perhaps I always have been.

The door swings open, snatching me out of my spiral. Casper stops when he spots me, and we lock eyes for a moment before he sweeps to his wardrobe to pull out his suitcase.

"Finally giving me my room back?" I joke with a forced chuckle.

"If football doesn't work out in college, you could try stand-up," Casper says, not looking my way as he flips the suitcase over the bed and sets about packing, "since you're so funny."

I shut the window. Even with it closed, the room feels cold.

Casper tosses his shirts and pants into his suitcase, pausing to think about which book to take.

"Going home for the weekend?"

"Halloween is important to my family," he says.

"I should've known."

He locks eyes with me after plopping *Doctor Zhivago* on the pile of shirts. "What do you want from me, Rowan?"

I don't know how to respond. Why do I need to want something in order to speak to him? I shake my head. "I'm just trying to make conversation."

"Good talk," he says, turning back to the wardrobe. "Catch you in another week when you glance my way again."

Okay. I get it now. I sit down on the edge of my bed to appear at ease, but I feel even more tense when I say, "I know I've been hot and cold, and you have every right to be hesitant. I've thought a lot about what you said the other night, and yeah, I get my way a lot. But I didn't mean that *you* are dangerous."

"Then what is?" Casper looks at me again, and I'm taken aback. I don't think I've ever seen his eyes such a light shade of blue. He looks so vulnerable.

My heart picks up speed, my chest tightens, and my knees tremble. I suddenly feel sick. My bones hurt, and my brain is nothing but a burnt-out sponge. I want to have out with it and tell him he's beautiful and that I can't help but notice.

I'm pretty sure that I'm gay. Say it, Rowan. No, I'm sure. I'm gay, and so are you, and we share the room, and I think you're the most obnoxiously pretty guy I have ever seen.

It's the truth, so why is it so difficult?

"What's dangerous, Rowan?" Casper asks. "You can tell me.

You kept *my* secret."

Say. It.

"What time is your ride getting here?"

The Sponsor pulls the discreet black car into the expansive grass yard currently serving as a parking lot. My stomach flips, and I breathe deep to stave off the panic about to combust inside me because we've arrived at the one place I shouldn't be: Casper's home.

I should have come out to him. He'd keep it to himself since I kept him being a vampire to myself.

But I chickened out one too many times, and he's never going to give me the time of day again. And that's for the best. It's dangerous enough that we were somewhat friends, if adversarial. The best-case scenario is that he never knows why, never learns that there are a group of guys who already know what he is and want to impale him.

"We're here only to observe," the Sponsor says, his voice warped and monotone beneath his black full-face mask as he adjusts the tip of his black-and-silver three-cornered hat. "The Belamy Feeding Ball is an annual attraction for vampires all over the eastern seaboard. If they're having it in Mockingbird, we must ensure that no one is killed, or worse—turned."

I fiddle with my white satin cravat that feels more like a noose. I feel ridiculous in this getup—a jacket and vest and breeches with boots, like I just escaped *Bridgerton*, my face hidden by a black mask that covers my forehead and nose, leaving only my chin and lips visible.

Casper was long gone when I emerged from our room and went to the kitchen to force-feed myself some lunch. When I returned with a bowl of instant ramen and six individual-sized bags of chips stuffed under my arms, I found the message slipped under my door, informing me that I'm required to do this to "prove my allegiance".

But if I'm here where I can see everything, I can make sure Casper is safe.

"Don't speak to anyone for longer than you must," the Sponsor says moments later when we walk past the Belamy manor, rising atop its little hill. "They'll know we're mortal; there's no hiding that. Therefore, they'll assume we are willing to be bitten. Do not allow a vampire to taste your blood. And don't eat or drink anything."

He leads us past the front gate, where a woman in a red historical ballgown with black Victorian print directs guests to the back gate. My mouth drops when I spot the numerous two-pointed incisions marking her neck. She's a cask.

"Don't stare," the Sponsor quickens his step, and we round the corner and jot up a side yard toward a black-velvet-roped queue. "Here." He reaches into his black 18th century overcoat and thrusts an embossed invitation into my hands. "One of them works at the all-night gym. He didn't receive his invitations this year."

I focus on calming myself while we wait our turn. Inside this party is a massive hoard of vampires. Bloodthirsty, immortal, lethal vampires. I don't know how many mortals like me will be in there, but I'm definitely outnumbered, and that thought is scary as hell.

This must be exactly how Casper feels at school. No wonder he's irritable—this feeling is awful.

Moments later, an undead guard with luminous golden eyes inspects our invitations and gestures to the open gate that leads into the backyard. The Sponsor nudges my shoulder with a hint of encouragement as we pass through and—

Vampires, vampires, and more vampires, with glowing, hungry, jewel-like eyes of all colors, dressed like they've won the Revolution (French or American, I can't decide), most of them in masks of their own, fill the backyard with undead glee. They laugh, show off their fangs, and prowl in search of wrists and necks. The mortals I spot seem eager to bare their throats, as though to shout, *Pick me! Pick me!*

The more I look, the more I see that *backyard* was the wrong word. This is a lush garden, with hedgerows and scores of rose bushes encircling black fountains, the stone carved with cherubs and demons. Red lights in the basins make the water look like blood as it shoots into the air. Torches and plump jack-o'-lanterns light our way as the Sponsor and I wander.

"Marvelous taste," a vampiress in a Medusa mask says as she licks her lips. She holds the wrist of an incredibly relaxed man with a euphoric smirk on his lips.

I shudder but remember what Casper told me about the casks: They are willing volunteers. They want this. Even if it's creepy as hell.

The Sponsor regains my attention by saying, "I trust you won't do anything stupid. I'm going to explore. Remember, observe, and if you see our classmate, don't approach him."

I nod, and the Sponsor leaves me to the hoards.

I inch along, keeping my wrists crossed in front of me and trying very hard not to brush against anyone as I head toward the end of the garden nearest the house.

"They've done such a lovely job with the place," says a vampire with a voice that belongs to another time. He takes a sip of bright red blood from a champagne flute. "We're lucky his majesty resettled here."

I pause and cock my ear. Did he just say "his majesty"?

"I agree," a woman says, her accent like something out of a BBC period piece. "There is a better sense of community than in that sterile Manhattan penthouse. Besides, I have it on good authority that her majesty always preferred the countryside."

Her majesty. His and her majesty . . . what was it Casper said his parents do again?

I move on before the pair senses me eavesdropping, stepping carefully to avoid running into a very large man with flaming orange eyes, his fangs out and dripping with freshly taken blood.

At the other end of the garden, a handful of vampires and casks dance a cross between a waltz and swing, to the music of an undead band set up on a small stage. The lead singer is a vampire with emerald eyes and long black braids, crooning out some strange melody. I make my way past that to the large stone steps that lead up to the back patio of the house. I bound up them two at a time until I'm a little over halfway, and I turn to get a higher view of the party.

My stomach flips over. It was macabre enough walking among them, but from up here, it's nothing but a sea of gothic horror. Bloodstained breeches and ball gowns. Shining teeth piercing unbroken flesh. I can't stop staring.

It's all so messed up but . . . entrancing. Once you get past the blood and the fact that everyone is a creature out of a horror film, it feels so natural. It's *their* world.

The band finishes its song to a wave of applause, and I clap on instinct. A trumpet sounds behind me, making me jump. I rush back down the steps to get out of the way as two vampires dressed as heralds march forward continuing to sound their alarms. When at last they finish, one steps forward.

"His majesty," he calls out, "King Malcolm Leopold Justice of the House of Belamy."

The garden falls silent in breathless awe as Casper's father appears at the top of the stairs. His face is kind but businesslike as he nods to his guests.

Casper's father is a king . . .

"Her majesty, Queen Camille Rowena Carlotta of the House of Belamy."

Queen. He definitely said queen. And Casper's mother has certainly dressed the part, in a large white ballgown that looks more like she's going to a wedding at Versailles. She smiles and takes her husband's arm. They descend the steps, standing tall and graceful, more graceful than any mortal could ever hope to be.

Casper's parents are royalty. Vampire royalty. His dad is a king, and his mom is a queen, which means that Casper is—

"His royal highness, Prince Casper Malcolm Johnathan of the House of Belamy."

My mouth drops open. What the fu—

Casper appears at the top of the stairs as the guests *ooh* and applaud. My roommate, *Casper*, is a—my brain doesn't want to think it. A pr . . . a priiiiii . . .

His jacket, black with silver brocading, and tight black breeches and boots fit better than they have any business to. He isn't wearing a mask, and his pouty lips and pretty face make me simultaneously happy and devastated, and I don't know why. It's painful to look at him, but a good kind of painful. How dare he?

He reaches the foot of the steps, and I back my way deeper into the crowd, fearing he'll spot me.

"Thank you all for joining us on this special night," Casper's father proclaims. "Tonight is our son's very first Feeding Ball, and we have been anxious for you all to meet him."

Everyone applauds. Casper keeps his eyes on the ground, wrists crossed in front of him. I wonder how he feels in this moment. Is he elated? Or is he nervous? Terrified?

"His royal highness has been studying this semester at Mockingbird Preparatory Academy. A strange challenge, we are aware." Mutters trickle through the crowd. "But he has been doing an excellent job and soon shall take his place among us. As such, the time has now come for the First Feed."

Another *ooh* rings out, and I tense. What's happening?

Casper's eyes search the crowd, and for a moment, I worry he's seen me. But he keeps scanning back and forth. His right eyebrow twitches, his lips twisting ever so slightly. No one else would notice, but I do. He's thinking through everything, readying some sort of performance.

"Will the selected cask please step forward?"

My heart plummets into my stomach as another guy, about our age and better looking than me, I think, steps forward proudly. The crowd applauds and shouts praise at him. Casper looks at the guy with a small smile.

Hold up. Are they a thing?

The guy bows to Casper and proudly kneels facing the crowd. He removes his jacket and cravat and unties the top of his white peasant-style shirt as Casper's father places a hand on his son's shoulder. His mother kisses his temple and whispers something in his ear. I take a small step forward, squinting to see.

Casper slowly places two fingers beneath the boy's left ear. He's going to bite him. Right in front of me. And I care about that way too much.

I scan for the Sponsor, but I don't see him. It's only me and Casper and a crowd of the undead preventing me from stopping this whole thing.

Casper tilts the cask's head to the side and kneels behind him. He takes a moment to look over the neck, long and muscular, waiting. The cask's eyes are closed, his breath held, bracing for what's about to happen. Casper parts his way-too-pink and way-too-full lips, and his fangs drop down.

A short, sighing note escapes my throat, and I purse my lips. I . . . I just *moaned*.

Casper lowers his head, plunging his fangs into the guy's neck, and all gasp as two trickles of dark red blood run down the casks's throat, over his chest, staining the pure white of his shirt, and sending my entire world crashing into the depths of . . .

Damn it. The depths of jealousy.

A tear pushes its way into my left eye, and I blink it back. Casper removes his fangs from the guy's neck, his chin covered with blood that isn't mine, and helps him to stand. They join hands and raise them high. His parents join them, clapping them on the back and proudly waving as everyone erupts into rapturous applause. I break away, pushing my way to the back of the crowd.

I have to get out of here. My heart is hammering so hard it hurts my chest. My stomach is so hot I think I might roast from the inside, and my own body is betraying me in these breeches. I pull my jacket tight to hide the stiffness I shouldn't have.

Because I'm not into that . . . except . . . God, I am so into that.

I dart behind a hedge and fall to my knees, pushing the mask off me as though removing it will help me to breath. I dry heave, but nothing comes up. Hot tears run down my cheeks and drip from my chin to the grass.

That was my dream. That's what, for whatever reason, deep down, I've wondered about. And he did it to someone who isn't me. And that will never be me. Even though it's better that it isn't.

Hands grab my shoulders, and I fling myself back. The Sponsor looms over me.

"I told you to only observe and not get too close," he says. "Where's your mask?! Get up."

"No," I say.

"Get. Up!" He lunges at me, and I swing my fist at him.

"I'm not okay!" I shout, "I am the least okay I've ever been, so can you back the fuck up?!"

He reaches into his overcoat and pulls out a walkie talkie. He's going to tell the Blackthorns about this, and who knows what'll happen then?

I lunge for the walkie, dragging him down. We roll over the ground as I desperately pry at the Sponsor's fingers, but his grip is too tight.

"Let go!" he commands.

He kicks me off, sending me sprawling onto the grass. I sit up, brushing myself off and whirl around in time to see—

Diego, scrambling for his hat and the mask that's fallen to the ground.

My brain turns upside down as I struggle for a breath. "*You?*"

Diego drops the mask. "Rowan, let me explain—"

"*YOU!*" The word scrapes over my vocal cords as I crab walk backward to a hedge. "The whole time?! You were sending me morbid presents and shoving a sack over my head—you. It's *you*. My best friend."

Diego puts his hands up in surrender. "Rowan, I've wanted to tell you for so long. And Reed. But as you know, the Blackthorns are very secretive, and I couldn't risk it."

"I can't—can't process—" I grab at the cravat, which is suddenly strangling me, ripping it from my throat. But I still can't breathe. I'm going to pass out. I'm going to die. I'm going to—

"Calm down, buddy." Diego pushes against my shoulder, forcing me to lie down. "I know it's a lot. Just breathe. It's fine."

"How?" I push out, rubbing my temples. "Why?"

"I got pulled in last year and learned everything. Our families are descended from the original slayers of Mockingbird. You're related to Constant Young, so I knew you'd be asked to join eventually. But when Casper showed up, and you had to room with him, I had to get you in fast."

I force a breath. A thousand thoughts spin around my head, but the most prominent right now is that at the very least—the *very* least—Diego is in on it. I have a friend, and he seems like he feels bad about hiding it. But I need to know another thing—

"Do the Blackthorns want to hurt Casper? You're not planning to stake him, are you?"

Diego shakes his head. "No. Slaying vampires . . . I don't know how to explain it. It's in the past. Civilized vampires haven't killed humans for over a century, at least not here. We keep tabs. And we keep mortals from falling into *this*. I mean, have you seen those freaks who *want* to be fed on?"

He looks disgusted, but it all seemed fine to me. It's their choice, so why do we think it's our place to decide for others? But I don't want to get into it, so I ignore that part and focus on the other bit. "So, it's peaceful."

"Yes. But we don't want them to know that we're watching. That could escalate things," Diego explains. "Hey . . . are you okay?"

I'm sick to my stomach, my temples are killing me, and Diego saw me having a meltdown over a boy I'm not supposed to be attracted to. I shake my head.

He stands. "We need to go before anyone sees you."

He offers his arm, and I hook my hand around his elbow to hoist myself up. I wipe my wet, tearstained faced with the back of my hands, and my jaw starts trembling again as Diego takes a few steps, leading the way out. My shoulders shiver, and my chest tightens. I bite my lip.

"Diego?" I say, my voice broken. I shouldn't say this now. It's not the time, and what if it makes everything worse? What if he hates me? But I feel so heavy, and so broken, and like my skin is falling off my bones, revealing the shriveled, scared kid that's starving inside of me. "I'm gay."

Two words, ones I wasn't planning to say, ones I have never said out loud in that order.

Diego blinks, processing, studying my face as though seeing me for the first time.

"I said I'm gay," I try again, hoping it'll break his silence.

He lifts his mask to his mouth and turns on the walkie talkie. I tense. "Sponsor with report, do you copy?"

"We copy," an identical monotone voice crackles through the walkie speaker. "What is it? Over."

"The Sponsor reports nothing. Thirteenth Son succeeds. It is a harmless Halloween party. Over and out."

He shuts off the walkie and cocks his head. "Thanks for telling me, brother. Let's screw the rules and go trick-or-treating; then you can tell me about guys."

CHAPTER FOURTEEN
CASPER

The cask, who's reminded me every chance he's gotten that his name is Xavier, has a slightly bigger right eye than his left and a strawberry seed stuck between his two front teeth. He's a year older than me and dropped out of college in hopes of finding a wealthy vampire to *keep him*.

Also, his blood tasted like the inside of a hiker's left sock in July, and while I'm thankful that Malcolm and Camille chose someone who wouldn't tempt me to keep drinking, I can't get that awful taste out of my mouth, no matter how much sweet blood I sip from my champagne flute. To make it worse, he won't stop making eyes at me like a hungry mountain lion.

He's barking up the wrong tomb, so I dart into the crowd, allowing vampires I've never met to shake my hand and congratulate me on a fine First Feed.

It hasn't been all bad. Actually, it's been thrilling to see so many people like me, fangs out, unashamed, unhidden. These are my people, and after going from a lonely attic to a school of mortals, the lightness that I feel far outweighs the nerves I had about making my debut, about drinking from a stranger while everyone watched.

If only Xavier would get the hint.

"Thought I'd lost you," he says with a grin, daring to brush my elbow with his fingernails that desperately need a trim.

Oscar shifts his weight behind me with a grunt, the quiet signal that all I need to do is ask and he will whisk Xavier away. But I'm also not convinced Oscar wouldn't snap him like a popsicle stick, and that's no way to prove I'm a budding diplomat. So instead, I force a smile and shrug.

"So did I," I say. "You know, you don't have to stick with me. I'm sure there are several vampires who would love to meet the guy who gave me my First Feed."

"I'm interested in *you*." He winks, and I fight not to cringe. I thought the first time a guy was smitten with me would be more magical, like in books. I don't expect violins and roses, but I'd at least have liked it to be genuine.

"I'm going to be very honest with you," I say. "Your blood was disgusting. It tastes terrible because you're not a good person. You just want my status, and I believe you were chosen so that I wouldn't drain you completely. So the next time a vampire does bite you, I do hope you'll have reflected on your intentions, because our tastebuds can tell."

He gapes at me, dumbfounded, before his forced smolder twists into a scowl. "Fine, then. Ugly."

Oscar comes between us, and the guy stumbles back. Guests are watching this unfold. Xavier might want to go back to school because no vampire is going to keep him.

"Your duties. Finished," Oscar says, baring his fangs. "Leave now. You must."

Xavier looks like he's going nowhere, puffing his chest out like he's going to fight my very large, very muscular, very old vampire bodyguard. But Oscar has never been opposed to tossing me around, so he certainly isn't going to hesitate with a rude cask. In a matter of seconds, he has Xavier over his shoulder, and he makes a spectacle of him as he carries him to the gate.

Everyone cackles and cheers, and I can't help but be entertained. If only I could bring them all back to Mockingbird Prep with me.

Malcolm approaches me with a kind but firm expression, Camille tsking on his arm. I start to explain, but he raises a hand. "Be benevolent," he says. "Enough people in this world think we're monsters; let's not ever give them an example that we are."

"He called me ugly," I say, and I hate that I even care.

"Never was a bigger lie told," says Camille. "Remember, darling, you are the leading example. See how everyone fell in line? They follow us."

I grunt and rake my fingers through my hair. "Of course. I understand now. I'll keep that in mind."

Camille takes my face in her hands. "That's my fine boy."

She kisses my forehead, and if I could blush, I'd be as red as the blood stains on Xavier's shirt. I glance around, noticing the vampires and casks discreetly eavesdropping, and I suddenly feel like a tiny child. I pull back and give a smile before making a gesture to indicate I'm walking away from this conversation.

"Oh dear, I embarrassed him." Camille winks.

"He's at the age, my love," Malcolm says. "May he never grow out of it."

With an eye roll, I march away from them. Malcolm thinks he's being hysterical, but considering I'll never *entirely* grow out of being "at the age", it's a vamp-dad joke, and I don't appreciate it.

My eyes fall on a piece of dark fabric left on the cobblestone path leading through the garden. Someone has dropped their mask.

I stoop down to pick it up, thinking that perhaps if I do find the owner, I can use it as a conversation starter to show Malcolm and Camille what a good host I can be. It's a classic masquerade mask with two plain eyeholes, made of satin and lace pulled tight over its bones.

But the longer I look at it, the more I notice the subtle detailing, the stitches of embroidery running over the forehead and cascading down the temples. It's the same branches that were carved over the headstones in the cemetery. An unmistakable symbol—for what, I haven't been able to learn, as the books I took out from the library proved little use, but this is too much of a coincidence.

I scan the crowd, but everyone around me has their mask. Up ahead, I spot bright red hair and rush to the long tables piled with fruit for the casks. Scarlett is perched on the end of one with a crystal goblet, pointing her finger at a group of mortals who seem entranced by her.

"My-maker-told-me-to-sip-the-very-best-cask-and-you-are"—her finger lands on a handsome bare-chested man with tan skin and a well-kept black beard—"it."

I hold the mask behind my back and wait for Scarlett to finish. "*Mmm*, pineapple," she says, and her casks laugh.

"Thank you, Ricky. Now, mix up, and you know what? Cis men step out this time. Hmm, batty-ratty-spider's–web—"

"Scarlett!" I call out before she can get too far in. She snaps her eyes to me with an enraged fury.

"No, you may not snack on my pantry," she says, "These are *my* casks, and you're underage."

"Can I speak with you a moment?"

She pouts her lips before sighing and waving her casks away. "Don't go too far, little pastries." She watches lovingly as they make to leave, giving us the space to speak freely. "Don't tell me you've come to mope. It's my night as well."

"No," I grunt, holding out the mask. "I found this on the ground. Look at the stitching, do you see it?"

"Branches," Scarlett says as she studies the mask. Her posture stiffens as she notes the detailing. "Ah."

"You know what it is?"

Biting her lower lip, she nods. "It's a blackthorn branch. More specifically, it's *the* blackthorn branch."

Knitting my eyebrows together, I lean in to look at the mask again, attempting to memorize the berries that seem almost to wink back at me. "So, it *does* mean something?"

"You said you found this on the ground?" She looks at me, and when I nod, she rolls her eyes. "I guess someone thought they were being funny. But you were good to bring this to me."

"I don't know what it means."

Scarlett glances over my shoulder to ensure no one is listening in. She leans in and drops her voice to a whisper. "Blackthorn is a very strong, sharp piece of flora. A lot of people think the crown of thorns Jesus wore was made from it."

I sigh with relief. "So, it's just a religious symbol." If that's the case, then that would be why it's all over those graves.

"That's only a piece of it." Her eyes gleam. "Many also believed it could ward off certain creatures of the night. And good material for . . . well . . ."

"What?"

Her tongue flicks over her lip. "For making stakes."

My mouth drops open. "You mean it's a—"

"Slayer's calling card."

I suddenly feel queasy, and not just because of the foot-odor blood I drank from Xavier. Why is this on a mask at a vampire ball, and on graves at my school?

"You mean to tell me"—I swallow—"there are vampire slayers?"

"They're known as The Order of the Blackthorns." Scarlett's tone has the lilt of someone telling a ghost story on a campout. "It was formed when the first settlers of this country were only just arriving. There have always been vampires everywhere, but the most feral, the most dangerous, the kind that eventually died out, arrived on a ship carrying Puritans from England." She raises her voice with each word, slowly raising her hands, as though telling a ghost story to a child. "By the time the ship arrived, nearly half of the passengers and crew were either *dead* or *turning*. Constant Young formed the order to fight back against those vampires."

"Young. As in . . . as in my roommate Rowan Young."

"Yes." Scarlett grins. She must note how tense this makes me, because she drops her story voice and rolls her eyes. "He's probably a descendant, but that means nothing, Casper. The order is long gone. Malcolm and Camille would not send you to a school run by the descendant of a vampire slayer if it weren't."

"Then what is this doing at our ball?" I point to the mask. "How are we certain the order is gone?"

"Because they're dead," Scarlett says, seemingly assuring herself as much as me. "Malcolm led the charge, and we put an end to the slaying. They've been defunct for well over a century now, and there've been no slayings in recent memory. Things like that"—she gestures to the branch—"like *this* are only an offensive relic now, and we should hide this to destroy later. Do you have a pocket inside your jacket?"

"No," I say, "But I can smuggle it up to the attic."

"Do that," Scarlett says. "I think it's a sick joke, so let's treat it that way. I don't want to escalate something that may mean nothing."

I'm not entirely convinced that this is only a sick joke. How could it be? Why would anyone do that here? I tuck the mask under my arm and leave her to continue the game with her casks.

Before anyone can approach me, I zip through the crowd and bound up the steps to get this into the house before someone sees it. But as I reach the back door, the party a dull roar behind me, I can't help but stop to look at the mask again, running my fingers over the stitches, the thorns and berries.

I lift it closer to my face to inspect it further, trying to see if there are any hidden details, any subtle clues that can tell me more about the Order and if they are, in fact, defunct.

A scent fills my nostrils, and I almost drop the mask as my mouth waters.

Woodsy, traces of vanilla, a pure, good sweetness that waters in my mouth and makes me even angrier.

Rowan Young wore this mask tonight.

CHAPTER FIFTEEN
ROWAN

"Your name is Rowan."

I sit up in bed, awakened by the voice I've become all too used to in dreams like this. But as my eyes adjust to the dark, and Casper's pale face fades in through the moonlight, I realize this isn't a dream. He's still in his costume from the party. His hair is disheveled yet perfectly tousled, as though he's wrung his hands through it repeatedly.

What have I done now? A couple of hours ago, I was full of Halloween candy, and my stomach was warm and happy because Diego knows my sexuality and now it feels right to say it. I felt light, seen. Now I'm being looked at with revulsion by the one guy I can't have and whom I couldn't tell Diego about.

"Uh, yeah," I say, my voice quivering. "And you're Casper."

I reach out for the lamp on the nightstand, but Casper is at the edge of the bed in an instant, showing off his vampire speed. "Do you know what your name means, *Rowan?*"

My fingers pause on the light switch. A chill sweeps up my spine.

"Little redhead," I say. "They didn't choose it for its meaning."

"Rowan is also a type of tree." The light flicks on. I yank my fingers back, realizing he's done it for me, and his own cold fingers almost burn the pad of my thumb. "I looked them up. Did you know they were once used in some places to make crosses and to ward off vampires?"

"No?"

"Can you think of any other trees that were used to hurt people like me?" he asks, smirking.

I gulp. He knows. Casper knows about the Blackthorns.

"Casper," I start slowly, "I know what you must be thinking, but really, it isn't what you—"

He tosses something black at my chest, and I gape at my mask as it tumbles into my lap. "Oh . . . I forgot about that."

"What were you doing at my Feeding Ball, Blackthorn?"

"I am not going to hurt you," I say. "No one is out to hurt you."

"This place is littered with the graves of vampire slayers, and you show up at my house wearing a symbol that means killing me and mine, and you didn't think there was any harm?"

"I only just learned about it," I say, pushing the covers off my lap, daring to stand as Casper takes a step back. "That's why I've been so stressed out. I was forced to join and then made to crash your ball to see if any mortals were being drained. That's it. They told me that no one is slaying. That's not the purpose anymore, I swear."

"Why didn't you tell me?" Casper asks. "Don't you think that's something I needed to know?"

"I don't know who's a Blackthorn and who isn't." This is partly true. I know about Diego now, but I don't want to throw him under the bus. "I don't know much about it—yet."

"The Blackthorns slayed every vampire they could for centuries," Casper says, pushing out each word as though he'd like to ram it through my skull. "They're the bad guys. We only want to live our undead lives peacefully and be left alone. *I* want to be left alone. I don't run down the hallways shouting about my vampirism. I play the mortal game. Mortals get that part of me. But . . ." He swallows, and his eyes become glassy, as though he's about to cry. But no tears fall as he says, "How dare you think you have any right to *every* part?"

A tear rolls from my right eye in lieu of his. He's right. I should have told him. But how was I supposed to do that without revealing why I cared so much? Without explaining that I can't not see that side of him because it's the side that I'm falling for?

"I'm sorry," I say.

"You're sorry," he snorts. "I should still be there. That was my night to be me, and instead, I'm here justifying my existence to *you*."

"I wanted to tell you, but I—" I cover my mouth with closed fists, but it does nothing to stop the next words from tumbling out, and I'm deafened by my own pleading, whiney voice. "I know that I've been hot and cold with you, and we didn't get along when we first met, but why do you still hate me so much?"

He purses his lips, his hands balling into fists. Glaring at me the same way he did when we first met—that look of unadulterated disgust. "Because, *Rowan*, you confuse me."

A singular "ha" cannons out of my stomach, and I raise an eyebrow at him, daring a step closer. "And what do you think you do to *me, Casper*?"

His eyes soften, only a bit. I know I shouldn't say any of this. I can't afford to. But he's right there, and I'm right here, and tonight is the same night I finally let myself be me. I *need* him to know that he's not in danger with me. He needs to know why.

Even if it makes everything else worse.

"I dream about you every night," I say, the words bubbling on my tongue. "And in those dreams, we do everything on this planet that there is to do. Do you know what I mean by that?"

He nods, the blues of his eyes going from aqua to navy to teal and back again at a head-spinning speed.

"I wanted to dislike you," I say, "so badly. I didn't want to find you so, *so* beautiful. But I do. And you don't trust my intentions. And I know that you're mad I kept the Blackthorns from you and crashed your ball. But all *I* can think about"—I choke as another tear emerges—"is why, when you sank your fangs into a boy's neck and drank his blood, why couldn't it be *me*?"

There it is. Everything I shouldn't say, standing between us like a sign at a crossroads. Two ways this can go, and no road behind us to retreat down.

"Because I hate you," he says, every syllable a dagger in my jugular. "You just said so."

"No," I say. "There has to be more than that. We were getting along. Yes, I ignored you; yes, I hurt your feelings. But you know I'm not that awful of a person. You checked on me when Dad and Coach were screaming at me. Something made you care. What was it?"

"Nothing," Casper says, dropping his eyes to the floor. "Thank you for your honesty. But it's nothing."

"Nothing." I take a step closer. "Why do you cringe every time I get closer?"

"It's nothing," Casper says again, squeezing his eyes tight.

A moment later, I'm so close to him my lips could easily touch his. I study the tiny lines in his wrinkled nose. I hear the small, tiny inhale of breath that I don't think he wanted to take.

"Is it my scent?" I venture, the pieces falling into place. "Is that why you didn't shake my hand? Or why you refuse to be in the room with me for long? Because I smell so good?"

His hand pushes against my chest, making me stumble back. "You're infuriating," he says. "And if this is some demented joke—"

"I think the fact that it isn't a joke scares you more. Maybe as much as it scares me."

"I'm not scared, Rowan," Casper says. "I'm telling you right now, this means nothing. It has to. I'm going away at the end of the year. I'm going on my tour, once I've gotten through high school *without biting anyone*. I'm not jeopardizing that because you want to experiment."

"It's so much more than an experiment, *your highness*," I say, and

Casper's eyes light up. "I'm not the only one who kept things back."

"This conversation is over," he says, and he heads toward the door. "Thank you for telling me that, but nothing can ever happen. Ever."

He pauses when his hand reaches the doorknob, and his head tilts. My heart hammers so loudly I know he hears it. He hears how much I want this.

"*Why*," he sighs, "did it have to be *you*?"

Then his lips are on mine, his hands around my back, every inch of him pressed against me as our faces smash together, safely hidden in our dorm, and finally, *finally*, I know what those pouting pink lips feel like against mine as his tongue parts them. My fingers run through his hair as we stumble through the room. He pushes me against his bookshelf, and a paperback tumbles from its place, knocking my shoulder on its way to the floor.

His flesh is so cold against mine, his chin so sharp on my jaw as he kisses the corners of my mouth, my temples, each bit of contact making it more and more ridiculous that I've never kissed a guy until now.

I don't want to kiss any other guy or girl or anyone else ever again, because there is nothing that could ever make me feel as incredible as kissing Casper Belamy.

A moan from me encourages him as his lips tug my ear, and my right leg instinctively wraps around his. He pushes me harder against the bookshelf, and I reach up to steady myself, grabbing shelf after shelf, brushing along the weathered spines of Casper's favorite books.

"I didn't plan on this," I say. "I was going to stay away from you."

"This is dangerous," Casper reminds me. "If anyone finds out—"

"No one is going to find out," I say.

Then he's kissing me again, and now *I'm* the one hunting for his tongue. I can't get close enough to him. I need every part of him so that I can discover if it's how I dreamt it would be.

My hands keep grabbing at the shelves as he lifts my legs completely around him. The room is spinning and upside down. This is the highest I've ever flown. I'm—I'm—

I'm on the ceiling.

We are on the ceiling. Casper has somehow picked me up, and we have levitated against the plaster. I gasp, peering over his shoulder at the floor.

"Casper," I breathe. "How are you doing this?"

"I don't know." He shakes his head. "I was told I'd be able to eventually but . . . I guess you brought it out of me."

He presses his face against mine again, and we're rolling over the ceiling, him holding me up as he moves gracefully, like a beautiful beast with hollow bones, while our classmates sleep in the dorms outside, no idea what is going on in Room 410.

CHAPTER SIXTEEN
CASPER

My eyes open to a sliver of gray light running down the wall. Sunrise is here. I need to get out of Rowan's bed and into the wardrobe before I'm hurt. But doing so would mean slipping from Rowan's arms, and I don't know whether sunburns or the cold absence of his touch would be worse. So I'll stay put, half-drunk on his scent, as the memories of last night bubble up and fit together.

He snoozes, his body melted around me. I don't question whether or not this is real. Everything last night really happened, and we can't go back. My body tenses as I wonder what he'll think when he wakes up.

What do *I* think?

I liked it. Way too much. His lips on mine, his fingers on my back. I liked the way he sighed in my ear, and how his leg wrapped around mine. It was like a glove fitting perfectly on the first try.

Just one sip.

I can't stay put anymore, not with his heart beating against my back and his blood calling. As slowly and quietly as I can, I slide against the mattress and remove myself from Rowan's right arm. He rolls over but doesn't wake up.

Outside, morning birds are singing on their way to somewhere warm. The first breeze of November wafts around the basswoods. My breath catches in my throat, and my knees tremble.

"Up early, son?" I remember a voice somewhere in the back of my head.

I remember gray light, the air already heavy and warm, and a man who isn't my father finding me on what I think is the concrete slab of a playground. I think it must've been December. It's the last sunrise I saw before turning. As soon as it flashes across my mind, it's gone, plummeting back down into whatever well it came from.

Memories of the former me are beginning to wake up.

My throat is dry yet full of molten lead. My chest is frozen tight, and my eyes hurt as a million tears well up, yet none fall. My fingers tighten. I've grabbed the curtain in order to steady myself.

Levitating and past lives. I'm growing into my full vampiric self. I wonder . . . do I still burn?

Before I can change my mind, I yank the curtain back and push my hand against the latticed pane. I wince but hold it there until the promise of smoke appears over the rapidly burning flesh on my arm.

Hands knock into my shoulders, and I tumble, falling over my bed. The room plunges into darkness as Rowan closes the curtain.

"What are you doing?" he asks.

"Seeing if I can stand the morning light yet," I say, cradling my arm. "Not quite there."

He rubs his face, trying to wake up more completely. I can almost see his own memories of last night flooding his mind. I tense, waiting for him to freak out or to tell me that it all meant nothing and to get out of his sight.

He paces around, eventually heading to his wardrobe to pick out today's outfit. I stand and retrieve my books, which all fell to the floor during our escapade. I place them back on the shelf one at a time.

"Are you mad at me?" I ask.

Rowan spins around, his eyes big with surprise. He sighs. "No.

Why would I be?"

"You can't be happy about what we did," I say.

"Casper," he says, and my stomach flutters, "I meant everything I said. Maybe I'm supposed to feel awkward about it, or whatever someone is supposed to feel after making out with their vampiric roommate, but I'm too relieved that you don't actually hate me to worry about it."

"Okay, but we might have started a war. You know, royal vampire? Slayer descendent?"

"We'll have to be careful."

I shake my head. "What are you saying? That this is going to happen again? Rowan, it can't. Your dad and the Blackthorns and—my parents, Rowan!"

"I know," Rowan says, biting his lip. He takes a few deep breaths, rubbing his forehead with both hands as he thinks over it all. "Which is why we'll have to be careful."

I gawk at him. How can he be so cavalier? "Twenty-four hours ago, you'd have told me what a danger I am. You were keeping away from me. Now you're wanting to keep something going that both of us know we shouldn't?"

Rowan doesn't answer at first. He leans against his wardrobe, running his thumb back and forth across his chin as his lips twist. Then finally, in a whisper, he says, "I came out to Diego last night. I'd never said it out loud until then. But I said it. I said 'I'm gay' and knew it was the truth. It was like . . . like being born again. You know?"

"Yes," I say. Another dormant memory reawakens: A night sky. A thousand stars, though you can't see stars in the city. When I opened my vampiric eyes for the first time. "I imagine so."

"Everything about last night, what I saw at the ball, coming out to my best friend"—his hand reaches out, and his warm fingers brush the thumb of my left hand—"kissing you . . . everything we did and said . . ." His lip trembles. "It was like seeing colors I didn't know existed. I didn't know that for seventeen years I hadn't been *me.*" His wide-eyed face looks at me like a puppy left in a box on the corner. "I know you're going away. That I might never see you again when we graduate, but you're here now. And now that I've been me"—his hand squeezes around mine, and I make the choice not to pull back—"when I'm around you, I want to be *me.*"

This is a bad idea. A dangerous, possibly deadly idea.

"I want to be me, too." I'm supposed to keep away, stick with other vampires, keep my eyes down and not ever let mortals know that I'm capable of more than they could ever imagine.

But I don't want to stay alone just to placate the mortals.

He saunters forward, bending and pressing his forehead against my chest, wrapping his arms around my waist. I brush my hands along the soft hairs at the nape of his neck as he sighs. And I sigh, too.

"No one can know about this," I say. "Ever."

CHAPTER SEVENTEEN
ROWAN

"Stop staring at me." I glare at Casper when I pass his lunch spot under the oak tree outside the dining hall, making my way toward Reed and Diego.

"You got in my line of vision!" Casper shouts back, pushing himself to his feet. But Quentin and Sophie stand to block his path toward me.

"Back off," says Sophie.

Dakota drops a playscript and shoots me the most disgusted look I've ever received. "Get lost, Rowan."

"Then tell your friend here to stop being so creepy."

"Tell *Mr. Young* that he isn't king of all he surveys." Casper hardens his expression and takes a step forward, his chest pushing against Quentin's outstretched arm.

"It's not worth it, man," Quentin says to him.

I smirk. To everyone who isn't Casper, it would appear I'm being smug. Actually, I'm breaking a small smile because Casper's eyes have remained their usual shade of blue. If he were actually mad at me, they'd be darker. I add a grunt for good measure and storm off.

Diego stands from the bench he and Reed claimed for us, his

hands in fists. "Is that Victorian ghost messing with you?"

Reed, who's more invested in his phone, says, "Not to start anything, but it's been, like, three months. Get along."

"But he's insufferable." I drop onto the bench.

With a sigh, Reed stands up and heads toward the dining hall. "I'm getting food."

"What's his problem?" I ask when he's a few feet away.

Diego shakes his head and sits next to me. "You and Casper have been at each other's throats since Halloween. He doesn't know the reason we have to put that thing in its place."

It? Heat blossoms from my chest to my neck and ears. I relax my fist and slowly breathe in through my nose before Diego can notice he's pissed me off.

"Yeah," I say, but my mind is drifting as I watch Casper leave his friends and make his way across the grassy area that leads to the science building, shooting a raised eyebrow at me before he disappears through a side door. "I know . . . I think I need to go cool off. Catch you later?"

"Don't let it ruin your day." He claps my shoulder before I stand.

How can Diego be so backwards about this? He was so great when I came out to him, but with this, he has no understanding. Casper might be a vampire, but he's a human being, not an "it".

I curve around the front of the science building so that Casper's friends don't think I'm following him, and by the time I'm coming up the front steps, I'm so angry from the whole exchange that I push through the door with too much force, and it bounces on its hinges as it ricochets back.

"Young!" My chemistry teacher shoots me a warning glance. "Watch it."

"Sorry," I spit out and cut down the hallway that leads to the side door.

When I reach the door to one of the supply closets, I double check to make sure no one else is around and yank the door open.

Casper spins around, his eyes locking onto mine.

"I thought I told you to stop staring," I say.

"You're still in my line of vision," he spits back.

I rush at him and sweep my arms around his waist as our lips smash together.

Confetti bursts inside me. I can't get close enough to him, and he seems to feel the same, his fingernails scratching along the back of my neck as my fingers latch into his shoulder blades.

"How are you so good at this?" I ask as his mouth sweeps down my chin, finding the sweet spot where my jaw meets my neck. An involuntary moan threatens to give us away. Casper remedies this with two fingers against my lips.

"I'm a vampire," he whispers. "I'm designed to do things well."

A bottle of Windex and a stack of towels plummet to the floor as he steadies himself against the top shelf of the closet. My head bumps the ceiling and narrowly misses the light bulb.

"What are we fighting about next?" I ask, grabbing the chain to the light and tugging it so that the closet falls into darkness.

"It's your turn," he says, tugging on my tie. "You tell me."

I kiss him as hard as I can in response. My tongue, my teeth, nothing can fill the empty ache in my chest. Or make me feel better about the idea of hurting him, even if it's staged.

"I'll figure it out," I say when I finally take a breath. "Can you just kiss me?"

"Until you say stop."

His lips instantly find my neck again as he settles on top of me— or under me I guess, considering I'm lying on the ceiling, watching the thin slice of light beneath the closet door and hoping against hope a shadow doesn't move across it.

"Hey Rowan," says Casper as he enters the Young House rec room, and I stand, clutching my pool cue like a nightstick and morphing my laughter into a disgusted grunt. "Can I speak with you for a second?"

Ben Ruthven rolls his eyes and sighs much more loudly than he needs to.

Diego takes a step forward while Victor Cress slowly makes his way around the pool table. "Don't you bother him enough in your dorm room?" he asks, his tone polite yet stilted enough to suggest danger.

"It's *about* our room," Casper says, but his eyes are locked on Victor's wrists as he rolls up the sleeves of his dress shirt. He glances at me, and I almost betray us by asking what's wrong. His eyes have darkened. He rolls up his own sweater sleeves before flicking his eyes back to Victor's.

"He doesn't want to talk to you," says Victor.

I should stop this, but I can't. Because now I see what Casper has seen. On Victor's outer wrist, so small you'd miss it if you didn't know to look, is a tattoo of a blackthorn branch.

"When will you learn that none of us want you here?" he asks.

Casper plunges his thumb into his mouth.

"Are you"—Victor laughs, cueing Diego and Ben—"Are you *sucking your thumb*? He is! He's sucking his thumb like a big baby!"

Casper blinks, his eyes violet. But Victor is still going, laughing in Casper's face. I want to run my pool stick through him for baiting Casper like this. If he's a Blackthorn, then he knows damn well that Casper is trying to keep his fangs from coming down and killing Victor in front of all of us.

"Go on then, baby, cry," Victor says, getting so close to Casper's face that he may as well stick his head into the mouth of a python.

Casper pulls his thumb from his mouth, and I notice the trickle of blackish blood where he had to bite himself.

I should say something, stop this before Casper is any more humiliated. But I can't. If I do, then I'll out us, and that could be more dangerous. Staying quiet is how we stay safe.

How would any of them understand what this is like for us?

They've never hidden their relationships because they don't feel safe. They have their club where they tell themselves they're the ones being preyed upon. They don't know what a real predator looks like because they've never seen their reflection.

"Have something to say?" Victor asks. I can't believe he's still going. It's like he *wants* Casper to attack him so that he has a reason to retaliate. "That's right, little babies can't speak."

"Knock it off!"

Mr. Abadi appears in the archway, his scowl enough to relay his disappointment.

Victor quickly rearranges his expression into one of confused innocence, and the rest follow his lead. But it doesn't matter what they do, because Mr. Abadi's eyes are locked on mine. Heat prickles my cheeks, and I shrink into myself.

"Don't act like you don't know what I mean," Mr. Abadi continues, but no one drops the confused look. "Oh, right. Babies don't speak. Casper, since you're the only *non-child* in here, why don't you tell me what just happened?"

But Casper whirls out of the rec room, his shoulder knocking against Mr. Abadi's on the way. I want so badly to throw my pool stick down and follow him. But—

"Rowan, come with me."

Mr. Abadi zooms out of the rec room, leaving me to the gaping *awws* and *oohs* of my so-called "friends". I shake my head at them. I didn't even do anything, and they're going to let me take the fall for it? This used to be my crew, my best buds. I don't recognize them anymore. Right now, they look to me more like three piles of old, white dog crap.

Out in the hall, Mr. Abadi makes it to the kitchen doorway before whirling on me with a fury I've never seen out of him. "What's wrong with you, Rowan?"

"I didn't do anything! I wanted them to stop too!"

"No stance *is* a stance," Mr. Abadi says. "If you didn't like it, you should've said something."

"And let them turn on me, too?"

I rush outside before he can stop me and set out to find Casper. I don't have to think too hard to find him. I only have to answer the question, *If I were a vampire, where would I go?*

I find him perched on the stone thigh of Elizabeth Gorham when I reach the forgotten cemetery, a weathered leather book propped on his knees, though he isn't reading it.

"You don't have to pretend," I say and make my way down the slope toward him. "I'm sorry about what Victor said."

"I'm not thinking about what he said," Casper says, still in his own world. "I'm thinking about how grotesque and slow I'd make his death if I weren't trying to prove I'm not that kind of vampire."

"Is it very grotesque?"

"I blanch to even say." He finally makes eye contact. "He's a Blackthorn."

"I found out when you did." I sit next to him and gently take the book from his lap. When I close it, I see that he's once again reading *Frankenstein*. "I'm sorry."

"It makes it different, knowing who some of them are. It makes the danger more real."

"I don't want to fake-fight anymore." I want to put my arm around him, but I don't, in case there are any spies out in the trees.

"I agree. It's egging them on. It's not great, but we should probably avoid each other during the day. Keep everything to the room at night."

"You're probably right," I sigh. "We have different classes, different extracurriculars. Avoiding each other should be easy."

"And safer."

I gesture to the forgotten cemetery and chuckle. "I love that we're navigating our secret forbidden relationship over the graves of slayers."

"They deserve it."

CHAPTER EIGHTEEN
CASPER

I remember sheet music, and snow. It's cold, and my yarn-knit gloves are too thin to keep my hands warm. It's Christmas Eve, and I'm in some sort of pavilion in the city. The man thinks I'm nervous because I don't want to carol with the other kids, but actually, I'm elated, because I'm about to escape—

"Do you need a moment?"

Mrs. Spencer's voice pulls me to the present. I'm staring at the sheet music for a song called "Corner of the Sky". We're in a dressing room backstage, and she and Mrs. Kitchen, who's agreed to help judge auditions, are staring me down while a student pianist gawks at me.

I swallow down the tears that can't fall anyway and nod. "No . . . yes . . . no. I'm good. I, uh, I don't sing."

"You'll be fine," Mrs. Spencer points a ballpoint pen at me as though casting a spell. "Just nod when you're ready."

With everything going on between Rowan and me, I'd nearly managed to block out auditions. I don't want to be in this show. I don't want bright lights shining in my face and half the mortal population of Mockingbird staring while I make a fool of myself on stage. But I *do* want to pass so that I can flee this place, so here we go.

"Okay," I nod. "I'm ready."

The next two minutes are a blur: just my croaking voice and thoughts of escape, of the loud, shrieking kids I must've once known fading as I hang back and duck into an alley. My voice breaking on the last note, an impossibly high one, as I remember talon-like fingernails and sharp stabs in my neck.

"See?" Mrs. Spencer mercifully cuts the pianist off. "You did great!"

"I'm happy to only be an usher," I say, laying the sheet music on the piano and backing away.

Mrs. Kitchen chuckles, but Mrs. Spencer offers a sad smile. "I'll make a note of it. Thank you, Casper. We'll need number twenty-five, please."

I waste no time in getting out of the dressing room and shuffling past the few remaining students nervously waiting in the stage wings. "Number twenty-five," I grunt and zoom out to the stage and down the side steps that lead to the seats.

"You did it!" Sophie rushes up to me and pulls me into a tight hug. I shove my hands deep in the pockets of my blazer.

"I'm so freakin' proud of you!" Dakota play-slaps me on the shoulder.

I offer a wry smile so as not to offend them, but honestly, all that just made going off the grid and being feral again sound like a great idea. "Thanks."

"Who's in there now?" Sophie asks as we make our way to the third row.

"I don't know," I grumble. "Twenty-five."

Dakota plops into a seat with a groan, and I note that her right eye twitches. "Oh god. That's Quentin. Hurry, everyone manifest his sudden case of laryngitis."

With a manufactured sigh, I flash a gentle smile to show I'm listening. At some point between Rowan and I giving in to our feelings and all the pretend fighting, Dakota broke up with Quentin. A few nights ago, Sophie and I found ourselves sitting at the foot of the Mocky statue on the front lawn while she cried it out and knocked back four airplane bottles of Fireball whiskey that Sophie sneaked onto campus.

"*You* broke up with *him*," Sophie reminds her. "Let him exist."

"He's trying to get cast as Pippin," Dakota says.

"Every boy here is."

"I'm not," I interject.

Dakota groans again. "You don't get it. He's been texting me about it nonstop. Like I'll be *so impressed* and come crawling back. He knows how badly I want to play Catherine, and if I get it, then I have to kiss him. If I don't, then he'll play the jealousy card. Mark my words."

Sophie squeezes her shoulder. "You're absolutely going to get Catherine, and he's *not* getting Pippin. Remember when we were all driving around singing with the cast recording? He can't hit that high note in 'Corner of the Sky'."

"That doesn't matter," Dakota rolls her eyes. "No one can hit it."

Behind us, the doors of the auditorium swing open.

"Am I too late?"

I do a double take. What is going on? Why is *Rowan* loping down the aisle, waving a page of sheet music?!

A hushed whisper, half excitement and half suspicion, falls around us. Drama kids aren't used to guys like Rowan showing up at drama club.

"Oh god," Dakota groans yet again, sinking further into her seat.

"Hey." Rowan stops just short of us and smiles at Sophie, making a point of ignoring me. Which is good, because with the glare I'm giving him, he might turn to stone were he to make eye contact. "Am I too late? I was at fencing practice. By the way, what is this play even about?"

Sophie's fingers curl into her palms. "It's not a *play*; it's a *musical*. At least respect the culture."

"Everyone just sit down," Dakota says through an explosive cringe. "People are staring at us."

Rowan retreats to the back and drops into a seat in the back row. Once he's settled, I whip my phone out.

What are you doing in here? I text him, then add, *We're not supposed to be in the same room, remember?*

A few moments later, he sends his response. *I know, I know. I'm sorry. But the few minutes we get at night just isn't enough. And I thought this way we would have a good reason to be around each other.*

I resist the butterflies in my stomach and respond with, *You're infuriating.*

Yeah, you're kinda cute, too.

I shove the phone in my pocket and take a seat behind Sophie and Dakota. It's not that I don't want Rowan around—I *always* want him around. But this is so risky. One accidental glance and someone could put it together. But I can't be completely mad at him when he's being such a retriever.

The last few to sing emerge from the wings. Quentin trails behind them, his face smug when he spots Dakota. Mrs. Spencer appears, Mrs. Kitchen and the pianist flanking her. Her face is twisted into an expression of deep consideration.

"Before the dance portion, are there any others who haven't sung?"

"Me!" Rowan squeaks from the back row, and everyone gawks at him as he stumbles into the aisle. "Hi! I haven't."

Mrs. Spencer's eyes light up. Clearly, she's never seen one of the "popular" kids around here, either. "Interesting. Follow me."

Now *I'm* the one sinking into my seat as Rowan makes his way to the stage, a murmur of students and a grunting Quentin breaking through the auditorium as they disappear backstage. This is such, *such* a bad idea.

I shake my head. There might not be any reason to worry. We'll wait for the cast list.

"She said *what?*"

Rowan shrugs from his bed. "She said I'm the only one who can hit the high note."

I drop my phone onto my pillow. I can't read it anymore. The cast list came in about two hours after auditions, and since then, my eyes have blazed with three dreaded words in bold: PIPPIN . . . ROWAN YOUNG.

"*Of course* you can!"

"It's not my fault I'm the only one." Rowan props himself on his elbows. "How was I supposed to know that I'd get the lead? I thought I'd be in the background or asked to do crew instead."

"Because you're *Rowan Young.* You get *everything.*"

He thinks about it with a smirk, as though he's only considering this for the first time. "I do, don't I?"

I toss my pillow at his head, and he lets it hit, falling onto his back as though the blow killed him. He laughs. "I'm sorry, okay? I thought it was a good idea. I just wanted to be close to you."

He reaches his arms out for me. I shouldn't reward him for throwing a major wrench in our "stay apart" plan, but he's so damned attractive when his face is flushed that I can't resist getting off my bed and into his, sinking my weight onto his chest as he envelopes me.

"For the record," I say, "I'm actually proud of you. Who knew you could sing?"

"Not me," he says. "Except maybe in the car. But hey, I'm proud of you, too, ensemble."

"I'm *in* the ensemble, not the *whole* ensemble. And don't remind me."

"I can't congratulate you without reminding you." He kisses my cheek. "You're supposed to be blending in and taking part in the mortal world, right? This'll be extra credit."

He's right, of course. I know that. But it still doesn't make the idea any easier.

"And with Sophie as Leading Player, I'll get to know your friends better," Rowan says, thinking up every reason why I shouldn't worry. "Her name's above mine, so I'm assuming it's a bigger part? My biggest worry is not being allowed to kiss you in front of everyone."

"Am I supposed to find that aww-worthy?"

"Is it working?"

"A little."

Moments later, we're back on the ceiling, my face in the crook of his neck, his soft moans in my ear, and I'm trying desperately not to take it farther than just making out.

But my god, it's getting so difficult.

CHAPTER NINETEEN
ROWAN

Between midterms, fencing, keeping up appearances, and now the play, Casper and I have found even less room-time for each other. But now that it's officially winter break, and we're back to our houses and away from the constant threat of the Blackthorns, we get to make time.

I pull the car up to the corner of Main Street where the houses stop and the businesses start. An inflatable snowman flashes me an apologetic smile with its painted mouth. Winter break also means the school year is halfway done. And so is my time with Casper.

That sad thought flees, however, when Casper appears from behind the snowman and makes his way over. I grin. Though it's only been a few days since we've seen each other, it feels like we're reuniting after months.

"Hey sweetheart, you lookin' for a date?" he asks as he crunches over the snow that fell this morning and pulls the passenger door open. He looks like Halloween ate Christmas, a black corded sweater and long black wool coat, pale and haunting against the lit-up snowman.

"Don't make it sketchy," I laugh.

Casper slides in, and I can't not wrap my arm around his shoulder and pull him in for a kiss.

"You smell so good," he says. "You *tried* to do that, didn't you?"

"No," I laugh. "I mean . . . a little."

Casper cracks his window. "You know that's dangerous. I suggest you drive."

With another laugh, I pull the car from the curb and head for downtown. It looks like something out of a cheesy holiday romance movie, with multicolored lights crisscrossing the streets, the shop windows dotted with tinsel and bows. Casper reaches over to brush my knuckles with his index finger, and my heart feels like a sigh as it relaxes.

"What are we doing tonight?" he asks. "You didn't say."

"That's because it's a surprise."

I turn down a busy side street and park across from the movie theater, a showing of *It's a Wonderful Life* announced on the marquee.

"The movies?" asks Casper.

"Nope," I say. "That's a decoy. We're going over *there*."

I point my thumb over his shoulder, and he looks behind himself at the window display of books nestled in Christmas ornaments, the frosted sign on the pane reading *Next Page Books and Wine Bar*.

"Nuh-uh," Casper says.

"Uh-*huh*." I grin at him. "You're going to pick out an obscene number of books, and I'm buying them."

"You can't do that!" he protests. "You know I like hardbacks."

"Oh, I know." I wag my eyebrows at him. "And I assure you, I *can* and *will* do that."

His face goes stoic, and I grin even wider, because now I know I've got him feeling mushy. I try not to laugh as he shrugs. "We'll see." But he kisses me, long and hard enough to betray his expression.

A moment later, I'm opening the car door for him and hoping he doesn't notice that I check over my shoulder to make sure we aren't being watched. Inside, the shop smells like paper and coffee. Old-school Christmas music pipes through the shop speakers in the corners. Laughter and chatter break out from the small bar in the back, where people sip from wine glasses and coffee mugs.

We pass a pair of stressed-out-looking men perusing spines and romance covers. "Next year," one of them says, "her gift is shopping here. I'm not guessing anymore."

"You're already better at this than someone's husband," Casper whispers and tugs at the hem of my sweatshirt.

"Remember that if we ever fight."

Casper sounds a "*hmmph*," and examines the nearest stack, his finger gently brushing the spines. Occasionally, he pulls a book down and studies its cover before glancing at the blurb. He only reads a few words before putting them back, until finally, he pauses on the blurb of one particular book.

His lips twist as he considers it, opening to a random page and reading a few sentences before snapping it shut and tucking it under his arm.

"You chose the first one," I note.

"I didn't choose it; it chose me," he says with an embarrassed, half-cocked smirk.

Grabbing the nearest book, I flap the cover up and down so that it looks like a mouth. "Casper," I say, making my voice sound like it's filled with helium. "Pick me! Pick me!"

He laughs. "It doesn't work that way."

"I say pick me!" I make the book "bite" his neck. "Pick me!"

"Quit!" He laughs, knocking the book away, and I'm tempted to keep going until I notice someone at the bar looking at me. I quickly shove the book back on the shelf. That could easily be someone my dad knows, and then we'll be caught.

"Sorry," I say.

"You're ridiculous." He crooks his finger under the hem of my sweater to tug me along, but I remain still until his finger loses its grip. Casper's shoulders tense, but he doesn't acknowledge it. I didn't want him to not do that. I want so badly to put my arms around him and hold him while he shops, to be part of these imaginary worlds he inhabits. But what if someone sees?

I hurry to catch up behind him.

"Thank you," he whispers to me, halfway through the blurb of another book. "This was the best idea ever. But I'm not letting you pay for them."

"Nope," I say. "You heard that guy. I'm the better husband."

He stiffens, and I take a half-step back. I hadn't meant for that to sound so intense. But there it is, and I can't take that back, so I say, "Not literally."

"Oh, I know," he says, his eyes meeting mine. "I get what you meant."

I should officially ask him to be my boyfriend, right? Right here in the bookstore, with Bing Crosby noting how it's beginning to look a lot like Christmas? It's the perfect place. It's only a few words. I just have to ask them, and—

"Oh!" Casper notices something over my shoulder, and I step back so that he can reach for the book that, I guess, has chosen him. "I've been wanting to read this one."

He places a copy of *The Thirteenth Tale* on top of the other book and sticks them under his arm. He looks so freakin' amazing in his sweater and coat, arms full of books, the dark waves of his hair falling to the side of his perfect head. The blues of his eyes are bright and cheerful, the corner of his mouth lifted in a smile that would make the Mona Lisa say, "Just forget it", and rip herself off the wall.

I *want* him to be my boyfriend. Not just a guy I'm fooling around with, but my all-caps *BOYFRIEND*. How could I not? This beautiful, smart, fearless guy who so arrogantly went out of his way to test me. Who's opened up and shared his biggest secret with me. Who saves injured opossums and has helped me figure out this school musical thing.

I want him; I want him; I want him.

"Hey Casper," I begin, my heart lodging itself in my throat. But

Casper doesn't hear me, zipping around the stacks and leaving me no choice but to catch up. I won't ask him now, then. Let him get his books, and then, when we're in the car, and the Christmas lights are twinkling, and people are leaving the movie theater, and Santa is ringing a bell for charity, I'll ask him.

Maybe carolers will even show up and make it extra special.

"We have to go." Casper spins around so suddenly he knocks against me, dropping his books.

"What? Why?"

"That lady at the bar? With the black hair?" He cocks his head, and I spot her, winking at a man as she tugs her turtleneck up higher. "She's one of Scarlett's casks. If she sees us, we're caught."

"Okay," I say. "You go. She doesn't know who I am. I'm going to check out."

"You don't need to—"

"I'm buying these for you!" I insist. "No book left behind."

Casper looks like he's about to protest, but he flees, and the bell jingles as he rushes out the door. I gather the couple of books he was able to find and head to the counter. I was so pleased with my idea I hadn't considered that there are people Casper has to avoid from his side. A vampire easily could have been working here.

So much for carolers and Christmas romance.

When I exit the store, the books wrapped in silver paper with red and green ribbons, I find Casper with his back to the window of the hardware store next door, under a sign urging people to repaint their kitchen in time for Santa's arrival. His head is drooped, his eyes somewhere else, kicking at an icicle that's fallen on the ground.

"Are you okay?" I ask.

"I'm tired of hiding," Casper says, crushing the icicle beneath his boot.

"I know," I say, reaching for his hand. He pulls away, running his fingers through his waves and stepping into the street. "I hate it, too. I hate it at school, and at rehearsal, and now I hate it here."

"Everyone else gets to stay in there and have a good time." He stops, balling his hands into fists. "But *I* have to run while *you* clean up my mess."

"It's okay—"

"None of them have to look over their shoulders. None of them think twice before loudly talking about their wives. Meanwhile, some of us can't go down the street without risking injury or worse, and I'm tired of it!"

"Easy," I say. "What's brought this out?"

"When I became a vampire, I thought I'd finally be free of hiding, of having to fit in with people I don't care about. But here I am, undead royalty, and I've never felt more hidden."

"You're not always going to be here," I point out, trying to help. "In a few months you'll be—"

"I'll be stalking through shadows and hoping there aren't even more dangerous vampire hunters where I'm going," he says. I lift a finger, about to shush him, but he's unstoppable. "Why do human beings make up all these games and conflicts for everyone else to deal with? You see that, right? It's all made up! Vampires versus slayers and vice versa because someone somewhere decided that's how it's going to be. And—and marriage! Decided by someone somewhere."

"Casper—"

"And school, and who wears pants and who wears skirts, and business casual-and-who-can-kiss-who-and—"

"Casper—"

"And-they-think-*I'm*-the-monster-well-*they*-are-the-monsters–"

"*Casper!*" I almost drop the books as I thrust my hands up in an attempt to get his attention. He purses his lips. Red rings have appeared around his storm cloud irises. "Nothing will get better by word vomiting."

"I would rather choke on word vomit than die from silence."

My stomach clenches, and air pushes into my closed mouth. I

shouldn't be laughing right now. He's being serious, but—I let out a huge cackle.

"What?" he spits through gritted teeth. "What is so funny?"

"You," I say, my squeezing shut. "How long have you had that sentence saved up?"

When I open my eyes again, his little smirk has returned, and his eyes have lightened a bit. He's trying to act like it's not funny, but it's no use. I can tell he's starting to see it.

"A while," he admits. And then he laughs, and I'm laughing, and we must look pretty silly standing in a gutter, laughing in each other's faces.

Finally, after we're able to breathe, Casper shrugs. "Why do you mess with me?"

"I don't know," I say. Words are bubbling up, and I don't know what order they go in. I've never said this to anyone. Usually, I freak out and run. I'm freaking out, but I'm not running. "I want more than messing with you, though."

When I get the courage to look at him again, his face has gone rigid, locked in that stoic expression. He's afraid of what I'm going to say. Maybe I shouldn't say it.

"I kind of thought maybe," I keep going, "I could be your boyfriend."

Boom. My heart pulses, and I know he can hear it. But his expression gives away nothing as he says a quiet, "Oh," and shoves his hands in his pockets.

That can't be good.

"That's okay if you're not feeling it. What we have is good. Perfect, even. We can forget the whole thing—"

"Stop talking." Casper holds his hand up. "I'm trying to process this . . . I've never had a . . . I've never been . . . do you mean that?"

I shrug, feeling like I'm standing in my underwear out in the snow. "I feel like we already *are* that and just haven't said it."

Casper nods once. Then again, and again, until his eyes practically glow a shade of teal, and for a second, I think he's going to levitate by the way he pushes onto the tips of his toes. "Okay."

"Okay?"

"Yes." Casper smiles, and if I didn't know any better, I'd think he had a faint blush on his cheeks. "We can be boyfriends."

Sweet relief fills my chest, and my shoulders relax. Wow. That was it. I did it, and he said yes, and now we're not just fooling around. We're a whole *thing*.

Something warm and glowing snakes through me. The closest I've felt to this is when we kissed the first time. But one thing is worrying me.

"You don't seem excited about it," I say.

Casper forces a blink. "I'm still processing. But I'm excited. Happy."

I hold out the books. "Merry Christmas, Casper."

He takes them, smiling sheepishly at the wrapping. "Thank you. I think what's missing is that big magic 'we're together' kiss, you know? I know we can't here, but . . . it's hard to be here."

I pause, and it's like the sun itself flips on in my brain. "Wait . . . I know a place."

CHAPTER TWENTY
CASPER

Rowan Young wants me.

Of course I knew that he *liked* me, that we enjoyed kissing in our dorm room when no one was around. I knew that he made a game of making me laugh, and that for however long this was going to last, he was there to explore it with me.

But he wants to be my boyfriend, and that makes it a bit more difficult. I want to be his, too, and now there is no way this can end well. Not when I get on a plane and he goes to college, and with vampires, casks, and Blackthorns all watching.

But . . . *he's my boyfriend.*

I take in his silhouette as we drive down the winding moonlit road that wraps around Lake Mockingbird. The expensively cut sand-colored hair I used to loathe. The green eyes I'd have gladly poked out. It's like looking at him for the first time. Where is that boy I couldn't stand? How did we go from there to here, and when will I wake up and be burned by the sunrise?

The other thought I can't shake, the one I can't keep myself from thinking about any longer, is that he is mortal. Since he first said those four words that led to us speeding down the backroads, he has aged twenty minutes. I have not. In the matter of our bodies, he has aged four months since I first met him. What about in four years? Twenty years? Sixty?

"There we are." He takes a sharp tour onto a snow-covered path. "Welcome to Castle Young."

The moonlight bounces off the snow, illuminating a lake house as clear as daylight. Two floors and pointed roofs painted blue, every bit the epitome of a New England waterfront home, complete with wooden steps that make their way down to a large dock that stretches out over the frozen lake.

Rowan stops the car and puts it in park. "We can't get up the drive with this snow. We'll have to hoof it from here."

"I don't mind the cold." I smirk and slip from the passenger seat, my feet crunching into the undisturbed white blanket.

He plods around from the driver's side, zipping up his winter coat. "Shall we?"

He gently tugs me along, and as we make our way up the path, I look up at the iced branches of the trees. The heartbeats of animals burrowed under the ground fills my ears, triggering my thirst, and I press my tongue against the spot where my right fang remains hidden. Rowan's pure, woody scent radiates off him like steam in this snow.

"Of course you have a vacation home," I say to distract myself.

"Don't you?" he asks teasingly. "*Little Prince?*"

I wrinkle my nose. "Don't ever call me that again. And yes, we have a penthouse in Manhattan. But of course, *you* have yours in the same town."

Rowan pauses in the snow, and his face may as well be made of spinning gears as he thinks. "It's been in the family since the 1900s . . . . Casper, I think I just brought you to a slayer-paid retreat."

I tense and survey the house, worried I'll suddenly see signs everywhere that this is slayer land. But it's only an old house—a beautiful one.

"That's okay," I squeeze his hand. "Tonight, it's not."

Rowan's shoulders relax, and he resumes walking, leading me until we come to the front door. Pulling his keys from his coat pocket, he flips through a few until he comes to an old brass one.

"We haven't been here in years. I don't know if Dad's kept it up," Rowan explains as he slips the key into the lock. "It might be a mess."

"So long as we're alone," I say. "You don't think there are security cameras, do you?"

"No." He turns the key. "There's never been those. Now that I think about it, it's probably because this was . . . well, you know."

"Slayer land." I nod.

Rowan half-snorts, tensely, as he pushes open the door and reaches around the side to fumble for the light switch. A second later, the entryway is glowing yellow, and we step inside.

It's just as cold in here as it was out there, the clouds of Rowan's breath continuing in wisps as he gestures to the open, cabin-like room, all the furniture covered with tarps.

"Here we are," he says. "I know it's not exactly up-to-date, but it's ours tonight."

I stop, his words bouncing around my skull. It wasn't so much the words as it was his tone: warm, a bit mischievous. *It's ours tonight.*

He turns to the large window that looks out over the lake, white and frosted beneath the moon. His breath becomes quiet as he takes in the view, and I notice his hands shaking. He has to be freezing, so I look around for a thermostat, but when I finally find it, it's locked under a box.

"Is there a space heater around here?" I ask, peeking into a closet but finding only cleaning supplies and an abandoned flannel jacket. I pause, noting it's smaller size. This must have been Rowan's when he was younger. It might be a bit of a tighter fit now, but at least it's another layer. "Here," I say, pulling it off the hanger and rushing over to Rowan, who's still lost in the view. "Put this on under your coat. I'm going to find blankets. Might have to use the tarps if I can't—"

I lower the jacket to see Rowan's face. It's almost unreadable, his eyes distant and a little less green than usual. He's not present.

"Are you alright?" I ask, slipping my arm around his shoulder.

His eyes slide slowly to me. He blinks. "Yeah. I'm fine."

"Do you want to sit down?"

He nods, once, and I gently crook my index finger around his and lead him over to one of the tarps, hoping there's some sort of seating under it. As the fabric pulls away, a large well-worn green couch is revealed. I help him sit down.

I can't just sit here and watch. I slide my hand over one of his knees and squeeze. His eyes close with a huge whoosh of air through his mouth as he lays both of his hands on mine and sinks over so that his forehead rests against it.

"I'm sorry," he whispers. "I didn't expect the memories to be so '*bam*'."

"Don't be sorry," I say, using my free hand to drape his old jacket around his shoulders like a blanket. "You don't have to explain anything."

He takes a deep breath before continuing, scooting in closer so that our hips are touching, "I haven't been back since my mom left us."

I move my hand over his shoulders, back and forth, a signal that I'm here as he slips into the past.

When he speaks again, his voice is tighter, shaky.

"She loved the lake. I've told you she's gone, but what I didn't tell you is that she lived here most of the time. She and Dad were through, but they wouldn't just say it. Actually, *Dad* wouldn't say it. I used to wish all the time that they would divorce, because then it would have made more *sense*. It never did, why she was here, and I was at home with Dad, or why she'd come get me and I'd spend weekends here. I never knew whether I was coming or going because there was no custody plan. Because they wouldn't tell me anything.

"Mom was a lot more spirited, I guess. She never liked our

family's status, and I guess after a while, it became too much. One week in the summer a few years back, I expected her to show up and steal me away like usual. But she never did. She was gone. Dad and I came to live here until school started, waiting for her to show up."

My hand lifts off him as the weight of what he just said pushes against me. I knew his mother wasn't in his life anymore, but I didn't know the details. Now all I can picture is a fourteen-year-old Rowan staring out the window, waiting for his mom to reappear.

"I try not to think about it much or let it bother me," he says. "I get why she couldn't do it anymore. I . . . I kinda wish she'd talk to me, you know? That's it, I guess. You don't remember who you were before, and I don't remember what I'm supposed to feel about my own mom deleting me from her life."

"Have you and your dad talked about all of this?" I ask, and Rowan shakes his head. "I think you need to. Clearly, it's hurting you both."

"Dad doesn't hurt, and therefore neither do I. You heard him outside the field house when I was cracking." His lip twitches, and his eyes glass over. But boys are like vampires—they don't cry. It might as well be stamped on his forehead. "Sometimes, I really hate him for it. I still love him. But I don't feel as close to him as I used to. Since she left, it's like he's checking boxes with me and making sure I can't leave him too. He's my father, but he's not my *dad*. And now I know I'm gay, and . . . what if I'm not his *son* anymore? Mom didn't want us; what if he doesn't want me, either?"

"I'm sure he would still want you."

He nods, taking a deep breath. "Maybe . . . I'm sorry. I really didn't intend to go into all of that. Being here just brought it all back, you know?"

I don't know, not really. "I'm glad you opened up," is what I can honestly say. "You know you're allowed to do that with me, right?"

"Yes," he says and stands, heading for the stairs. "And thank you. I think I just need to get out of this room. Come on, there's some old games in the loft cabinet."

"I'm going to rip your hand off!" I shriek as Rowan places yet *another* draw-four on the Uno stack. "Take that back right now!"

"I can't," he explains, wagging his eyebrows. "It's already been played."

"But I don't want it to be a draw-four," I say, batting my eyelashes and trying my best to do to Rowan what Camille does to Malcolm. But he doesn't budge, shaking his head and tapping the draw pile.

"I'm starting to remember why we hated each other," I say, counting out four cards.

He snorts, rolling onto his stomach. "Hey, do you remember when you gave me *Tale of Two Cities* and said it was basically about a guy being too douchey to live?"

I instinctively cover my mouth with my cards as I laugh. "Yeah. I thought you'd be too obtuse to realize."

"It was *so* rude!" he says before hopping to his feet to walk rigidly around the room, impersonating me. "You were all, *'Ooh, I'm so smart! I'm from Belgium! You've never heard of it!'*"

"I assumed you'd heard of Belgium," I argue. "I wasn't *that* pretentious."

"*Ooh, I read all these classics just to say I have!*" He cracks himself up, doubling over, unable to breathe. "You were such a *creep!*"

"I'm still a creep, thank you!" I throw my arms around his legs and try to drag him to the floor. He steadies himself on my shoulders.

We struggle, me trying to push him to the ground and him trying to pull me up, until finally, his knees give out, and he comes tumbling on top of me in another peal of laughter.

"I'm not a douche!" he argues.

"Oh really?" I clear my throat as I roll so that my arms lean against his chest, and he giggles as I launch into my own impersonation of him. *"Ugh, I'm Rowan. I'm so popular. Keep away, keep away—wait a minute—what's that—oh! The way you drink that guy's blood is so hot! My turn! My turn!"*

"Shut up!" he cackles.

"I'm so hot and popular; I have a neck for days! And you're all beautiful and stuff. Chomp chomp!" I snort, patting his chest. But Rowan has stopped laughing, gazing up at me with eyes that seem to dance in thought as his hand rakes over the side of my head.

"You are, though," he says. "Beautiful, and stuff."

He brushes his lips against mine in a gentle kiss. Then again, harder, as our lips part and close, finding all the ways they fit together. My body instinctively presses against him.

Wood and vanilla take over my senses. The throbbing of his veins, the sweet, pure aging of his blood like wine waiting to be uncorked as I hold him tighter and tighter.

I pull away. "We should cool down."

"I'm freezing," he says, pulling me in again.

We're at it again, and it hurts because my heart can't crawl inside of his. I'll never feel close enough. He flips me so that he's on top, his mouth finding its way from my lips to my jaw and down the side of my neck.

"Is this okay?" he asks.

"Yes," I whisper, my fingers latching into his shoulder blades.

"Are you comfortable?"

"Well." I grin. "I *am* on a stack of Uno cards."

He laughs and sits up, offering a hand. "Follow me."

"Where?" I ask, suspicious.

"In here." An impish gleam takes over his face, and he pulls me through the nearest door and flips on a dusty lamp. The room is furnished with a twin bed surrounded by posters for superhero movies, the characters seemingly winking at us. This must have been Rowan's room.

"And what"—I cross my arms—"did you think was going to happen tonight, Mr. Young?"

"Nothing, Mr. Belamy," he says, pulling my wrists from my chest and leading me over to the bed. "But you can't deny it's more comfortable."

He sits and makes to pull me over him, but I step back. "I don't know if I'm ready for that."

"I'm not trying to have sex with you," he says.

"Really?"

"Really," he says. "That's not why I brought you in here."

I nod. "Good. Okay. Carry on."

He pulls me over, my legs straddling his waist as we resume kissing. A few minutes later, when I sense he needs air, I roll to his side.

"I'm wondering though," I say, "and you don't have to answer, but . . . I mean . . . have you thought about . . . us . . . you know?"

"Yeah, a lot. Have you . . . us?"

"Yes."

"When you think about it . . ." he starts with a small cough, ". . . are you . . . ? Or . . . ?"

"You mean which position?" I ask.

He nods.

"Well . . . I mean, I don't know for sure yet. But . . . I think about both, I guess."

"Which are you usually?"

"I guess, usually . . . I'm on the top, actually," I admit, and his eyes get a little bigger. "What, because you're the jock, you assumed I'd slip to the bottom?"

His smirk gives him away, and he lets out a breathless laugh. "Yeah," he says. "I'm usually on the top too, when I think about it."

"Usually?"

"We don't have to talk about this right now," he says. "It doesn't matter . . . we're not doing anything."

"Right," I say. "No, we aren't going to do anything. So . . . keep kissing?"

We do, and our hands continue to meet each other, as they always do, discovering every area through our clothing. After a few minutes, he's pulling off his coat, and I don't stop him. He must be warming up and able to handle the cold. My hand slips beneath the back of his shirt as his hands do the same beneath my sweater.

He pulls it over my head, and I set about unbuttoning his shirt.

"If we aren't doing anything," I say, "then I guess this is okay."

"Absolutely!" he says as his bare skin presses against mine. "This is where we stop."

But we *don't* stop there. More rolling over each other. More kissing. We're getting to a point where there is no going back. I don't want to go back. I never want to go back. But is this the time and place? Is this a *smart* idea? If we do this tonight, then we are going to do it again. And probably again, and at some point, we could get caught. And then not only are we dating, but we're sleeping together. That's hard enough when you're just two guys, but we're talking centuries old rivalries.

If I sleep with a mortal slayer, I am *so* dead. And him, too.

His tongue leaves a wet patch on my throat as he pulls away to look at me pinned beneath him. His eyes drift to my lips.

"I want to see your fangs," he says, his tone firm. Almost a command.

"Why?" I ask.

He swallows, his jaw twitching back and forth. "Because I want to see all of you."

I kiss him as hard as I can, willing my fangs to drop down, then I smile at him. His eyes widen, and his body twitches.

"Wow," he sighs. "They're beautiful."

"Why do you find this beautiful?" I ask. One thing I cannot fathom.

"Because." He squeezes me tighter. "I feel like they were made for me."

Made for him. My fangs are *made* for him?

"You don't want me to bite you," I say. "It would be *so* painful. And I can't be sure that I would stop. Or that once I've had a taste of your blood, that I won't say anything to get it. You do not want this."

"Casper," he says, his chest swelling. "Don't make decisions for me. I want this. I've wanted it since I learned what you are. It's all I've dreamt about for months. Ever since your Feeding Ball . . . I've seen you do it. I want you to do it to me."

I shove him back and get off the bed. How could he want me *that* close to him, and how could he not see what danger that would put him in? And me.

"Even if I did stop," I begin, "even if I never did it again, what if a Blackthorn saw the mark?"

"You *will* stop," he says, standing up off the bed and only stopping when his face is inches from mine, "because you were able to stop for the cask. As for the mark . . ." his mouth breaks into that cocky grin that makes me instantly infuriated and enchanted. "You can heal them up."

I lose count of the seconds spent staring into his eyes, of the faltering breaths in my lungs. I'm so overcome by his scent, by the pounding beats of his begging heart. By the carnal, raging bloodlust of my primal nature, and of the sheer impossibility that a vampire could ever decline blood that is offered freely.

"I hope to your higher power," I say, dark urges bubbling through my body, "that you know what you are asking for. Turn around."

The grin falters just for a moment before it appears again. "Really?"

"Turn around, Rowan. And take a deep breath."

What am I doing? This is a terrible idea! This might be the worst idea I have ever had, but when Rowan turns on his heels and faces the opposite wall, waiting for me to take him in my arms and drain him of an ounce of life, I eye him up and down, and all I can think is—

Fuck it.

I step behind him and wrap an arm around his chest, pulling him back against me. He gasps. "Are you giving your blood willingly to me?" I whisper, reciting the questions that any ethical vampire would ask a mortal.

He nods.

"Say it."

"Yes."

"And you come to me of your own free will to offer your blood?"

"Yes."

My fangs drop further as my jaw lets loose. "Good."

Rowan cries out as my fangs enter his strong neck. I relish the satisfying pushback of his flesh as they pierce him. My grip around him tightens, my body pushing against his back as my mouth fills with warm, fresh blood.

Not just any blood. His blood. And it's . . . it's the best I've ever tasted. So pure, sweet, and complex. It's better than any wine, any chocolate—hell, any drug or vice you could find on the upper crust of this planet.

His heartbeat hammers against my palm, his pulse shooting blood cell after blood cell as he cries out.

Our feet leave the floor, and we're floating, our bodies entwined, as I let his blood wash over my tongue, reviving my eternal youth and my power far better than an animal's ever could.

I need to stop. I *have* to stop. But I keep sucking, and sucking, while his body relaxes.

You're taking too much! I scream inside my head. *Stop! Stop! You're going to kill him!*

I need more and more. All of him. Every drop. Every bit of what makes Rowan so wonderful.

STOP!

I grab a fistful of my own hair and pull my head back, taking care to remove the fangs correctly as we plummet to the bed. I stare at the ceiling, heaving, his blood washing down my chin and my chest, dripping from my fangs.

I want more. Give me more.

Rowan's face is . . . it's euphoric, a relaxed smile on his lips, his eyelids drooping. Blood stains his skin.

"I'm going to get something to wipe this off," I say, standing and heading over to his drawers. All I find are old T-shirts. "Um—"

"Use them," he whispers, and I wipe my chin before handing it to him.

"I'm sorry," I say. "I took too much."

"No you didn't," he says. "I don't think you took enough . . . How did I taste?"

"Amazing . . ." I admit. "I'm sorry that I hurt you."

"Hurt me?" He sits up on his elbows. "Casper, you . . . that felt *so good.*"

"What?!" I take a step back. "Rowan, I almost didn't stop. I could have lost myself, and you'd be dead. I shouldn't have done it. I won't do it again."

"Casper, enjoy this with me." He reaches his hand out. I take it, though I can't look him in the eyes. He makes me lie down next to him, and he presses his forehead to mine. "Skip the 'I'm a monster' bit. I loved that."

He kisses me, and soon we are right back where we started.

But our activities are cut short by a pounding at the front door.

CHAPTER TWENTY-ONE
ROWAN

My heart pounds in my ears.

Boom. Boom. Boom. They pound the door again, louder.

"What do we do?" Casper whispers, his fingers squeezing my upper arms.

"They know we're here," I say. "How did they know we were here?"

Boom-boom-boom-BOOM.

Casper rolls off me, rushing to his discarded clothing and stooping to toss me mine.

"The window," he says as he pulls on his jeans. "I can get us to the ground, then we bolt."

"Okay." I try and fail to steady my hands as I put my shirt on. "But . . . Casper?" I gesture to the blood stains that have covered the sheets of my old bed.

With lighting speed, Casper rips them off and balls them under his arm.

"We'll have to burn them," he says. "Come on."

I follow him to the window, he pulls open the curtains, and—

We scream at a pale face with eyes like glowing embers staring back through the dark glass.

"*Oh no,*" Casper says as he unlatches the window.

"No!" I pull at his shoulder, "Don't open it!"

"I have to; it's—"

The sash shoots up, and a woman with hair as red as her eyes flies through, knocking into Casper and pummeling him to the ground. All I can do is stand as still as a mannequin, watching as this vampire attacks my boyfriend.

"You *idiot!*" she screams, "You—lying—two-faced—treasonous—little—shit!"

Casper bucks her with his feet, and she's flung back toward the window. She grabs the curtain to keep from tumbling out, pulling the rod down with her. She tosses the curtain aside as Casper pushes himself into a hunched stance, his hands outstretched, ready to fight.

"Let me explain," he says, his voice as dark as the sky beyond the window.

"Explain how you're sleeping with the enemy?!" The woman shrieks and points a long fingernail at me. I recognize her now as the woman who was sitting on the banister that night I took Casper out. His aunt, Scarlett. "Do you have any idea who this boy is?"

"Yes!" Casper shouts, "His family were slayers. We discussed this."

Scarlett opens her mouth to respond but stops. She sniffs, looking me up and down as though I'm an animal to be slaughtered. A smile of disbelief shatters her statuesque expression. "Are you kidding me?!"

Before I can even blink, she's on me, grabbing the back of my hair and pulling my head back.

"Get off him!" Casper screams, his fangs dropping.

Her free hand rips the collar of my shirt, and she drags her nose along the spot where Casper's fangs entered only minutes ago. "Drinking from a slayer?!" she shrieks, "Are you *trying* to get us all staked?!"

"It isn't what you think," Casper says. "Let him go."

"No," Scarlett spits back, her grip on my hair tightening. "You've started something, and it has to be finished. If you don't kill him now, he's going to run to his little Blackthorns."

"I won't run to anyone," I whisper.

"Shut up!" She pulls my hair. "Casper, you do it or *I* will."

"You don't understand," Casper pleads.

"What is it, then? Why are you hunting him?"

"I'm not!" Casper shouts, and it all comes out, "We're dating, okay? We're *together*!"

Scarlett's grip slackens enough for me to slip away, and my knees give out. I crawl to Casper as he stoops and wraps his arms around me like a blanket of protection. He doesn't take his eyes off Scarlett as she shifts her gaze between us.

"You," she says, slowly, taking a step back, "and *you* . . . you're . . . oh, for fuck's sake."

"He's not like them." Casper moves his hand to my neck, and I wince. It tingles and itches. When he pulls his fingers away, I see the fresh blood on his fingers where he's pierced them with his fangs to heal the bite mark. "He's not going to hurt me."

Scarlett lets out a wry laugh. "They always hurt you."

"I'm glad you know," Casper says. "It isn't what was supposed to happen, but here it is. We're going to be together. I hope you can accept that."

"Aren't you suddenly so mature?" Scarlett sits on the bed, gripping the edge of the mattress so tight her fingernails stab the fabric. "Do you really think vampires are going to accept you being with a slayer? Do you think the Blackthorns will be okay with you noshing on their prized descendant?" She points at me, and I shrink. "Don't think I haven't been looking into your family. I know *exactly* what stock you come from."

"He wasn't even born," Casper spits back. "Neither of us planned this. Please try to understand."

"Oh, I understand. What *you* don't understand is that the two of you are not special. You're not the first vampire to slip fangs into a slayer." We look at her, watching as her expression shifts between anger and disbelief before ultimately settling into resignation. "Her name was Anne Thatcher."

My gaze slips to Casper's, but he doesn't look at me; he's fixed on his aunt.

"It was 1926," she continues. "In those days, the term 'Jazz Vampire' had a different meaning for some of us . . . My favorite speakeasy was called Mama's Bite, hidden five feet beneath a barber shop. It was a redbrick labyrinth of tunnels and hidden rooms, crawling with thirsty vampires and lovelorn casks. That's where I met Anne. I assumed she was a cask. What I didn't know was that she was a slayer, there to gather intel. She finally told me after three months, but by then, our affection for each other was undeniable. And you know what? I didn't care. Malcolm and Camille didn't either. By that time, tensions had died down considerably, vampires sticking to nightlife and decadence, feeding only on willing casks or animals. Slayers had become a benign presence to be tolerated.

"We thought Mama's Bite was a safe location. That so long as she was passing harmless bits of information to her fellow slayers, none would question the frequency of her visits. We were fools. While she was supposed to be trailing me, a slayer was trailing the both of us. They caught us in the farthest back room, where no one would hear the screams.

"I easily could have been staked, but do you know what those bastards did instead?" She looks to us, but neither Casper nor I respond, watching as her lip trembles, emotions from a hundred years ago returning in full Technicolor. "They killed *her*. To teach *me* a lesson. Staked *her* through the heart while they made me watch."

She stands and paces, quickly, as though outrunning her memories.

"Scarlett . . ." Casper begins, his voice breaking.

"I vowed never to fall in love again." She puts her hands up to silence him. "I don't want to. There will never be another Anne. I like my casks. I don't worry about losing them because I don't fall for them. But if you two do this, it's not a matter of *if* you'll get hurt; it's a matter of *which one of you* will be hurt. The Blackthorns might be your classmates, and your father might run the school, but that doesn't mean they wouldn't kill you if they thought it would hurt us. Do you understand that?"

I don't know how to respond. I've been worried about Casper getting hurt. Thinking of how much I want to protect him. I hadn't thought about them coming after *me*.

"Yes," I say. "I understand."

"He shouldn't *have* to understand." Casper stands, and now *he's* the one pacing, his hands balling into fists. "Why should anyone care? We're always hiding!"

"And what do you expect, Baby Sheik?" Scarlett asks.

"To be together in peace," Casper sighs. "Someone . . . I don't know . . . If anything will ever change, someone has to be first. Right?"

"You're right," Scarlett says. "Someone *would* have to go first. But not you." She turns her gaze to the window, out into the night. "That out there is our best friend, Casper. You're safer there, in the night, where the wrong people can't see you."

"That's wrong."

"No, it isn't. This sort of thing ends poorly in the light. If you don't want to lose each other, you'll keep it in the dark."

CHAPTER TWENTY-TWO
CASPER

"Do you think she's right?" Rowan asks, his voice barely audible as he pulls up to the curb where he picked me up.

I shrug. The taste of Rowan's blood is already haunting me. Those first pure, sweet drops that exploded on my taste buds. The complex notes coming together in a symphony of flavors. The warm, comforting aftertaste of him, tempting me for one more sip.

Saliva pools on my tongue. Once wasn't enough—I'll need it again and again until I've had all of him. But something else is snaking through my mind, something unfamiliar and yet all too true. After a second, I understand what it is. Shame. Not only for drinking his blood, but for things I don't remember.

"Are you in there?" Rowan asks. I blink, keeping my eyes trained on the snow-plowed street ahead.

"Sorry," I say. "Was thinking . . . I suppose Scarlett's right. But that doesn't mean *it* is."

"Do you want to taste my blood again?" he asks, and I sense hope in his tone. "If it'll make you feel better?"

I grab his hand as he reaches up to pull his collar down.

"We shouldn't do it again," I say. "We made things more

dangerous by doing that. I want my tour. I want to be trusted. But now I want more. I can't stop thinking about it."

"So have more."

"No!" My voice rises, but I catch myself. "I could kill you. When the thirst takes over, I can't stop. I'd drain the life out of you." My heartbeat picks up speed. The taste of him scares me. "And I would enjoy it."

He's quiet for a moment as he studies my fingers against his. Then he forces a snort. "Okay, creep."

"I'm a *vampire*!" My voice rises again. "It's my nature to go to that place, and when I go there, there is no going back. I don't want to kill you. Okay?"

"Okay," he sighs. "Fine. I understand. But I want you to understand how incredible it was for me, too. I also want more."

Guilt prickles the back of my neck, and I rake my fingers through my hair. I should have known this would never be a one-and-done thing. There's a reason casks exist. The high of being fed on is incomparable to any drug. The only way you could ever be satisfied after surviving a bite is to become a vampire yourself.

And now I've gotten Rowan hooked.

"I'm sorry," I say. "I should have thought twice. But I wanted you so badly, and . . . I don't know what I'm doing. I'm barely a year into this. I had one simple job— get through the school year and don't bite anyone. And I couldn't manage it. The closer I get to you, the more I risk, not only for me, but for every other vampire here. And *I don't know what I'm doing*. All I know is that I don't want to get left in the dark, or whatever Scarlett said."

"Casper." Rowan swallows. "How did you become a vampire?"

Up early, son? I remember a voice.

"Hmm?" I ask, lifting a hand to the left side of my neck, which suddenly itches.

"I went into the wrong alley in NYC and ran into a feral," I say, offering the part I do know for sure. "A vampire who'd lost their humanity. He grabbed me and pulled me further into the dark. He stopped draining me at some point and cut his arm open and made me drink from him. Who knows why? Maybe he saw how young I was, or maybe he thought he could keep me as a pet. Ferals are twisted and impulsive beings with no obvious motivation."

The itchy spot on my neck burns. My fingernails push against it, but it won't be soothed.

"I laid there all night, my veins burning and my body thirsting for something I couldn't name. At sunrise, I figured something strange had happened to me, because I was badly burned. I couldn't speak. I couldn't think in words, only in needs. The need to hide. To . . . to drink blood. I hid in a dumpster until dark, feeding on rats. Malcolm and Camille heard reports of an infant vampire stalking the subways and came to investigate. They found me in an abandoned tunnel. I couldn't speak or understand anything, only that they were taking me with them. I didn't know who I was. I didn't remember anything about myself. The me that exists now is something that was created. Something *I* created."

Rowan tries to take my hand, but I yank it away, too gone in the past to let myself be touched.

"They kept me in a soundproofed panic room in their penthouse so that my inhuman screaming couldn't be heard by the mortal cleaning crew," I say, "with a chain around my ankle so I couldn't wander. Distraction was the key. One day, when I was particularly difficult to deal with, Camille had an epiphany and had a TV and an old-school VCR that she'd collected from a mortal thrift shop brought up.

"That's when I was reminded, via a near worn-out tape, of the existence of *Casper the Friendly Ghost*. I'd seen the world in black and red for so long that the colors of the cartoon hypnotized me. It was like seeing and understanding the world for the first time. I sat crisscross on the floor drinking from a sippy cup of blood, like a screwed-up toddler with a morphine addiction."

Rowan's eyes light up. "That's how you got your name."

"Did I tell you Malcolm made up our surname from the French

Bel Ami?" I smile. "It means beautiful friend."

"No, you didn't tell me that," Rowan whispers.

"There were other tapes—*Looney Tunes, The Flinstones*—but I liked Casper best, and his witch friend Wendy, because I felt they were a bit like me. Something that was supposed to be frightening, yet I wasn't. I couldn't be. It's hard to be taken seriously when you're drinking from a sippy cup."

I snort.

"Casper Belamy. I liked the ring of it. I watched that *Casper* tape so many times the video wore out. From there it was other old shows. *The Munsters, The Addams Family.* And *I Love Lucy,* and *The Dick Van Dyke Show,* and over time, as my thirst became more manageable, and my sippy cup graduated to a coffee mug, it occurred to me, as Camille sat with me, laughing at jokes she'd heard a million times, comparing the way Lily Munster spoke with the cadence of her voice, that she had designed herself on these characters. And that meant I could, too.

"The Belamys purchased our new home the moment I could be trusted outside the panic room, abandoning their Manhattan penthouse for the quiet, small-town town life with their "newborn" son. It was when I explored our new home that I found my new self.

"The library and its books had been abandoned along with the house. I like to think that the books knew I'd find them, so they waited for me. On a table next to a Louis XV sofa was an old leather-bound copy of *Frankenstein.* The pages were so yellowed and dry that I had to hold them very carefully so they wouldn't crumble in my fingers. And the smell of it was so strong and cozy that it blocked out the omnipresent scent of blood."

"That's why it's your go-to."

"I didn't intend to read the whole thing in an hour. Or at all. But my vampiric speed and ability to take in large amounts of information proved themselves, because that's exactly how long it took. I was so amazed by the story, and my newfound ability, that I read it again, this time in forty-five minutes. And then again.

"I was smitten. Here I was, this manufactured *thing*, told that I would be feared by everyone else, peeking through cracks in windows to watch the mortals living out happy ever afters, raging all the time that I'd have to figure out a different way to be fulfilled.

"When the clock struck two in the morning, and I finished my sixth reading of the book, I decided to try out another. Then another. And by the end of the week, I'd read thirty-five books, most of them twice. All old classics, all requiring me to keep steady hands so as not to damage them, all with that insanely amazing, papery smell."

I pause, and Rowan sits quietly. Another snowfall begins beyond the windshield, the only noise the gentle hum of his car engine.

Finally, I shrug. "That's me. I'm bits of made-up people to create an undead, made-up person. I imagined their voices, their inflections, the way I thought they might move and react. Somewhere along the line, the act became reality, and I emerged, with a want for autonomy outweighing my want for blood.

"And I like the me I created. Even if it was something I came up with, it's still *me*. But there are days I wonder who I *was*. If I'm still that boy, too. Lately, he's creeped in here and there."

"Casper, I'm sorry—"

"I should let you get home," I say, straightening my coat. "Your dad is probably wondering where you are."

"You do know I'm glad about tonight, right?" Rowan asks sheepishly. "What we did?"

I nod, unbuckling my seatbelt. "I know. And . . . I'm glad. And I'm glad you're my boyfriend."

He shoots me a small smile. "I'm glad, too."

After I leave the car, I wait until he's pulled away before I turn around and stab my fangs through the inflatable snowman in the yard behind me. I watch with angry glee as it deflates along with my bubbling memories.

I'm haunted by the memory of sheet music as "Angels We Have Heard on High" croons from Malcom's phonograph. It taunts us demons as we sip blood from crystal glasses and pretend its eggnog. It makes the memory hurt all the more.

So does wearing this fuzzy red Santa hat Camille made me put on, complete with green pajama pants dotted with candy canes. We're all in them: me, Camille, Malcolm, and Scarlett. Oscar is the only one dressed differently, clad in red velvet with white fur lining and shiny black boots. We're gathered around the twelve-foot Christmas tree, strung with ornaments and trinkets collected over centuries. We're surrounded by mountains of presents, black and red gift paper torn to shreds. It's a picture-perfect vampiric Christmas morning.

But I can only think of a terrible Christmas Eve.

A stack of crisp new books and rare first editions are piled next to a couple of designer jackets and dress shirts on the floor next to me. I should be happy. Getting into the spirit as goofily as Camille and Malcolm are, continually finding reasons to stand under the mistletoe. And I would be happy—

If not for all the mental images. Of sheet music. Of a concrete playground that Christmas morning. Of a man who isn't my father standing too close, and the feeling of discomfort attached to the memory.

For three long nights, ever since I bit Rowan, I have been accosted by the echoes of that day. Hearing snatches of dialogue heard by my mortal ears.

"More bloodnog, darling?" Camille asks me as she reaches for my glass.

"Oh!" I clutch it with both hands like a small child, bringing it to my chest. "No. I'm . . . I'm still working on it."

They made the kids from my group home go caroling, I remember, telling us to smile and look happy to do it, and afterward, this man told me he'd saved me a seat on the bus. So I hung back.

"Sit with me, baby boy."

"Are you alright?" Camille's finger brushes my chin.

"Perhaps he overindulged in the bloodnog," Malcolm says, perching on Oscar's knee as Scarlett snaps a picture through the 1920s camera Camille gifted her. "Isn't that right, sport?"

"Who wants me to sit with them?" I whisper, lost in thought.

"Casper?" Camille asks. "What is it?"

I shake my head. "Nothing. I'm fine; just can't decide which of those new books I'm going to devour first."

She smiles, placated, and sets about wadding up the discarded gift wrapping. Needing something to silence my thoughts, I stand and look over the massive Christmas tree.

One new ornament, a legitimate Hallmark collectible, catches my eye. I study the New York City skyline in the tiny globe that hangs from its pine branch.

"I'm going to find my family." A voice, light and crackly, enters my mind.

My grip around the glass tightens. I could've sworn that was *my* voice. But my voice isn't that crackly, or as light. It's smooth and deep, and—vampiric.

I remember a clap on the back. The squeeze of a finger in my right shoulder blade. Bile runs cold up my esophagus.

"Oh!" Camille gasps, reaching into a gap in the Christmas tree. "What is this? It seems Santa Claus hid another one!"

Scarlett grunts. "He isn't a toddler, Camille."

"Get stuck in a chimney," Camille snaps. "Look, Casper! I believe it's yours."

It's a red gift box, the size of my fist. I trade it for my wine glass and lift the lid of the box, dig through white tissue paper. My fingers run along a smooth glass orb. It's an ornament, red as blood. I hold it to the light as I make out the glittery silver writing on the side:

BABY'S FIRST CHRISTMAS.

It was Christmas Eve. And I didn't want the man to find me.

"I would adopt you if I could, Michael. You're my favorite."

"I didn't tell anyone."

The ornament drops from my hand and shatters on the floor. When I open my eyes, a circle of concerned vampires are standing around me.

"I'm so sorry." I drop to my knees to scoop up the shards. "I'm sorry-I'm-sorry-I'm-sorry—"

"It's alright—Casper, stop!" Camille stoops, an arm wrapping across my chest as she pulls my head to hers. "It's only an ornament. What's wrong?"

"I'll get him a fresh drink," Scarlett says darkly, and I hear her footsteps somewhere beyond the memories as she makes for the kitchen.

"Let it pass by," Malcolm says, his hand touching my shoulder.

"Don't touch me!" I scream at him.

"Shhh." Camille takes my face in her hand. "It's only Malcolm. Where are you in there?"

I can't speak. My mind is flashing with images. Bunkbeds. Cold concrete. A Bus. Lit signs. An alley. And faces. So many faces, laughing and snarling and shouting at me. And bunk beds. Cold concrete. A bus—

Michael. The man said *Michael.* That can't be me. I'm Casper.

"Here," Scarlett says, thrusting a glass of warm, sloshing blood to Camille. "What's wrong with him?"

"I think his past is coming back," Camille says, as though I'm not sitting right here. "Casper, drink your blood."

She tilts the glass to my mouth, but I swat it away. I can't control myself as it plays in my mind over and over again. And I feel it. I'm trapped, not good enough and—preyed upon.

"A tiny, little sip, champ," Malcolm says, his voice instantly calming. He's trying to control me. "Just one, and we'll let you go."

"You're not my father," I spit at him.

He sighs, a small, broken breath.

"He doesn't know what he's saying," Camille says. She tries the blood again, and I let her pour the liquid into my mouth. It tastes like pineapple and spice. She lets me go, and I lay back on the floor, my head brushing a branch of the Christmas tree.

"I understand," Malcolm whispers.

"Oscar, let's get him to his casket," says Camille, her voice breaking with a mother's concern. "Don't worry, Casper. We'll all be here when it's over."

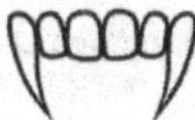

In the darkness of my closed casket, it all comes together. That last day as a mortal. Each time it replays, it becomes clearer, more chronological, more precise, as though it all happened only yesterday. It begins with the man asking, *"Up early, baby boy?"*

Then I recall it's the morning of Christmas Eve. I'm watching the sky get light on what will be my last sunrise, sitting on the concert slab of a fenced-in playground. Just me, my hands brushing along the chain-link fence. Should I climb it? Should I get away now?

I can't get away now. Because someone joins me. And on this go-through, I remember we all called him Mr. Kyle.

"Not running away from us, are you?" he asked.

Michael cannot be my name. The little flashes of this kid who was supposed to have been me? No way.

"You only have a few months until you're eighteen, unadopted, unwanted. I thought I could keep helping you. But hey, if you're unhappy with my help . . ."

"I'm not unhappy." That light and crackly voice came out of my mouth. *"I'd just like . . ."*

The eyes aren't right. I have bright blue eyes; this kid has dull gray ones. And I'm as pale as the snow falling outside the attic window. This kid is tan, and he has three freckles on the left cheek of his face, which is a lot fuller than mine. I don't have freckles.

"What would you like?"

"To know who I am."

"You're Michael Mortenson. You're a clumsy mess who walks like a humpback. Your father was a junkie, your mother didn't want you, and you're here because every family that fostered you didn't want you, either. You're always going to be this kid, no matter how successful you get. All you have is your great heart."

I absolutely refuse this as my past. This is a trick. A nightmare.

"I didn't tell anyone. About—"

"I would adopt you if I could, Michael. You're my favorite. You know that, right?"

The coffin lid bangs against the wall, I shove it open so hard and fast.

"And don't you ever make me get up this early to track you down again."

I spit bile onto the floor.

That *was* me. I was there, and now I am here.

Now I know why I hung back and slipped into that alley. I couldn't last another month in that group home, with *Mr. Kyle*. I'd been in and out since I could remember. I never knew who my biological parents were. Now I never will.

It doesn't matter because I'm Casper, and I *like* my new family. And I'm away from *that*.

Right now, more than ever, I wish vampires could cry.

The house is silent below. It's almost sunrise. Across town, people will be waking up from stupors brought on by too much turkey, scratching their heads as they try to find places to shove their gifts.

I can't help but wonder what my old parents are doing. Before I think better of it, I'm on my phone and clicking to Facebook, typing in the name I *think* is right. Kyle Hale.

No—Kyle *Hail*.

There he is. A man in his late 30s, looking overly happy in front of an oak tree. I click on his picture and scroll through post after post. Bible verses and memes about self-acceptance. I almost drop the phone.

Almost a year back, there's an old picture of me, with freckles and a tan, plastered on a missing person's graphic.

I keep scrolling, and scrolling, reading posts from social workers, from him. There are articles about my disappearance. The most recent say I'm presumed to be dead.

I click the phone off and toss it into my casket and leave the attic.

Creeping through the halls, I try to force the memories to subside, but they won't. I'll never forget who I was again.

And I hate who I was. I hate knowing what I'd rather have stayed hidden inside me. I don't want to be who that person was. To have gone through what they went through. I don't want to sit with traumas that I don't fully remember.

I'm Casper Belamy, Prince of the Vampiric East of the United States, and that is all.

As I wander the ground floor, I feel myself drawn to the kitchen, where the door to the basement seemingly calls to me. I've never been down there before, nor do I know what's kept there, but something in my core tells me to find out.

The door creaks when I pull it open and descend the rough, dusty steps. It's nothing more than an unfinished, gravel-filled room that must have been more of a cellar when the house was first built. Barrels and crates are stacked atop each other, filled with relics of my parents' pasts. I pass a pair of gloves and a long, black cigarette holder sitting atop a hatbox. They must have belonged to Scarlett.

A faded blue gown, Edwardian in style, so old it looks as though it would fall apart were I to touch it, hangs on a dusty mannequin. That must be Camille's. And here in this box—sheet music, yellowed, the words in French, and rusty opera glasses. Malcolm.

The entire basement is a collection of pasts shoved deep below.

My eyes fall on a newer cardboard box. I have a feeling I know what I'll find in there. But I don't want to look. Just leave it all where it is, and get back to Casper, to finding out who he's going to be in the end.

Except . . . I can't resist walking to the box and pulling it off its shelf.

With a short, sharp breath, I pry it open.

An oversized blue hooded sweatshirt. A pair of ripped jeans. Both are covered with rust-colored stains and smell of the metallic, salty scent of old, dead blood. A yellowed eye-tooth in a Ziplock bag. This must have been mine before the fangs came in—

I remember now. After that feral left me bleeding in the alley, scared off by sirens, I woke up burned by the sunrise, and I made it into the dumpster, then the tooth fell out. I'd pocketed it.

A rat tail in another Ziplock. And another. That's right. I was surviving on them. Why would I have kept the tails? As souvenirs?

They'd found me feral, right before I reached the point where I'd never recover.

Red hot embers within me ignite in an explosion of anger as I throw the box, enjoying the satisfying crunch as it makes impact with the wall and busts at its weak cardboard seams. That me will always be gone. Mr. Kyle was wrong.

I will never be that kid again.

CHAPTER TWENTY-THREE
ROWAN

"Heads up!"

Reed's snowball explodes against my coat in powdery flakes. He shouts a *woot* before squatting down to make another, and I have to hurry to beat him to it, plunging my bare hands into the snow on the quad.

The healed area of my neck where Casper bit rubs against my shirt, and I resist the urge to scratch it as I form the ball in my hands.

"Too slow!" Reed's fresh snowball slaps against my beanie, and I tumble onto my back.

Perhaps I'm being paranoid, but all I've been able to think about since that night is it happening again. Just as Casper craves blood, I'm learning the hard way that I crave the bite, the forbidden pain I wanted so badly. And now that I've had a taste, I'll never be satisfied until I have more. And more. Until a Blackthorn notices how off I am.

"Earth to Rowan!" shouts Reed, "I'm feeling generous! You gonna throw that?"

I blink myself into the present and stare at the snowball in my hands. My palms are red from the cold, but I don't tremble.

Actually, I can barely even feel the snow. The cold doesn't get to me so much now. I throw the ball as hard as I can, missing Reed by about seven feet.

"You okay?" he asks, watching as the ball disintegrates on the ground.

"Yeah!" I respond too quickly and too loudly. "I'm good."

I'm anxious to see Casper. We haven't seen each other since that night. Since the first bite. His texts are usually short; he prefers not to talk that way. But since then, I've barely heard from him at all.

What if Scarlett told his parents about us, or the thirst for my blood has driven him feral?

I catch up with Reed, my heart racing as we make our way to Young House among the strings of classmates lugging suitcases through the snow.

"Get anything good for Christmas?" Reed asks.

My dream come true.

"Bunch of clothes I don't want. Dad's already curating my college wardrobe. A *lot* of suit jackets."

"Don't remind me about college," Reed whimpers as we reach the steps to the dorm. "I'm not ready for the year to end."

The common rooms are crowded. I barely manage not to crash into anyone as I chase Reed to the stairs. But when I bound up the first landing, I nearly trip over the one student I truly care about.

"Woah!" I stumble, narrowly missing Casper, who sits with his legs crossed on the floor, a thick book open on his lap. "What the—"

Casper looks . . . different. His eyes are somehow even bluer against the dark circles that have appeared around them. They no longer just make my knees turn to mush—they pierce me, like an icepick through my own eyes.

His face is narrower, more angled. I wonder if it's possible for a vampire to lose weight. And . . . is he *paler?*

He's dressed in all black, from his turtleneck to his suit jacket, all the way down to his boots.

"Hello," he says, and my stomach flips. His voice is deeper and more hypnotic. Almost inhuman. He flips the book closed, and I make out the title, *The Vampire Lestat*, beneath his black-painted fingernails. "How was your break?"

He arches an eyebrow at me, and I shake my head, unable to process what I'm seeing. Casper isn't even bothering to hide his vampirism. Any Blackthorn that might be watching could spot him from a mile off. What is he *thinking?*

"What'd you say to him?" Diego pops his head around the landing, and I jump at his sudden presence. Next to me, Reed grunts.

Casper rolls his eyes before standing up. "I said 'hello'; is that permissible?"

Diego cringes at him. "Who the hell hangs out in a dark stairwell?" He mutters something about Casper being a psycho before disappearing up the next staircase.

Casper tilts his head and shrugs, his eyes piercing me yet again. I want to tell Diego to apologize. But if I do that . . .

"I, uh . . ." Reed scoots his luggage along the landing, heading for the corridor of dorms. "I'll catch you later, Rowan."

Casper waits for the sound of Reed shutting his door before scowling. "Did you hear the news? I'm a 'freakin' psycho' now."

"Go to our room," I say, not even looking at him. I can't—his eyes hurt mine too much. "And wait for me."

He starts to say something else, but I'm gone, marching to Diego and Reed's door. I pound on it.

A second later, Reed is gaping through the crack. "You scared me."

I push the door open all the way and storm in, locking eyes with Diego, who's draped over his bed, tapping mindlessly on his phone.

"Stop it," I say. "All of this with Casper. Just stop."

"He was being a creeper," Diego says through gritted teeth.

"This is our last semester here." I ball my hands into fists. "Ever. We won't be bullies. Leave him the hell alone."

"I can agree to that," Reed says, and I notice for the first time that he's backed himself into the corner, as though trying to escape the tension in this room. "It got old months ago."

"Casper is *incapable* of having feelings." Diego swings his legs onto the floor and stands up, staring me down so hard I shrink about two inches. Heat rises in my cheeks. "Why do you care, Rowan?"

"I . . ." My voice will barely come out. Why is he looking at me like that? His eyes are so detached and cold. This isn't the Diego I've known for years. "I don't think it's right."

"You and I know very well what is right and what isn't," he says. "Is there something you'd like to tell me? Because I know you're not that stupid."

"What are you talking about?" Reed asks.

Diego knows. Somehow, he's figured it out, and he's testing me. How could he know? I take a step back. "They're changing you," I say.

"*You're* the one who's changed." His spit splatters my chin as he pushes the words through clenched teeth. "I don't care what you do with who, but it better not be with *that thing*—"

"I slapped the crap out of Diego."

Casper pulls his arms from me. "You did *what*?"

"I think he's onto us," I say. "And he won't stop harassing you. I'd had enough. But now he might tell the others, and I don't know what to do—"

He pushes the covers off us and leaves me in his bed as he paces the floor, practically hovering. "*Rowan!* Violence isn't the answer. How could you be so—what do you mean, he might tell the others?"

I wince, rubbing my forehead. "He's a Blackthorn . . . I've known since Halloween."

"And you didn't tell me?"

"I came out to him when I found out," I say, reaching my hand out for his. He doesn't take it at first. "And he was so great about it. I didn't think it was right to throw him under the bus. But I couldn't take him being such a jackass anymore. I blacked out."

Casper folds his arms, considering. "I'm all for a hero defending my honor, but violence still isn't the answer. What if you set him off?"

"I know."

"What if he retaliates by outing us to the whole order? If he knows . . . what if all of them already know?"

"Sorry," I say again. "But hey, it's not like you're bothering to hide anything."

"Excuse me?"

I gesture to the black nails, the clothing, the changed face. "What is all *this*?"

Sighing, Casper pries his hand from mine and rakes it through his wild hair. "I'm just being me, Rowan. Is that a problem?"

"Don't turn this on me." I crawl from the bed and pace to my side of the room. "That isn't fair. It's one thing to be you; it's another thing to push it too far. There're Blackthorns everywhere."

Casper gives a half shrug, casting his eyes to the floor between us. "So are we. I'm hardly the only guy with painted fingernails when it's not a school day."

"This isn't about nail polish! Are you *trying* to look more, well, vampish? To see what happens or something?"

"Maybe," says Casper. "Perhaps I'm tired of putting on someone else's face every day. Aren't you?"

My stomach flips. "That wasn't called for."

"I'm sorry." Casper joins me on my bed, laying his head against the pillow. "Really. I didn't mean it like that. I know I'm hiding myself a little less. I had an . . . *interesting* Christmas. I got my memories back."

"Oh!" I sit up on my knees, ready for Casper to share. But he averts his eyes by looking up at the fencing swords hanging above him. "Oh . . . not what you were expecting?"

"I'll tell you the details at some point, but for now, let's just say that becoming a vampire was the best case scenario for me."

"Wow, okay." I nod. "Anyone from the past I need to backslap while I'm on a roll?"

He snorts. "Down, dog."

With a sigh, I lay my head on his chest. "For what it's worth," I say, "I really like this new vibe. You're sexy as hell."

"Don't distract me from my melancholy."

"Too late," I say, kissing his cheek. "You look too cute when you're melancholic."

His finger traces over my collarbone, looking at me as though deciding where to plunge his fangs next time. "*You* look too cute when you're riled up."

"And you're welcome to do what I think you want to."

He jerks his finger away. "What? No, Rowan. We talked about this. I can't. If I keep drinking your blood, it's never going to end. Not until you're dead or a vampire."

"Don't worry about that right now."

"How can I possibly not—"

"I make my own choices. If you're going to be more of a vampire," I say, crawling and planting my hands beside his shoulders so that my neck hovers just above his lips, "then you kind of have to do what vampires do."

"You're a terrible influence."

"I know."

His fangs enter the unbitten side of my neck.

CHAPTER TWENTY-FOUR
CASPER

When I push through the library doors, I see that even a room full of books isn't safe for us anymore. There he is, my favorite classmate: the boy who could tempt me into giving up my tour for one kiss.

But there's also the fencing team, sitting in the farthest-back study table, whispering about him. Like they've been doing since he and Diego had their fight. All I want to do is rush at him, leap over the table, and show all of his teammates what real making out looks like. Then I'll make them sorry for shunning him.

But I can't.

Before the temptation gets too strong, I duck into an aisle and lose myself in R–S. I only need to find a few books to keep my mind occupied, and then I'll leave. It hurts too much to be in here, between him and them. Soon, I'm staring off into space, thinking of all the things I'd do to protect him if only I could.

A moving shadow pulls me from these thoughts, and my eyes drift to a gap in the shelf at my waist. Someone is walking behind the stack, pausing just beyond the books in front of me.

Slowly, a familiar hand appears through the gap, palm up.

Rowan's scent permeates the aisle.

With a sigh, I put my hand on his, and he closes his fingers, squeezing tight. He pulses once, then twice. I pulse twice in return.

We remain silent, holding each other's hands through the stacks. I rest my head against the spines of the books and pretend that it's his body. He's only three feet away, and yet I miss him so much—

"You asleep?"

I jerk back, my hand pulling from Rowan's, and I stumble against the bookshelf behind me. Several books on the top shelf are knocked out of place and rain down on me.

"Woah!" Mr. Abadi rushes forward. "I'm sorry, I didn't mean to scare you . . . Are you alright?"

I look at the gap in the shelf. Rowan is gone. I wince when I hear the door to the library close. "Yeah," I say and pretend not to hear the snickers of the rest of the fencing team as they follow Rowan's lead. "I'm fine. I'll get these."

"Don't worry about it," Mr. Abadi says. "I'll help you."

"No," I shake my head. "It's *my* mess. I'll get them back up."

Mr. Abadi nods and points to the end of the aisle, as though to say *I'll be over there*, and disappears behind the stack.

I push my tongue against the spot on my gums where my left fang lurks. That was so close. Too close. Mr. Abadi could have easily seen us. Then we'd get what we originally wanted, which was to not share a room together.

Shaking my head, I stoop to gather the fallen books and return them to their spots alphabetically. Stohler, then Stone—

Where is Bram Stoker?

There's something off about the spacing of these books. I slip my fingers between two, right where *Dracula* should be shelved, and push the books on the right over until there is no more space. A perfect, book-shaped gap is left. Right where I found it the first time I was in here.

I spin on my heels and march out of the aisle to the circulation desk, where Mr. Abadi has settled in with two hooks and purple yarn, knitting.

"Did you ever hear back about that book you pulled?" I ask, planting my hands on his yarn.

"What book? Oh." Mr. Abadi slowly sets down his needles and reaches for his tea mug. "*Dracula*? No, like I said, it wasn't in the catalog, so it must have been someone's personal copy."

"It had a sticker, and the cover was laminated, and there is a gap where it would go on that shelf."

"Have you read *Rebecca*?" He drops his knitting, reaching for the desktop mouse. "You would devour it. Gothic mansion, a bit thriller, a bit romance, a bit ghost story. It's iconic."

"I've read it six times, seen every film version, and listened to the German musical cast recording. Hey, I don't want *The Little Stranger*," I say, noticing the title he's typing in on his computer. "I want to know where that copy of *Dracula* is."

We're interrupted by the clomping of the fencing team as they make their way from the study tables. Victor Cress snarls at me as he passes. I grip the edge of the circulation desk because otherwise I might chase down and attack him. Mr. Abadi raises an eyebrow at me once they've gone, and when he speaks again, his voice is noticeably more soothing.

"I understand," he says, raising a hand as though to calm me. "I don't have it."

"What about *The Vampyre* by Polidori? *Carmilla*? *Queen of the Damned*?"

"Why the sudden interest in vampire books? It isn't spooky read season," Mr. Abadi challenges me, squinting one eye. "And no, we don't have any of those. I'm sorry."

I bite my tongue so hard my fangs descend, thinking it's time to feed, and I have to pull my tongue back before it's impaled. I turn around and gently push at my right fang until it retracts.

"Are you alright?"

"I'm fine," I say. "Never mind. What's *The Little Stranger?*"

But Mr. Abadi doesn't fill me in with the premise. He stares back at me, head tilted, waiting for me to spill. I give him nothing, maintaining my resting expression and hoping it's enough to throw him off the trail.

Finally, he sighs. "Follow me."

He makes his way deeper behind the circulation desk toward a door leading into his office, leaving me no choice but to go with him. But when I've stepped into a dim, windowless room, lit only by the blue glow of a computer and a wax warmer that makes the office smell like pies baking, he shuts the door behind him and leans against it.

"I'm not going to hurt you," he says, his usual hapless expression swapped out for a darker, conspiratorial one.

"What are you doing?" I make for the door, but he blocks my path, and a hiss swells in my chest before he says what I've dreaded hearing since arriving at this school.

"I know what you are." The words fall from his mouth in a rehearsed manner. He's been planning this. "I've always known."

I dart my eyes around the room, searching for anything that could be a weapon. But a brown ceramic mug of pens or thumbtacks stabbed into a cork board will hardly do the job. Closed hutches and file cabinets cram around me, and he'd be on me before I could turn them over. I'm trapped.

"I don't know what you're talking about," I say.

"Yes, you do," he shoots back, his trembling index finger pointing at me. "You're a vampire. Don't deny it."

How could he possibly know? Unless . . . Mr. Abadi is a Blackthorn. Which explains why he's been so keen on getting to know me.

"I won't," I say, forcing my shoulders back and my undead princely demeanor to take over, "if you tell me exactly what it is you're doing."

"I wasn't going to say anything," Mr. Abadi says, sighing. This would be my chance to push him out of my way and get out, but a new timbre in his voice holds me back. The accusation is gone, replaced with exhaustion. "I knew it was a matter of time before you noticed our collection has become . . . let's say *sanitized*." He gestures to the closed hutch next to me. "Please, have a look."

Keeping my eyes on him for as long as I can, I open the doors and take a look. There it is: *Dracula*. And *Salem's Lot*, *The Vampyre*, and every volume of *The Vampire Chronicles*. There are also non-fiction books on paranormal activity and vampire lore.

"Why are they here?" I ask.

"You know why," Mr. Abadi says. "They didn't want anyone putting things together. Or for you to get any ideas."

"*They* being the Blackthorns?" I ask. I can tell by his face that he knows who I'm talking about. "They made you pull these? Why did you? It's only a bunch of kids in a good boys heritage club."

"You think that's all it is?" Mr. Abadi cocks his head, folding his arms. "You don't think there are more out there? They have fathers, their fathers have fathers. They're only the young crop. And I can assure you, to these boys' fathers, it is *not* just a 'good boys heritage club'. Casper, I'm showing you these because *someone* needs to tell you what you're up against. Have your parents said anything about it?"

"No," I say, looking over the books again. "Scarlett—my aunt— did a little, but not that much. I don't think Malcolm and Camille know they're at the school."

"They should, and you need to know as much as possible to protect yourself," he says, as a chill fills the room. "You might want to consider leaving the school altogether."

Leave the school? Give up my tour? Give up Rowan? It's out of the question. "No one is going to actually kill me."

"They killed my husband," says Mr. Abadi, his lip twitching.

My eyes grow larger than I thought they could. I knew he lost his husband not too long ago, but I didn't know how. This can't be right, though. From what I've been told by Scarlett and Rowan, the

Blackthorns don't kill anyone anymore. Unless . . .

"Kevin was the love of my life," Mr. Abadi says, sitting down in his office chair and reaching across the desk for a picture frame that he shares with me. The photo is of him and a laughing man, the two of them in tuxedos. This must be their first dance at their wedding.

"You know, I don't think I've told you this, but one of my favorite things in this world are wildflowers." He smiles. "I'm not a nature person. That was Kevin's thing. And he used to make fun of me when he'd drag me out hiking with him because I'd have to stop to look at all the flowers. I'd get mad because he would pick a couple to be sweet, and I'd say, 'Well, now you've killed them.' So we agreed he could pick the wilted ones. That was our odd little thing— wilted flowers."

He takes a deep breath, scratching his thumb against his cheek as he flips through the memories in search of what happened next. "He was a talented artist—classical art, sculptures. There was nothing he couldn't do if he stared off into space long enough to get the vision for it. It was his dream to do it full-time. A month after we were married, he was offered a fellowship to study in Rome.

"While he was there, on a night he'd stayed out too long and was drunkenly wandering the streets, he was lured and bitten by some vampire feral. I suppose he must have sensed something in him, something that deserved to live, because instead of draining him, he cut himself and forced Kevin to drink his blood. He was undead by sunrise.

"He was gone for a year. I thought he'd abandoned me. But he was surviving in the catacombs, coming out to feed, trying to get himself under control. One day, I found wilted wildflowers in the mailbox. He'd come back to me. And I learned everything. And do you know what, Casper?" He looks at me, though I know he doesn't actually want me to respond. "I accepted him. Once I understood, once I believed, I accepted him.

"He never drank from anyone. Ever. Human blood never entered his mouth. He drank from animals, and never an endangered species." He laughs, but it is a hollow sound. His voice cracks as tears push into his eyes, and I feel my own lips tremble, watching this funny, jovial man transform into a broken child before me. "Turns out, they had been watching us the whole time. And that cowardly Blackthorn waited until I wasn't around to get an easy shot. A shot which planted a stake into my one-and-only's heart."

For a second, he can barely speak. He lays his hand on the desk to steady himself. I drop the book and go to him, but he holds out a hand to keep me back. I hug myself instead.

"He wasn't even feeding," he says, his hand slamming the desk. "My husband's murderer walks around free. *He* got to go home to his wife and kids, knock back a scotch, and congratulate himself. *I* get the memory of finding my husband crumpled on the ground, impaled by a stake"—he hiccups—"next to a bundle of wilted flowers."

He spins in his chair, hiding his face from me as he breathes, wiping the tears away so I can't see them, while I stand like an imbecile, unable to do anything, even cry with him.

"I apologize," Mr. Abadi says, slowly spinning back around to face me, his eyes dry but red and puffy. "I hadn't planned to tell you that. But this clearly is book banning. You can see them, right there, out of circulation. This is where it begins, Casper. It will go beyond books. And then where will we be?"

My eyes find the picture again, and I study the pair. Mr. Abadi and his husband. So happy and content. It seems like the end of a fairy tale: two Prince Charmings and a DJ. But the end of a fairy tale was the beginning of a nightmare.

Shouldn't I be permitted to have that fairy tale, too? Is there something so wrong about me that I shouldn't?

Two words, from deep in my gut, tumble out of my mouth. "Fuck that."

"Language," Mr. Abadi says.

"No. Fuck that," I say.

Mr. Abadi smirks, folding his arms. "I know this is a private conversation, but if you say that again, I *will* have to write you up. You're seventeen years old. You have an eternal life ahead of you; don't put yourself in a situation where that life is cut short."

"I'm not going to rage through the halls. But . . . I'm not playing their game either."

"Casper—"

"They're trying to erase me," I say. "I only just learned who I am. I don't want it taken away."

He lets me go without another word.

CHAPTER TWENTY-FIVE
ROWAN

The first *real* fencing practice of the year is held a week later in the athletic center. Up until now, we've just been getting back in shape, honing our moves. Today, we start getting *really* ready for competition. I've been looking forward to it, even if it does mean having to face the guys who've been giving Casper a hard time. Even if I *might* have to fight Diego.

I don't know how Casper's remained so calm since then. He's maintained that icy wall throughout the school days, pretending to eat lunch with Dakota and Sophie as though nothing is going on.

It's harder for me. I've been worried Dad is going to find out about me slapping Diego—and more. But all has been quiet, just me and the frustration. Fencing will be a welcome outlet for my anger.

Taking a deep breath, I push open the door to the fencing room, and—

The whole team is already here, gathered on the mat in a big huddle while Victor Cress whispers something to them. When they see me come in, the whispering stops, and they stare me down, arms crossed over their white uniforms.

"Hey guys," I say, trying my best to sound friendly and not suspicious. "What's up?"

Victor looks back at them before turning to me with a smug mouth. "Hi, Rowan. We need to speak with you."

"Um. Okay."

"We've all been talking it over as a team, and . . ."

Blood pounds in my ears, and I nearly drop my foil. I force a laugh. "You kicking me out or something?"

I can practically hear everyone's shoulders tense.

Victor sighs. "It's not fun for us. But . . . well, you've seemed really distracted lately. We don't want it to hold us back."

"I've had schoolwork," I say, the words barely stumbling. "And the play. I'm fine."

"We think it's best if you resign," Victor says, this time more casually, as though he's saying I need to have a drink of water.

"And I guess you're going to fill my shoes?"

He purses his lips.

"Well, nice try," I say, taking a few more steps into the room and setting about getting my stuff placed on the nearest chair. "It's not up to you. But good to know you'd all like to stab me in the back. Excellent teamwork, boys."

"We don't want you on our team anymore," Ben Ruthven says, and for a second, I think he's going to raise his sword. "This can be easy, or it can be difficult."

"See"—Victor walks, no, *saunters*, toward me; I resist the urge to kick his smug shin—"You weren't much of a good team member when you were smacking the shit out of Diego here."

My eyes lock with Diego's, who looks to the floor as quickly as he can.

"Is that what this is about?" I force a laugh. "You know nothing about that. But if it makes Diego feel better, I'll apologize."

"He's not even sorry," Ben says, waving his hand at me. "You're such a prick, Rowan."

"Let me put it this way," says Victor. "If you don't drop out of the team, we're going to tell Abadi and your dad, *and* Coach. I don't think suspension would be a good look on you, dude."

"Guys, you *know* me; we're friends—"

"We *were* friends," says Victor. "But we're sick of the Rowan Show. This isn't your team anymore. This isn't your school. You're done here."

I can't believe this is happening. All my school career, I've always been captain. Up until Casper came along, this was *all* I had. Now they're going to take it away because . . . because I'm with Casper. Because I'm not the *right* type of Blackthorn for Victor and Diego.

"Sorry, you can't be in here," Victor says, re-joining our teammates, who are holding their foils like they're ready to attack. "Team-only practice."

"Fuck you," I say, grabbing my stuff and storming toward the door. I lock eyes with Diego again, and this time, he doesn't look away. "Fuck all of you."

Diego's eyebrows dip, and he suddenly looks like a guilty thief. He steps forward, but Ben stands in the way, and he stays put.

"Hey, could you tell Coach and your dad that you're sick of fencing and quit on us?" Victor asks. "Save us having to fill out a physical assault report?"

The door slamming is my answer.

I walk as quickly as I can, but where to, I don't know. My mind buzzes, replaying the betrayal over and over. This was my life, my patch of earth. Now it's gone. Because I didn't want to be an asshole to my own boyfriend.

I feel weak and lightheaded; blood is surging through my veins, my fists longing to break something. I'm going to punch holes through the walls. I'm going to key all of their cars. I'm going to— cry.

Hot tears are running down my face before I can stop them. I'm a snivelling, pathetic mess. I pause at a series of black-and-white pictures of sports teams from the 1920s till now, the serious-faced swoopy haircuts trickling into greaser styles, then mullets and mustaches.

Statistically speaking, several of these guys were gay, too. I wonder if they ever got kicked off a team for being with someone they weren't supposed to be with.

"Rowan?" A voice pulls me away from the pictures, and I drop my helmet.

"Sorry!" Dakota says, stooping to pick it up. I stoop at the same time, and we nearly knock into each other. "I didn't mean to scare you."

"It's okay." I take the helmet from her and wipe my nose with the back of my hand.

"Do you need help with anything?" she asks. I spin around as fast as I can to dry the tears. "Hey, it's okay."

"What are you doing here?"

"I came to borrow some of the equipment," she says. "I don't like working out in the student gym where everyone can hear me huffing and puffing. I'll leave you alone. Hey . . . seriously. Are you okay?"

"I'm really good." I nod, but when my eyes meet hers, the tears pool up again, and my lips snarl against my will. "I'm fantastic."

"Okay," she says, her voice dropping to a whisper. She takes my hand and leads me to a girl's bathroom. "It's okay."

"That's the wrong room," I warble.

"It's a single stall; I don't even know why these are gendered. Pointless."

She pulls me inside and locks the door behind us, flipping on the water and gently moving my wrist under the faucet. "Cool off. You'll be fine."

I shake my head as the cold water hits my wrists. "Nothing's fine. I got muscled out of the fencing team."

"What?"

"Victor led the charge and kicked me out. I was captain, and now I'm not anything."

"They can't do that."

"They did." I lean over the sink, forcing two deep breaths in through my nostrils and out through my mouth. "My dad's going to kill me. And they're not going to stop. They're going to push and push and push until it all comes out, and then I'm *really* going to be dead."

"What's going to be pushed and pushed?" Dakota asks.

I shake my head. I've already said too much. If I say any more, then we'll have to add one more name to the roster of people who may or may not know about Casper and me. But . . . well, I could tell her part of it. I guess I need to.

"Dakota, there's a reason I ghosted you after we hung out those couple of times over the summer," I shut the water off and hop up on the sink.

"Ghosted is a strong word," she says. "Don't get me wrong, it kind of hurt for a minute. But it's not like I haven't done the same thing."

"I know," I say. "But I couldn't keep seeing you because I figured out why it would never work, and I couldn't tell you the reason."

Dakota forces a small laugh. "To be honest, the whole time I thought you might be closeted."

I lock eyes with her, my cheeks burning about 500 degrees. After a second, her smile drops, and her eyes widen. "Oh . . . *oh*. Rowan, it's okay!" The tears appear again. I sit still as Dakota rubs my shoulder. "I wish you'd have told me."

"You don't understand," I sob. "I'm *me*. And now I'm losing everything I've ever had. Except for . . . I'm *with* someone."

"You are? Who? Does he go to Mockingbird, too?"

"I can't tell you."

"Oh my god, he does, doesn't he? Wait. Rowan . . ."

I'm unsure how long we stare at each other, her putting it together and me watching the puzzle pieces fit into place. She raises an eyebrow. "Are you screwing your roommate?"

"N-not screwing . . . we haven't done that yet, but . . ."

"It's Casper," she nods. "You and Casper. That's why you go out of your way to torment each other when we're around."

I nod sheepishly. "Could you act like you don't know until I get the chance to break it to him? No one's supposed to know, and he'd freak out if you said something."

"Sure," she says, her smirk growing broader until she covers her mouth. "You're so teen Disney, and he's so *Addams Family*. It's adorable."

"Stop it!" I laugh through the tears. My face is going to singe off if it gets any hotter. "Teen Disney? How dare you."

"I won't tell him I know," she says, calming her expression. "I won't tell Sophie, either. But I hope you do tell people. You deserve to be happy—wait. Is that why they kicked you off the team?"

I shrug. I can't very well tell her about the Blackthorns or reveal what Casper really is. "It's . . . complicated."

"Remind me who's on that team? I know Diego and . . ."

"Victor Cress, Ben Ruthven, Skylar Long—"

"That's right," she says, her expression darkening. "Right . . . well, maybe getting kicked out of their little club was the best thing that could've happened."

I furrow my eyebrows. "What do you mean?"

She shrugs, taking a deep breath. "Nothing. We should probably get out of here before another rumor starts."

CHAPTER TWENTY-SIX
CASPER

"Should we invite him to sit with us?"

I look from my second reading of *The Little Stranger* to Dakota, who cocks her head toward the far window in the dining hall. Rowan sits at a table by himself, staring out the window at the snowfall. It's sad seeing him without anyone, not even Reed. Especially with all the red and pink paper hearts taped to the windowpane.

"I want to," I say.

"There's a group of us," Dakota says, though I don't know that she, I, and Sophie would constitute a group. "No one will bother you two."

Rowan told me the day he got thrown off the fencing team that Dakota put it together. At first, I was worried it would be the start of a flood of people knowing, but so far, so good. After a few days, we decided it would be best for Sophie to know too. I didn't want one friend to know and the other to not. Honestly, it's been a relief. The hardest part is—

"I'm sitting with him," Sophie stands up, lifting her tray of apple slices and yogurt.

"He said he wants to be alone." I reach to grab her arm but stop myself. If she notices how cold I am, there'll just be one more thing to explain. "He still has Reed."

"Reed went home for the weekend, and Rowan is there *alone*. You can't keep each other a secret like this." Sophie slaps her tray on the table. "You're going to wreck a good thing."

"Sophie, sit," Dakota calls after her.

"I want some air." Sophie makes for the door. Soon she's gone, heading out into the snow.

"It's not her relationship," I mutter. "Why's she so mad?"

"You forget she went through this at her last school," says Dakota. "Her ex-girlfriend did this to her. She's not seeing the uniqueness of your situation."

If only Dakota knew the full extent of my uniqueness.

Ever since talking to Mr. Abadi and seeing the hidden library of vampire books in his office, I've wanted nothing more than to go on a rampage. I can't look at Diego or Victor without seeing them as some grotesque *thing*. It's them who had those books removed. It's them who kicked Rowan off the team and have proceeded to make a spectacle of bullying him.

Oh, how I would love to torture and terrify them until I'm the only nightmare they'll have for the rest of their lives.

"I want so much to go over there and sit with him," I opt to say instead. "He hasn't been feeling great since the whole fencing thing, and—"

I snarl as I spot Victor Cress and Diego making their way across the dining hall. The clatter of plates and mindless chatter stops as our classmates notice the two of them reaching Rowan's table.

"What do they want from him *now*?" Dakota groans.

They're saying something to him, but I can't hear what. Rowan shakes his head, biting his lip. His face has turned the color of his own blood. Why can't they leave him alone? Still shaking his head, he flips his empty lunch tray and stands up so hard his chair teeters, threatening to fall to the floor. He steps back as Victor and Diego take the table over, beckoning the rest of the fencing team to join them.

"Are you for real?!" Dakota half-shrieks.

My heart cracks as Rowan leaves the dining hall, his silhouette fading into the thickening snowfall. I stand up and grab my untouched tray along with Sophie's.

"Where are you going?" Dakota asks, grabbing her own tray.

"To rip their vital organs out and hang them on the wall to shrivel."

Dakota grabs my sleeve, and I'm surprised by her strength as she pulls me back. "Casper, no."

"You saw what they just did!" I point, my voice rising. I take a deep breath to quiet myself, glancing around us to ensure I haven't caused some sort of scene. "Sophie's right. I can't just sit here."

"So don't," Dakota says. "Instead, do something that doesn't involve violence."

"Then I'll check on Rowan," I say.

Placated, Dakota lets me go, and I rush from the dining hall.

A few minutes later, I'm crunching over the snow, following the footprints Rowan has left. I find him near the main quad, punching a snowman in its pebble-nosed face.

"What was that about?" I ask.

"Sounds like you saw it; that's all there is to it . . . Did I used to be like them?"

"Only towards me." I offer a smirk.

"I'm so sorry," he says. "I was sorry before, but I definitely am now. That feels awful."

He shivers in the snow.

"This snow's picking up quite a bit," I say. "Do you want to go home?"

He shakes his head. "Getting snowed in with Dad would be the worst thing for me right now."

I could kiss him for being so obtuse sometimes. "I meant *our* home."

On Rowan's TV, Captain America does something action-y with a fancy gadget. Rowan's staring at me with a content, closed-lipped smile.

"What?" I ask.

"I never thought I'd see you watch one of these movies."

"You watched *Les Misérables* with me and only groaned ten times. I owe you." He opens the blanket around his shoulders, welcoming me in. "You're just going to get cold again with me in here."

"I like your kind of cold." He kisses me, and I wrap my arm around his waist, my fingers grazing the waistband of his gym shorts. We lie back on the bed, the sound of the Avengers getting violent with some villain drowning out the sounds of our kisses.

"Actually," Rowan says after a bit, "I . . . love it."

My hands freeze just as they slip under the back of his shirt. His body is incredibly warm. And his heartbeat has picked up, racing so fast it must be trying to escape his rib cage.

"Rowan?" I look into his eyes. Have they gotten *greener*?

"I love you, Casper."

I blink, though I don't need to. Did he just say . . . he couldn't have said . . . it was my imagination. I only wanted to hear it, so I plugged it into his mouth, and it replaced whatever he actually said.

"Sorry," he says, an embarrassed grin dimpling his bright pink cheeks. "I don't mean to freak you out; I—"

"I love you too," I say. I do. I love Rowan Young. He can't get close enough. I can't imagine being here without him. I love him as he is now, and when he's eighty-five and looks nothing like the boy holding me now, I'll still love him. Even if I remain the same.

"Yeah?"

"Yeah."

He kisses me, over and over, and eventually, our shirts and the blanket are on the ground. Under the covers, Rowan whispers in my ear, "Bite me."

"Sir, yes sir," I grunt.

His blood fills my mouth, and I sigh at the sweet taste as he holds on to me as tightly as he can, wincing. My eyes roll back and—

I remember a small orange flame, a white wax number on sugary icing. It wasn't the correct number because it wasn't just my candle. It wasn't just my cake. I had to share it with another kid. But we both got to blow out the candles because—

"What's wrong?" Rowan grabs the right side of my face as I pull my fangs from him and look up with a hiss. Another memory has returned. "Casper?"

"I just had another memory," I say, but this one makes me smile, and I let out a soft laugh. "Rowan . . . it's my birthday today. I'm eighteen."

"You old perv." Rowan pushes my chest, sporting an irritating, lopsided grin.

"Shut up," I laugh.

"I'm kidding. *Babe!* That's so awesome! You're getting it back. I'm glad I was here for it. Happy birthday," he says, pulling my face to his. "I'll get you a present."

I nestle my head in the crook of his neck and set about healing the mark. "You already gave me one."

Rowan moves his hand to mine, pulling my fingers from my mouth just before I pierce them. "Don't," he says. "Don't heal it."

My eyes slide to his, searching for some hint of a joke. "You're not serious. We have to heal the mark. If a Blackthorn sees—"

"But this one is different," he says, his eyes glassy. Begging. "I'm not ashamed. I'm not hiding you."

He's so adamant, so sincere, that I almost go with it and move along. But . . . it's *so dangerous.*

I pull my fingers from his and pierce the pad of my right index finger. "It's too risky. Maybe someday, but not—"

"This is the love bite," he pushes me off him as he sits up, and

I have to be careful not to get blood on the sheets. "You gave this to me when I said I loved you. On your birthday. I know we have to heal the rest, but . . . this one is *special*. I can hide it with stage makeup. I'll avoid the Blackthorns. This one means more." He rubs his hand over the bloodstained puncture marks, traces the two tiny holes with his fingers. He presents it to me, as though showing off a badge of honor. "I know we have to be careful. That we have to hide the evidence. But . . . I'm not ashamed. I don't want to hide it like I am. I'll be very careful. Let me have *one*. Please."

Slowly, I nod. "Alright. I won't heal this one. But Rowan . . . promise me you won't let anyone see it. Ever."

"I won't," he says. "This is *our* thing."

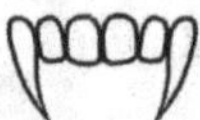

"When we return, I promise you a grand finale that you will never forget!" Sophie calls out over the empty, darkened auditorium with the air of a showman as she lifts her top hat and Rowan launches into the final notes of "Morning Glow", the finale of the first act of *Pippin*.

From my spot at the back of the stage, I do my best to give jazz hands that could be seen from Google satellite.

A hush falls over the stage as we stay posed, waiting for applause or a scream. What we get is a mix.

"That was *not* terrible!" Mrs. Spencer shouts, and all of us groan. "No, no! You did a lovely job! But we need *Broadway*. We don't have the pep yet! But that was a good start to tech week. Crew, you were phenomenal. Cast, hang up your costumes. If I find a single piece on the floor, I'm hiding it!"

Dakota ducks around two medieval soldiers high-fiving and zips toward me in a long peasant dress, pulling fake daisies from her fake blonde braid headband. "Hey," she says. "Do you have much homework tonight?"

"You know I get it done during class," I say. "Why?"

"Sophie and I are wondering if you and Rowan want to escape campus and go have dinner with us," she says, a hopeful smile on her face. "It's our tech week tradition. We break out each night and go somewhere different, and it'll give you guys a little break from everyone here."

"You forgot it's mandatory," Sophie says, zipping over and plopping her costume top hat on my head. "You can't give Casper an out—he'll take it."

"I'll have to ask Rowan," I say.

"Rowan!" Sophie looks up the scaffolding that's been wheeled out for the finale, where Rowan sits on a wooden throne painted gold, wearing a king's crown that's a little too big on him. "Wanna eat mozzarella sticks with me tonight?"

He smiles. "Yeah."

Sophie bops the top hat so that it falls over my eyes and whispers, "I already asked him between "War is a Science" and "Glory", when you were stuck in the green room."

Rowan climbs down from the scaffold, and I try not to stare at how attractive he is in his costume, a tight shirt made to look like chainmail. There is no collar. It shows off his collarbone and the tips of his shoulders—and my bite mark laid bare.

"Your makeup rubbed off," I whisper, resisting the urge to cover it with my hand.

"I'm on it." He zips backstage, and I follow. I know it could make us seem more suspicious, but I'm paranoid. We hadn't considered how hot stage lights would make the makeup streak, and now the undeniable proof that I fed on him is on display for the entire drama department. He makes it to the makeup table and sets about spreading on concealer. "I'm covering it, don't worry."

"Knoll!" Stella Harris, our student stage manager, appears around one of the curtains, hot on Quentin's trail as he barrels toward the stage door with a duffel bag. "Hang up your costume."

"I have to go," he says.

"Hang. It. Up."

Stella disappears as quickly as she came. Quentin grunts, slipping the bag from his shoulder and shrugging out of his Charlemagne robe.

Dakota, who's been busying herself with resetting her fake braid on its wig head, shoots him a suspicious look. "Where are you rushing to?"

Quentin doesn't even look at her as he says, "Oh, *now* she'll acknowledge me. If it's any of your business, I have plans tonight."

"Doing?"

"Uh . . ." Quentin glances at Rowan. "Hangout with the fencing team . . ."

Rowan's shoulders droop. He needs to blend the foundation on his neck better, but now is not the time for me to say so. "You're on the team now?" he asks.

"They had an opening," Quentin admits. "Just thinking about my resumes, you know?"

He slips to the costume room.

I wipe my own makeup off, taking care to stand close enough to Rowan to comfort him, but not so close that anyone would think something else is going on.

"You alright?" I ask him.

He finishes covering the bite mark, throwing his makeup sponge on the table. "I'm great. I don't care. Mozzarella sticks, please?"

"This Friday and Saturday at seven, and Sunday at two," Sophie proudly explains our performance schedule to our server as they take our milkshake glasses, mine still full of pink ice cream.

"Oh, I'll definitely be there," they say and nod to my glass. "Would you like a to-go cup for that?"

"Sure," I say. Rowan can drink it later, even if it isn't cookie dough flavored. I slide the glass to them, and they take it away, ducking into the kitchen.

"You know they aren't actually going to come, right?" Rowan asks. "They were definitely just being polite."

"We're the best advertisement," Sophie exclaims, pointing to the stage makeup she didn't remove before we left school. "Right, Dakota? . . . *Dakota?*"

Dakota, who had been staring out the window, comes to and lets out a sigh. "Sophie's right. Sorry, what were we talking about?"

"What's wrong?" I ask. "You've been zoned out since we left campus."

Dakota bites her lip. I try not to react when Rowan nudges his foot against mine under the table. We had to sit catty-corner to each other just in case another vampire, cask, or Blackthorn parent was here.

"I mean . . . aren't you all a little suspicious? Rowan gets kicked off the team and Quentin slides right in?"

My eyes flick to Rowan, but he's already staring back with a moody expression.

"I wasn't going to say anything," Dakota continues, "but it's getting too weird. I didn't just break up with Quentin because I wasn't feeling it. There was a big reason."

Sophie slides her hand across the table, but Dakota doesn't take it. She trains her eyes on the middle of the table, tracing her finger over the restaurant's branding etched into it. "He's in some sort of club. I figured it out pretty fast after we got together. It's like a secret society thing. I just figured it was an elaborate excuse to have a boy's night, so I didn't worry about it."

My eyes bore into Rowan's. Quentin's a Blackthorn and has been this whole time. Is that why he was friendly with me at first? To get intel?

"But it just got weirder. *He* got weirder. Super attached. Always going on about legacy and his family lineage, and on and on about the importance of keeping that up—"

The server returns with my to-go cup of half-melted milkshake and the check, and we all lean back, pretending to laugh at an unsaid joke. "Here you go!" they say, "And you just pay at the front when you're ready. No rush at all; hang out as long as you want."

"Thanks." Sophie smiles at them. The minute they're onto the next table, she leans back in, her expression hard. "He what, Dakota?"

"He kept hinting that he wanted us to get married. Like, *fast*. He didn't even care about my college plans or anything. He went on and on about how he's going to take over his dad's business and that it didn't even matter—"

"Woah, woah." Sophie waves her hand. "Excuse me?"

"Maybe I'm just grossed out by the whole thing, or paranoid, but I got the impression he wanted me to . . . drop everything and have kids with him."

"*What?!*" Me, Rowan, and Sophie all shout in unison.

"Shh!" Dakota says. "We need to go. I can't talk about this in here."

About five minutes later, we've paid, and we're waiting for Rowan to come outside after popping into the restroom. Dakota shivers, reminding me that it's late February and I have to pretend to be cold. I hug my arms over my chest.

"So, this baby thing," I begin hesitantly. "Did he try anything?"

"No, thank god," Dakota says, shaking her head. "But he kept bringing it up. Toward the end, he got really controlling and territorial—"

"Forget his car," Sophie says, "I'm going to key his face."

"And that's why I was freaking out when he was trying so hard to get cast as Pippin."

Rowan makes his way out of the restaurant and joins us, wiping the remnants of sink water from his hands and plunging them into his coat pockets. I wrap my arm around his shoulder as the late winter chill sweeps through his hair.

"All I knew was there was some sort of club, and he wasn't like this until he joined it," Dakota says. "So I sniffed around in the girls' dorm common rooms, and after a while, a good handful opened up about how intensely a few guys were coming onto them. Then I noticed the common denominator."

She beelines to her car, and Sophie is quick to follow. But Rowan and I hang back, sharing hard stares, as though communicating telepathically.

You know what the denominator is?

Oh yeah, I know what it is.

"Dakota Gibbs!" Sophie shouts, breaking our trance. We both run over to the car as Dakota reveals what's in her trunk. "You stole Quentin's bag?"

"He left it lying backstage," Dakota says. "I had to know what's in here. Rowan, all of these guys acting weird with their girlfriends are on the fencing team. It's the whole team."

"Yeah," he says, sounding ill. "I put that together."

"When they kicked you out, it hit me. You're gay. If they've got some sick, twisted MAGA-esque thing going, you'd be a risk, right?"

She's got it half-right.

"It makes complete sense," I say. "But opening that bag isn't going to make you feel better."

"What if they're hurting people, Casper? Look at the way they've treated me and the other girls, not to mention you and Rowan. What if they come for Sophie? Mr. Abadi? If there's something in this bag proving it, shouldn't we stop it before it starts?"

"Dakota, just wait a minute—"

Zip. She's got the bag open and pours the contents out. We lean in, and my hand wraps around Rowan's. But there's—

"Nothing," says Sophie. "It's just his uniform and a granola wrapper."

Dakota grunts and sits on the edge of the opened trunk. "I should have known he wouldn't be so careless. Great. Now I look like the crazy ex."

"No," says Rowan. "You're right. About everything . . . I was in the club."

"Rowan," I say, "you don't have to—"

"They're all about legacy, you're right. And I'm sorry they're going so far. I feel almost responsible for it. Maybe I've perpetuated it. They've always been douchebags, and I never said anything to them because I didn't want to lose them. Now it's gone off the rails. But they haven't met for months—"

"Yes, they have," Dakota says. "A *lot*. I've also been keeping track of how often girls get stood up by these guys at the same time."

"So, they've been meeting without me." Rowan nods.

"Hold on a minute," Sophie, who's been snooping through the wadded-up uniform, says. "Rowan, you know a lot about fencing, right?"

"Only everything."

"Then confirm," Sophie holds up a wooden stake. "This isn't gear for that, is it?"

My stomach curdles, and I swear I'm about to turn into ashes. How can we possibly explain that?

"Ew!" Dakota shrieks, prancing around as though the parking lot is suddenly made of hot coals. "Ew-ew-ew-ew-ew! He's a psychopath! What the *hell* are they doing?! Virgin sacrifices or something?"

"Or something," I whisper.

"What is this, Rowan?" Sophie demands, raising the stake higher. "It has to mean something."

"Everyone, calm down," he says, adopting his old golden boy voice. I clutch my stomach and wonder if vampires ever vomit. "Let me talk to my dad. He's the headmaster; he'll look into it."

"Rowan—"

"*Sophie*," he says. "I don't know what to tell you. But we need to get back to school. Please. Let me talk to him."

Sophie seems unsure but drops the stake in the trunk. "Come on, let's go."

CHAPTER TWENTY-SEVEN
ROWAN

"Should you tell your dad?" Casper whispers as we sneak up the stairs of Young House. "It's not like you can tell him much."

"I don't know anything anymore," I whisper back. All I know is that I want to get to our room and lock the world out.

When we near the top landing, music perks my ears up. The beat of a bass, piping from Victor and Ben's room.

"What now?" Casper mutters.

"Go to the room," I say over my shoulder.

"I'm fine—"

"Go to the room, Casper," I say. "Lock the door until I get back. Please?"

Casper looks offended but trails to Room 410 and disappears inside. I didn't mean that he couldn't protect himself, but . . . I guess I'm feeling a little protective *of* him after tonight.

I make my way down the hall and pound on the door. It swings open, revealing Diego, playing bouncer and holding a list on a clipboard. My heart drops from my chest. They're having the party I was going to have on move-in day. My dream party. And I wasn't invited.

I try to step into the room, but Diego blocks me with his arm.

"You're not on the list, Young."

"Hey, Rowan!" Reed appears behind Diego, waving. "Where've you been?"

"Hey, Reed," I say as happily as I can, attempting to get past Diego again. But he won't budge.

"Get lost, Young."

"Diego, stop," Reed shoves Diego's arm down and yanks me inside by the shirtsleeve before Diego can block me. "Whatever happened between you two, get over it."

"He's not supposed to be here—"

"Yo, shut the music off!" Victor calls out from the corner, and the bass stops. The entire fencing team stares back at me, Quentin sipping from a red solo cup.

"Are you *drinking?*" I ask. "Guys, if Mr. Abadi comes up here—"

"I'm glad you came, Young," Victor says, stepping forward. I notice his school uniform is perfectly pressed, and he's trimmed his hair and combed it into an oddly familiar style—I choke on my own breath. He looks like *me.* "We were just seeing if Reed here has what it takes to be a fencer."

I lock eyes with Reed. "No."

Reed deflates. "I didn't want to hurt your feelings by telling you. But, well, you and Diego have been fighting. And you're hanging out with the theatre kids now, and . . . I need something too."

Pursing my lips, I hold back a cry that's trying to punch through my throat. They're not just sticking with ancestry anymore—they're actively recruiting as many guys as they can. They already took Diego from me. They're not getting Reed, too.

"We can hang out anytime you want," I say. "The play's taken a lot more time than I thought it would. I'm sorry, Reed. But don't. Not these guys."

"What's wrong with us?" Ben, who's busy pouring drinks, asks. "You loved us until recently. What changed? Is it your new little friend you're always sneaking off with?"

"I think living with that freak's stained your brain, dude," says Victor. "Just admit it. He's gotten to you. We'll help you."

"Yeah," says Diego. "We'll help you if he's got you messed up."

"What does Casper have to do with this?" Reed asks before chugging whatever that is in his cup. He winces, and when I snatch the cup from him, I smell nothing but straight tequila.

"You're getting him drunk! You're all out of control!" I crush the cup in my fist and slam it on the ground. "Come on Reed. We're leaving."

"No. I'm not your crony anymore."

"Who said you ever were?!" I have to fight not to scream. "Reed, listen. This is not what you think it is. These guys aren't your friends. Please just come with me, and—"

"You better be real careful what you say next, Young," Victor says, standing so tall I feel like I'm shrinking in a shadow. "Unless you want *everyone* knowing the truth about your little fucktoy—"

My hands are around Victor's jacket lapels in an instant, hurling him to the floor. Then I'm on top of him. Everyone's shouting, throwing their hands on me, trying to get me off. But I won't be moved.

I want to plug his nose with my fist so he can't breathe; then he'll feel smothered and know exactly what the inside of a closet feels like.

Victor manages to get his hands on my collar and pulls it down. "What's under the makeup, pretty girl?" he spits.

I raise my fist.

"Rowan, *NO!*"

It was Casper who screamed. He must've heard the shouting and come down here. He shouldn't have. His hands pull on my shoulders. I struggle against him as he peels me off Victor and forces me to my feet.

Victor breaks into a fit of laughter, some of the guys joining him. I'll tear all of their faces off. I lunge for him again.

"Stop it!" Casper grabs my chin in his hands. "Rowan. Stop.

Right now."

All I see is red. And black. And more red. And—blue eyes pleading with me.

"Not like this," he says.

Hot tears blur my vision as I break into sobs.

"What a pussy," Victor says.

"Come on," Casper says, gently leading me to the door. "They don't know what they're talking about. We're friends, people. You don't share a room for months and not somehow become friends."

Snickers break out around the room. They know he's lying just as well as I do. The question is, what's going to happen next?

I pause as we go, sticking my hand out to Reed.

"Don't stay," I beg him one last time. "*Please.*"

Reed's lip twitches, and for a second, I think he's about to reach out. But he takes a step back and another swig of tequila from a fresh cup.

My face deflates again, and as Casper pulls me from the room, I hear Ben whisper, "*Lose-errrrr.*"

Casper is silent as we walk to our room. When he gets the door open, he waits for me to go in before he follows, bolting the lock behind him.

"Reed, too?" I crumple onto the bed, burying my forehead in my hands. "How did this get so out of control? We were so, *so* careful. How do they know?"

"Maybe it was a matter of time," he says, rubbing his forehead. "I should call Malcolm and Camille. We might be fighting a losing battle."

"No!" He opens his mouth to argue, but I shake my head. "You only have a couple of months—*we* only have a couple of months—before you get your tour."

"There's a cult of vampire hunters across the hall. I might be stubborn, but I can admit when I'm in too deep."

"I'm not letting you give up yet." I push myself to my feet and take his hands in mine. "You're too close. I've known these guys since kindergarten. I know how they work. Last thing they'll want to do is explain themselves. It's mind games."

"Do you really think so?"

"I don't know the future. But I know one thing: my dad won't let anyone hurt me. We have our differences, but he's still my dad. Maybe it's time I let him in a little."

"What do you mean?"

My heart finally feels a little peace as I say, "I'm going to come out to my dad."

CHAPTER TWENTY-EIGHT
CASPER

"Everyone's already headed to class," Rowan says as we cross the grassy field toward the main stretch of campus. "You slide in, and I'll head to Dad's office."

"Are you sure?" I ask. "You shouldn't have to come out because of me. It should be because *you* want to and are ready."

"I've never been more ready," he says, pausing to face me. "I'm not saying he'll be happy, but I'm his kid. He won't let these guys hurt us. It'll be a good thing. I think."

"I'm very proud of you," I say. He kisses me, and I offer him a small smile. "Alright, then. Let's go."

We make it to the main stretch of campus. Huddles of students walk, scrolling through their phones. They don't even notice Rowan and I walking together, our shoulders brushing.

Around a corner, there are more students with glazed expressions, more phones. The same audio plays in various spots on whatever video is going around.

"Did we miss something?" I ask.

"Hold on, I'm getting a text. Reed's tried to get hold of me—Casper?"

I've pulled out my own phone, which has been on silent, and see that I have over fifty missed calls. Some are from Dakota, others from Sophie. From Scarlett and Malcolm and Camille, too.

There are also voicemails.

"Hey," I say, "do you have—"

"Rowan? Where are you?" Reed's voice says through the speaker of Rowan's phone. "I'm sorry. I'm so sorry. I didn't know. If I'd known, I—Please let me know you're fine—"

Students peek up from their phones. A few of them spot us; they point and whisper.

I click the last voicemail I received, one from Sophie. "I know you're upset, but you have to let me know you're okay. Where are you? I'll come. Casper. Please."

The chatter of the students, the catcalling and laughing becomes insufferable. Rowan grabs my hand and pulls me toward Gorham Tower rising over the Student Readiness Center, all the while our phones blowing up with even more calls and texts.

Ding. Ding. Ding.

Buzz. Buzz. Buzz.

Ding. Ding. Ding—

Diego's face stares at us from the screen of the phone lying on the desk. There's a caption reading "Storytime" along with a hashtag for the school. It already has around four hundred hearts.

"My boy Rowan was a model student," Diego says. "And a great friend. Then he rooms with this guy, and they start getting weird together. Always sneaking off. It's not like him, and it never was, until this new kid started getting in his head."

Rowan's racing heartbeat is the only clue that he's still next to me. We can't look at each other or hold the other's hand while it all happens. They've wrenched away Rowan's privacy, ensured everyone knew before we could tell our story. Worse, they made me sound like a—I can barely think it—like a groomer. Like I coerced and preyed upon him.

They couldn't say I'm a vampire, so they cast me as a different kind of monster.

Mr. Young's finger swipes to the next video. One of Victor. It's clear these videos were all recorded last night after we left. Their words are slurred from alcohol. Rowan's heart is pounding so loudly I can barely hear the audio of it. My mind focuses in and out between the present and some silent, safe place in my brain. I manage to catch the end. "We all know he's creepy and off. But he's getting my friend to do some pretty suspicious things, and this just isn't the Rowan we all knew. I think he's been messed up and manipulated—"

"Have we seen enough?" Mr. Young asks, pressing his finger to his phone screen to stop the stream of TikToks.

"It's not true, Dad," says Rowan. "Casper isn't doing anything wrong—"

"I love posts about our school, when it's for a championship or the good work of a student organization. Not . . . not for *this*."

"They're lying!" Rowan shouts, standing up. His dad glares at him, but Rowan doesn't back down. "They're trying to make him look bad because—because—"

"Because why, Rowan?"

Because I'm a vampire, and you have some potent ancestry, and these guys can't just live and let live.

"It's alright, Rowan," I say.

"It's not."

"Rowan, wait in the foyer." His dad stares him down. "I need to speak with Casper."

"No."

"Foyer. *Now*."

Rowan doesn't seem like he's going to move, still staring down his dad with a fury I've never seen on him.

"Rowan," I say quietly. "It's okay. I'll be fine."

With a long glare between me and his dad, he slips into the foyer and shuts the door behind him.

"He's telling the truth," I say. "I'm not luring him into anything."

"I don't believe you," Mr. Young says. "You tell me why an entire fencing team would speak out with concern if there wasn't some truth to it?"

"Because they're after me," I say, barely hearing my own voice. "But what does it matter? You're just going to side with them."

"Why do you think that?"

"Because you already have," I find my voice again, but with it comes pent up anger. "*They* twisted things around and outed us, and *we're* in trouble?"

"My son was perfectly happy until you came along," Mr. Young says, picking up a pen and proceeding to click the end of it over and over. "Now he's confused. Shunning his friends. Spending all of his time sneaking around—with you. What am I to think?"

"You should talk to him," I say. "I know he wants to talk to you."

He stares me down, and I tense. He looks *so much* like Rowan. "Surely you understand why I'm concerned, learning about all of this. Yes?"

"I understand why you'd be upset." I tilt my head. "I don't understand why you automatically assume it's my doing."

"Malcolm and Camille," he says, pulling a drawer in his desk open and producing a folder, the same one he'd used when he welcomed me onto campus. "That's what you call those people?"

My eyebrows slacken as his dark expression morphs into a smirk.

"You don't think I believed they were your biological parents, do you?" he continues. "They clearly aren't old enough to have had you."

"We lived in Europe for most of my life," I counter. "Less

preservatives. Less burnout. A lot of people look really young for their age."

"Speak another language."

"What?"

"You just said you were in Europe most of your life. A school in Belgium? I know you said it was a school for American army brats or something like that, but surely you picked some up. Go ahead."

I gulp, though my throat is the driest it's been since becoming a vampire. "I don't have to prove anything to you."

"Can you at least prove the school exists?" he asks. "Because as it just so happens—it does not. Also, it turns out there is no Casper Belamy *anywhere*."

"Sounds like something you should have checked before accepting my application for enrollment."

"I *did* find the tiniest crumb, however," Mr. Young ignores me, opening my folder. "Added it to your file, see here? It's a crazy, modern world we live in. All of us are so connected, whether we want to be or not. While searching for Casper Belamy, I found this little guy."

He flops a piece of paper in front of me, and my eyes pound from the pressure of tears that can't fall. There I am, sun-kissed skin, a few freckles, round cheeks. On a missing person's flyer.

"Who is Casper, Michael Mortenson?"

"Give me that—"

Mr. Young snatches the paper away. He studies it. "You've changed. Quite a bit. So, who are Malcolm and Camille?"

"I was a foster kid," I say. "Malcolm and Camille are my parents now, and you're out of line—"

"No. They're not your parents now," Mr. Young says. "When I found this, I reached out to your old group home. They had no idea where you were and assumed you were dead—Don't worry, I didn't give them the truth. Yet."

I stand, the chair toppling over behind me. "You had no right to do that. You have no idea what I went through—"

"I knew something wasn't right about you. Now I know—you're a liar, and you're mixed up with suspicious people. And you're dragging my son into your orbit, and when I think of the awful things—You know what? Just give it to me straight. You say I don't understand what's been going on. Make me understand."

"You need to talk to your son," I say through gritted teeth.

"I'll get to him. What have you been doing to my son, Michael?"

Maybe I just want to watch him crumble under my stare for playing this twisted little game of "gotcha" with me. Maybe I want to hurt him for calling me the wrong name. I plant my hands on the desk and lean my face dangerously close to his, inhaling the musky smell of him.

"Whatever he wants me to."

My lip twitches as soon as I say it, and as his eyes glass over, his expression of fury replaced by disbelief. I shouldn't have said that. Why did I say that?

"That's not what I meant," I say. "That didn't come out right."

Mr. Young's fury returns. "It came out exactly right. You're suspended until we get to the bottom of this."

"You can't do that—"

"I've already called those people you call parents. They should be here any minute. Get out of my office and wait for them. Don't bother packing; we'll send your things. And by the way"—I pause, my hand on the doorknob—"stay away from my son."

I fling open the door, and it bangs against the wall as I exit.

Rowan rushes to me, grabbing my hand. "What happened?" he asks, "Are you okay?"

I don't respond; I simply head to the front door.

"Casper!" Rowan's hand leaves mine. Behind me, his voice breaks. "We'll figure it out. I'll talk to him!"

I stop. My chest is so tight. My throat is so dry I can hardly speak. But—no. I won't cry, though I desperately wish I could. Now these emotions can join the pile of others I'll have to hold in forever.

"It's okay, Rowan." I glance over my shoulder. "It's probably for the best. You'll be safe now . . . I love you."

Rowan makes for me, but his dad exits his office and holds him back. "Get off of me! Casper!"

"It's okay, son," Mr. Young hushes him, patting his chest. "You'll be glad later."

Rowan whimpers, his eyes a dark, mossy green as they well up. I don't think I've ever seen him appear so young before. "Don't leave me."

My vision blurs, and I blink, but the tears still won't fall as I force myself out of the building before I make things worse. Rowan's cries fade behind me as I make my way down the steps, toward the long black car that's arrived since we entered the building.

Scarlett waits at the open backseat, wrapping her arms around me when I get to the bottom step. "Let's get you out of here, Baby Sheik."

"I don't want to leave him."

Across the horseshoe drive, the Blackthorns, or some of them anyway, watch me, their smug faces all lifted in celebration. I know I'm lucky they only lied about me, instead of staking me. But a quiver in my stomach tells me this was only a warning.

"Where are Malcolm and Camille?" I ask, sliding into the back seat.

"I persuaded them to stay at the house. I thought you might need a minute before you see them. This will die down in a week or two; this stuff never holds interest for long. Do you want me to go in there and fight the headmaster?"

I shake my head. "I've caused enough trouble."

I've caused so much more than enough trouble.

CHAPTER TWENTY-NINE
ROWAN

"Big show opening tomorrow, huh?" Dad asks across our booth in a crowded steakhouse, stirring a packet of raw sugar into his iced tea. I sit with my own drink: plain water, untouched. The idea of drinking anything right now makes me nauseous, made worse by the smell of food and the idea that I'll have to pick my way through dinner. "How was the last practice?"

"Fine," I say, watching as rain picks up beyond the window, turning the snow on the ground to slush.

Everyone in the cast has referred to tech rehearsals as hell week. They're right. This week has been absolute hell. In class, I'm zoned out. In the dining hall, I sit alone. I pretend I don't hear the whispers about me and Casper. I don't watch as the Blackthorns clap themselves on the back for ruining our lives.

Dad got them to take the videos down, but he didn't punish them. Erased videos don't erase what happened. Everyone knows Dad's making me sleep at home and carpool with him. Everyone knows Casper and I were together, whether they believe he manipulated me or not.

"I wish you had told me you ended up in the play," Dad says, pulling me back to the present. "Why didn't you?"

"Musical," I say, still thinking of Casper.

"What?"

"It's not a play. It's a musical. I didn't think you'd like me being part of it."

Dad takes a sip of his tea through a red plastic straw. "I'd have worried there was too much on your plate. It's not really your thing, either, is it? A *musical?* I wouldn't have made you drop it if you really wanted to do it, though."

I start a game with my straw, trying to hold an ice cube to the bottom of the glass, failing as it slips and floats back to the top.

"Was it something Casper got you to do?" Dad asks.

"*What?*"

"Did Casper talk you into being in the play?"

I glare at him. "Musical. And no, he didn't." Letting go of the straw, I clamp my hands together between my knees. I feel so exposed with him questioning me around all these people. "There's a *lot* he didn't talk me into doing."

Our server arrives at our booth. "I think we need just one more minute, please," Dad says, and the server gives us a wry smirk before drifting away. Dad flips open his menu. "What are you hungry for? Perhaps I should try something new tonight. A lot of people are trying new things lately."

I pale. "It's not a new thing."

Flipping the menu closed, Dad fixes his gaze on me and waits until I manage to look him in the eye before saying, "I don't like these changes in you."

"This is me, Dad," my voice breaks. "This was always me."

"What was Casper getting you to do?" he asks. "Why are your friends saying what they're saying if this was you all along? It doesn't make sense. I'm okay with gay people. Hell, I hired Mr. Abadi, didn't I?"

"*What?*"

"But you were not gay," he says. "Not until Casper. What, were you two drinking and just being idiots one night, or—"

"I'm fucking done."

"Watch it."

The server is approaching again, so I take the opportunity to nod to her and give my order, which is the first thing my eyes land on. I don't like crab cakes, but it's not like I'm going to eat anyways, so what does it matter?

Dad orders his usual steak, rare, and I can't resist but enjoy the slight irony that he wants to consume blood. "Could I call him?" I ask, quietly. "Just once? You can take the phone right back—"

"Hey, you make your stage debut tomorrow. We should celebrate."

"Please. I need to know that he's okay—"

"Want to split a lava cake for dessert? You used to love it."

"I have an idea," Dad says, and I tense up in the passenger seat. "We haven't been up to the lake house in a while."

My heart booms in my chest. Does he know about Casper and I going there, too?

"I'm too tired," I say. "I have school and then the show tomorrow."

"Come on." Dad flips on the turning signal and whips down a side street. "For old time's sake."

"Why do you want to go there?" I ask. "You haven't been since Mom—"

"Maybe it's time we face it," Dad says, and my heart drops. "Together. I'm sure your mother wants us to move on and forget her."

We cross Main Street, and I catch a glimpse of the rooftop of Belamy Manor. Casper's only fifty feet away, and I can't get to him. My heart clenches in my chest, and every cell in my body wants me to smash the window so I can get out and run to him. But it's gone just as soon as it appeared.

I need him.

"Okay," I say, nodding. "Yeah. Let's go."

"Really?"

"Yeah." I smile. "Can we do something really stupid, though? Can we . . . can we drink?"

Dad considers, looking at the road. "Excuse me?"

"We've done it before," I say. "Remember? My birthday? We had a beer, and I wasn't an idiot about it. Can we get a six pack and go up there? Have a really good talk about everything. Maybe I *am* a little messed up."

Dad purses his lips, but finally, he nods. "You know what? Why not? Let's do it."

"Really?" I bounce in my seat. "*Yes!*"

I keep up my excitement as he pulls into the next gas station parking lot and turns off the ignition.

"Can we *each* have a six pack?" I ask.

"Don't push it," Dad laughs. "I'll be right back."

He gives me a closed-lipped smile before he gets out of the car, tilting his head to look me over. At this moment, he's proud of me.

I feel almost guilty about it when moments later, while he's inside the gas station, I fling open the passenger door and make a break for it, running through the rain. I slip on a patch of ice and tumble. I cry out as my palms skid over broken ice and gravel. I hiss at the sting, but I push myself up as fast as I can and keep running, and running, and running, until I reach the gate of the house filled with vampires, blood soaking my hands.

CHAPTER THIRTY
CASPER

Painful tears push the back of my eyes, unable to escape, and my chest seizes with a breathless sob. Then another. And another. Pulling a deep breath through my nostrils, I blink a few times and paint on a tight-lipped smile as the blue light of the old television washes over me. Dorothy Zbornak says something hilariously scathing to Blanche Devereaux.

There's no way out of this; I can only go through. I can only do what I can *when* I can. Right now, all this sad, traumatized gay boy can do is watch *The Golden Girls*. It's all I've been able to do at all. Not even books hold my interest anymore. I mindlessly sip cask blood from an IV bag and keep watching.

The door to the attic swings open, and Malcolm and Camille levitate in unannounced.

"I ordered Oscar not to let anyone in."

"We outrank you," says Malcolm, and Camille hovers over my casket before settling down next to me. I scoot against the satin-lined edge.

"We need to decide how to handle this," Camille says.

It wasn't easy, telling them what happened. I thought for sure they'd lock me in the attic themselves and save me the trouble of doing it. Or disown me. Or order Rowan's assassination without a second thought. But they did none of those things, opting to give me space instead. I suppose the time has come for them to handle this however they're going to.

"I'm sure I've lost my tour," I say. "What else will you do? Eternal house arrest? Make me drink his blood until he's dead?"

"This is a serious thing, Casper," Malcolm says. "How we address this with our fellow vampires matters."

"Over a century of peace could easily evaporate," Camille agrees. "For what? A boy?"

"A boy I love."

A boy I haven't been able to speak to since the whole nightmare. A boy who's been outed, who's in trouble, and I have no way to help or protect him. I sit up in the casket. "What if they've really hurt him? What about Dakota? And Sophie? Are they after them, too? I knew I shouldn't act on my feelings, and I did it anyways. I know I did a bad thing. I let him know what I am, and I didn't tell you. I drank his blood. Everything I wasn't supposed to do, I did. I failed. But—never mind."

"No." Malcolm steps toward me, his ears perked, eyebrows raised. "Continue."

"I failed, but . . ." I shake my head, willing the words to come into place. I've lost everything. My freedom. My friends. Rowan. But I need them to understand *why*. "It was just me. Only me around mortals for months and months. And I know you want us to blend in, and I know that you want to keep us safe, but I'm tired of trying to pass as them. I'm so, *so* tired of it, and . . . it was *so* lonely.

"Rowan understood me. He made me feel less alone. I wanted *someone* who understood and to feel like maybe I wasn't just there for some test. Like perhaps I actually belonged somehow.

"I messed up," my voice cracks. "I picked myself over every other vampire. What if I ever had to lead? I'd bring it all down! You should've just left me on the street."

Camille's lip twitches as she asks, "You really feel that way?"

"Why did I find Rowan, why did I get any of this, if it was all going to be ripped away? Any minute the Blackthorns could lay siege on us, right?" I ask, and their expressions tell me they've definitely considered this. "We could be killed because of me and Rowan being together. Scarlett told me what happened to her and the slayer she loved. And you're the ones who have to clean it up."

"Wait one heartbeat," says Camille, closing her eyes and waving a long fingernail. "What did Scarlett tell you?"

"What happens when vampires fall for slayers," I say. "Her and Anne. Didn't you know?"

"Yes, of course." Her gaze sweeps to Malcolm's, who is looking at her as though he's been caught in headlights. "That was a tragedy."

The door swings open, and Oscar leans in.

"Your majesty," he says to Malcolm with a small bow. "Young man, at the gate, to speak with the prince. He requests it."

My stomach lurches, and I jump out of the coffin. "Is it Rowan?"

Oscar nods.

I levitate from the casket to the floor. He's alive.

"Send him away," urges Camille, rushing to Malcolm. "What if his father finds him here?"

"Camille—"

"Send him away, Oscar."

"No!" I lock eyes with her.

"It's out of the question," she insists. "This is too dangerous, Casper. You can't let him in here."

"Let him make this decision," Malcolm says, a decree.

"Malcolm!"

"Camille, the house is surrounded by undead guards. We're safe. We have to allow him to make decisions, or he'll never learn how." Camille doesn't seem convinced by Malcolm's reasoning, but she nods. "What will you do, son?"

"Let him in." I don't even think about it. I need to see him. "Now."

Malcolm nods to Oscar, who disappears through the door. "Used to be," he quips, "they had to let *us* in."

"Don't make light of this, *your majesty*," Camille says, rubbing her temples.

I rush to my full-length mirror in the corner and check myself over. My hair is a mess, and my eyes are so dark and sallow. "I look like a med school cadaver," I say, cringing.

"If he can't look at you during your worst, then it isn't real love," Malcolm points out. "And if he looks any better, I'll be very surprised."

He's right, but I keep trying anyway, somehow making it all worse. Rowan is coming here, to my *room*, and the king and queen of the Vampiric East are going to watch the whole thing, and—

Vanilla. Wood. Love. I inhale sharply as Rowan's scent fills the room. In the mirror, just above the reflection of my shoulder, I spot a pair of forest-green eyes, wild and watching me.

"Rowan," I whisper as I note his dripping wet hair, rain running down his face. He's shivering.

"It sure isn't Captain America," he responds, and I whirl around, rushing at him. He holds up his palms, and I gasp at the sight of his blood all over them.

"What did they do to you?"

"I fell," he says. I prick my thumb on my fangs and set about pushing my own blood against the wounds, watching them as the skin comes together. "I had to get away from Dad. He's refusing to accept that we're together, and—" He glances at my parents. "Hello."

His eyes round to perfect circles, and he dips his torso, bowing to them.

"A slayer bowing to a vampire king," Malcolm notes. "The times really are a-changin'."

"Not now," Camille says through gritted teeth. "Hello, Rowan."

"I'm so sorry," I say. "I'm sorry I ever showed up at school and ruined everything. I'm sorry you got outed like this."

"It had to happen," says Rowan. "And if it hadn't, there's no telling where either of us would be. I can't believe it. He's my dad, and he won't even *try* to listen to our side. I'm his kid!" He turns to Malcolm. "You called me a slayer a minute ago. I'm *not*. I'm with you. They can suck—I mean—they can kiss my—I'm not a slayer, okay?"

"Okay," Malcolm says, totally unfazed. "And we vampires don't care what language you use so long as it isn't vampist."

"I don't see how you can be so devil-may-care about this, Malcolm," says Camille. She steps to the window and pulls back the curtain to look out over the garden, as though trying to spot the army of teenage slayers inevitably arriving. "You might as well invite him to next Christmas, the way you're taking this in."

"I likely *will* invite him," Malcolm says. "You act as though Scarlett is the only one who ever fell for a slayer."

Camille's grip on the curtain tightens, and she looks slowly back at him. "*Malcolm.*"

"Who else did?" I ask.

Camille and Malcolm stare at one another for what seems like an eternity. An argument of glances, ending with a sigh that makes the room temperature feel as if it's dropped four degrees. Camille lets go of the curtain, raising both eyebrows. *Go on then.*

Malcolm smirks. "I did."

Camille's eyes have locked on the floor, and I can almost see the cloud of memories she's wrapped herself in. "I have not been entirely open with you, Casper. I'm sorry. But if you had known everything, it would have been difficult for you to handle."

"What?" I ask, "What would have been so difficult to know?"

Camille swallows. "That I lived in Mockingbird Preparatory Academy when it was originally known as Blackthorn House. All of us slayers did. It wasn't a school, oh, no. It was a fortress."

"Your mother," says Malcolm, and he looks almost proud, "was the most prolific slayer of her time."

"I only did what I was taught," Camille says. "Thought what I was told to think. Believed what they decided was best for me to believe. And I believed vampires were evil. Soulless. I thought it would be impossible to even converse with one. And then Malcolm came along."

"I had just arrived," he says. "In the area, anyways. You see, I never believed we needed to kill each other. I thought, 'Well, there must be balance'. So where to begin my crusade except right at the top, with the young slayer known as Elizabeth?"

Camille flinches at hearing her mortal name, and Rowan and I lock eyes as we process. The woman's grave in the cemetery. The ornate one. The stone woman. That's . . .

"You're Elizabeth Gorham?" I ask.

"Not any longer," Camille says. "Malcolm was an excellent fighter. I nearly had him, too, except something about him gave me pause. And I realized, as I looked into his eyes, that vampires are just like slayers. We all want to live in peace. And what can I say? I fell in love."

"Of course, it was scandalous when she tried to convince her fellow Blackthorns," Malcolm says. "You might have almost started a war, Casper, but we not only started one, we finished one. I turned her, of her will."

"But if you aren't dead," I say, "why do you have a grave at the school?"

"Why do I—" Camille processes, and her eyes shine brighter. "None of those graves are real. They're monuments. You see, I wasn't the only Blackthorn who decided to turn and join Malcolm. Several minds and hearts changed. Having those headstones and vaults placed were our way of burying our old lives to begin the new. We're all still alive, finding our bliss in eternity."

I can't believe this. Here is a slayer who became a vampire. Who is now my mother. And a queen of vampires. And it's all hushed, swept away.

"People should know," I say. "The Blackthorns, other vampires. They should all know. We should all come out this way."

"It isn't that simple." Malcolm shakes his head. "There are many opinions and beliefs out there. We do not speak or decide for everyone."

"But don't you see how optional all of this is?" I insist. "It's happened before; why can't it happen again?"

"Casper." Rowan says. "I want to agree with you, but your dad is right. The most we can hope for right now is to get away from them. Who knows what the Blackthorns will do if they get their hands on us?"

"And you don't want to know," Camille says darkly. "Not if their practices are the same."

The door swings open again, and the sound of heels clicking against the attic boards draws our attention as Scarlett rushes in.

"Blackthorns at the gate!" she says. "Two of them. They want to search the house for the boy."

"What are their names?" Rowan asks.

"How should I know?" Scarlett rolls her eyes. "They're wearing masks."

"I knew they'd come here," Camille shouts. "I told you not to let him in!"

"Camille, stop it," Malcolm says. "Do you not see? Our son has found someone. That is the important thing. Slayer or not, he's ours now too. If he wants to be."

Camille considers, glancing between us. She reaches into the casket and pulls out a blanket, which she wraps around Rowan. "You poor thing, you're soaked through." She levitates to my dresser and rummages through it, retrieving a sweater and black jeans, which she brings to him. "Casper, take him out into the garden, past the weathered oak. You know exactly where I'm talking about. Stay there until one of us comes for you. They can't find him here. We have to buy time."

"Okay," I tug Rowan's hand. "Come with me."

"We can't go through the yard," Rowan points out, "Not if they're searching the house."

"We're not going through the door," I say, pulling him toward the window.

"And Casper," Malcolm says, "I suggest you both think long and hard about what you plan to do going forward. We will support whatever you decide, but this is *your* path to figure out."

I nod before signalling to Rowan to hop on my back and then jumping through the attic window.

CHAPTER THIRTY-ONE
ROWAN

I slide off Casper's back when he stops running, about ten yards past a gnarled and dying oak tree. Rain is falling steadily, and I tighten the blanket around me.

"Are you sure they won't find us here?" I ask as he stomps the ground randomly until a hollow thud echoes from the slush.

"They can't look here if they don't know about it," he responds, stooping and pulling open an old metal door in the ground, gesturing for me to go through it. He helps me as I find a metal ladder and start the downward climb. My shoulder brushes a cobweb as I descend, and I fight the chill it brings out in me. Continuously, I keep glancing up at the open door above me, expecting to see Dad or a storm of Blackthorns, until Casper climbs in and closes the door, plunging us into pitch blackness. I hear the yank of a chain.

A yellow bulb buzzes above us, illuminating the metal sidings of the room. There are cots, shelves of old canned goods way past their prime, and piles of blankets.

"It's a bomb shelter from World War II," Casper explains. "The family that lived here then must have built it. We've started referring to it as the crypt as a family joke. It'll keep us hidden."

My eyes fall on a rust-colored stain on one of the cot blankets. "Were they vampires, too?"

Casper inspects the stain, and he gives a strangled chuckle. "No. I guess Scarlett must have had a cask in here. Maybe let's sit on the other one?"

I nod, laying my blanket and the dry clothes on the opposite cot, and peel off my coat and soaked sweatshirt. Casper looks at the wall as I change.

"You know we're past that sort of modesty, right?" I jab while pulling on the jeans, which run halfway past my feet thanks to Casper's height.

"I might be a vampire, but I'm still a gentleman," Casper quips.

The sweater is also big on me, the sleeves hanging over my hands and the collar leaving my neck and a patch of shoulder exposed. But wearing his clothes gives me a warm sense of security that I didn't expect, and once I've settled in next to him and wrapped the blanket around us, my back and legs finally relax. It must have been two or three miles from the gas station to Casper's house.

If Victor or Ben or any number of Blackthorns are here to search the house, that means Dad reached out to them, looking for me. Resting my elbows on my knees, I bury my face in my hands. What a mess I made of this.

Casper's hand rests on my back, making me shiver. "Do you want to talk about it?"

I shake my head. "No. He thinks you made me gay or something."

"I know."

"I had to get away from him. It was fight or flight. We were at a gas station. I was afraid. I just ran . . . God, this is so messed up. We're literally stuck hiding in a *bunker.*"

I stand up, and the blanket falls from my shoulders as I pace, raking my hands through my hair. "How did it ever get this far? Who allowed this to happen?"

"Rowan?"

I kick the metal wall. Then I kick it again. And again with the other foot. My fists slam against it until the burst of anger dissipates, and I rest my forehead against the cold metal. "I was *Rowan Young*. I was the top guy. I was untouchable. And I'm *here*. We're both *here*, hiding in a *bomb shelter*. If I'm not safe at school, who is? I want to know whose fault it is. Who could have cut it off at the pass and didn't?"

"All of us," says Casper. And that's the end of his response.

Is this life now? Hiding out and hoping that neither of us gets hurt? Looking over our shoulders? How could either of us possibly go back to before? Is it just going to be us running forever? How is it ever going to stop?

The funny thing is, all I can think about is Mom. And Dad. Both of them, giving me advice over the years. Telling me what to do and what I want. I never questioned it. But now, it's up to me, and it's up to Casper. I can't just follow instructions and watch as it works out for me. But there *is* something they both taught me. And it's all I know to do.

I push off the wall, nearly tripping over the hems of Casper's too-long pants. "I'm not running away. I'm standing my ground."

"What?"

"I'm done," I say, shoving my hands out to the side as though it pushes all of our troubles away. "No more hiding. No more ignoring it and acting like nothing is going on. I'm not scared anymore. I'm not giving them that." Going back to the cot, I take his hands in mine as I sit next to him. "Aren't you tired of hiding?"

"You know I am."

"Tomorrow, I'm leaving here, and I'm going to perform in *Pippin* for the whole school."

"What about your dad?" Casper asks. "And Victor, and Diego—"

"I don't care," I say. "I'm not going to hide."

"Me either," Casper says. "I'm going to be there to give you a standing ovation."

I tilt my head. "What about your family? Don't you have a whole dynasty?"

"What kind of leader would I eventually be if I ran from my problems?" he asks. "And you're right. We can't be scared of them. We'll go."

"Right into a big crowd, where everyone sees us."

His eyes darken as he touches his forehead to mine. We sit quietly, the only sounds the beating of my heart and the slow, gentle breathing of his lungs.

"You know," says Casper finally, "in books, there's always this big 'gotcha' and a comeuppance for the bad guys. Our grand plan is just to walk into the building."

"It's already hard to do," I say. "It's going to have to be enough. Even if it means walking bravely into a hundred rooms. Every room we ever enter."

"You're right." Casper shrugs. "Then it's settled."

He kisses me, ending the conversation. I kiss him back.

"I wish we'd done everything together," I whisper. "Just in case."

"Neither of us are going to die," he says, sounding a lot like his dad. A royal decree.

"Still."

"Me too," Casper sighs. "But we don't have—" He pauses and blinks when he sees my lips purse in a sheepish expression. "We don't, do we?"

"We do," I say. "I might have put a couple of condoms in my wallet . . . when we went to the bookstore. I didn't know if we'd . . . I just wanted to be safe."

"And you've had them there this entire time?" Casper laughs.

"Yeah," I chuckle. "Presumptuous?"

"Very," Casper says, knitting his eyebrows together. "What kind of vampire do you take me for, Mr. Young?"

"The vampire I want in every way," I say, and it seems to suck all the humor from the room. Casper keeps staring at me, and I stare back at him.

"Is this . . . is it?" I ask, my stomach flipping. "The moment we . . ."

"I think it is," he says.

"Are you sure?"

"Yes."

"I don't know if I'll be good at it."

"Me either," Casper says, his fingers fumbling at the button of my jeans. I gently lay my hand on his wrist. He looks up at me, afraid, like I'm about to take it back. But my mind is flashing to what he said about it back at the lake house.

"You be the giver."

Casper nods as our hands move to undress each other. He's the first to see everything. I'm the first to see *him*. And this first time might not be perfect, it might not be the way I'd thought about it, but it is somehow exactly what I wanted it to be. It would be nice, I think, as Casper takes over and I finally, *finally*, feel him close enough to me, if it were like this for the rest of our lives, however long those might be.

CHAPTER THIRTY-TWO
CASPER

Gorham Tower looms over the horseshoe driveway, reminding me of a prison watchtower as Oscar pulls through the gates and turns onto the narrow drive that leads to the visitors' parking lot. But knowing that it's named for my mother, who has our backs tonight, makes it feel a little less scary.

"You're both sure about this?" Camille asks from her seat across from Rowan and me. "It isn't too late to change your minds."

Rowan's index finger crooks around mine.

"We're sure," I say. "No more running and hiding."

"I still think this is too dangerous," says Camille, more to Malcolm than to us.

"The boys are right." Malcolm squeezes her hand. "And if they're going to do this, it's best with all of us together and an auditorium full of witnesses."

"Are you okay?" I ask Rowan.

Sharply inhaling through his nostrils, he nods.

Oscar slows the car when we roll up behind the line of vehicles, trying to find a place to park. The show starts in forty-five minutes, and the lead is just now arriving.

"It's not fair you can't participate," Rowan says. "You worked hard."

"So did you." I squeeze his hand. "And whatever happens, I want you to have a good show. You're really good, and I can't wait to see you up there doing it."

His cheeks flush red. But then his eyes fall on the campus and darken. His grip around my hand tightens. "This is it, then. We're doing this."

I nod.

"Promise me you'll stay safe," Rowan says. "If you think for a second they might try to hurt you, promise me you'll get out."

"He doesn't have a choice but to stay safe," says Camille. "We're all here."

"They won't do anything with an auditorium full of parents watching," I remind him, though to be honest, I'm not so sure. There isn't a precedent for this. "Go get your moment. And Rowan"—I brush a finger under his chin—"you do you."

He nods. "And you do you."

I hiss, and he cracks up, one moment of relief before whatever happens . . . happens.

"There you are!" Mrs. Spencer says when she spots us in the corridor outside the auditorium. She rushes to us, taking Rowan by the shoulders. "Your father told me you were violently ill."

"Oh?" Rowan asks, disconnected. "People say a lot of things."

"Are you sure you're able to perform? If you're sick—"

"I'm not sick." Rowan escapes her grip. "I'm great, and I'm going out there."

"Atta boy," Mrs. Spencer says. "Quentin will be relieved he doesn't have to go on with a script."

Rowan's eyes slide to me. "I'm sure he will be."

"Go on, get backstage, get ready! Places in thirty!"

"Thank you, thirty."

He keeps hold of my hand for as long as he can as he heads down the hall that leads to the backstage door.

When he's gone, Mrs. Spencer asks, "Are *you* okay?"

"No," I say honestly. "But I'm here."

She pulls me into a hug before I can stop her, and I don't fight it. "You're brave. *So* brave. Can I take you backstage? The cast has been worried—"

"They have?"

"Yes! None of us believe any of it."

This makes me feel a *little* better. I'd like to at least see Sophie and Dakota, but now isn't the time. I don't want to draw any more attention to myself than I have to. "I should stay in the audience. I don't want to take away from their moment."

Mrs. Spencer huffs, obviously disagreeing with me. But she drops the subject by looking over my shoulder at the vampires standing guard. "This must be your family. Hello, I'm Mrs. Spencer, the theatre instructor."

"It's nice to meet you." Camille extends her hand, glancing around the corridor for anyone who could be watching. "I'm Camille, Casper's mother. This is his father, Malcolm. Thank you for taking him in the way you all have."

"Well, of course. We're the weird kids; we stick together—"

"Where do we find the entrance?" Scarlett asks. "Sorry. I'm Casper's aunt, Scarlett. And I really don't want a scene with him being here."

Mrs. Spencer blinks. "Oh. Yes. I completely understand. You just go down this hallway and turn right. Box office is next to the auditorium doors."

I lead the way. Without Rowan, it feels like I'm missing the right side of my torso, a feeling which intensifies when we come upon the crowd of parents and students here to see their kids and friends perform. I'd told myself not to pay attention to anyone, but my eyes betray me, scanning the crowd for Blackthorns.

"Casper, have you seen this?" Camille asks and points to a black foam presentation board on a table. The cast photos are glued to it. I stare at Rowan's picture. He's the cutest black-and-white cheese ball I've ever seen. "I can see why he caught your attention. He's just as handsome as your father."

"Shh." I nudge her away from the pictures. "Not now. We need to get seated."

"Let her finish complimenting me first," says Malcolm, playing the part of cringe-worthy dad.

A phone camera clicks nearby, and I spot a first year boy snapping a picture of me as he heads into the auditorium. Must be alerting his classmates of my presence.

Don't let them know you're scared. Don't let them know you're scared.

"Casper?"

Mr. Abadi elbows his way through the crowd. When he gets to me, he places his hand on my shoulder. "What are you doing here?"

"I couldn't stay home and cower," I say.

He smiles before his face drops into a solemn expression. "Are you absolutely sure this is the best idea?"

"For me, it is," I nod. "Rowan and I *both* need to do this."

He looks over my face, slowly putting it together, a light fading up in his eyes. "So you two *are* . . . well, it all makes more sense now. Probably better I didn't know until now, or I'd have had to switch room assignments on you. That's *definitely* against school policy." I snort. "I'm glad you're not hiding. Just be careful."

"I will."

He pats me on the shoulder and gestures to my family. "Go on then. By the way, you were my favorite student. If you tell anyone, I'll call you a liar. Dig?"

"Dig," I smile, nodding to him before joining my family.

The auditorium is already packed, people chatting and taking pictures of their programs against the projection of the *Pippin* logo that pops across the royal blue curtain.

Once we're seated, I try pretending to read my program, but I keep scanning the faces of everyone around me. The entire fencing team is seated six rows back. When I spot them, my already-slow heart stops beating for five whole seconds. Diego's eyes drift from the stage to me, and he sits up with an instant-red scowl. I spin around.

"They're all here," I whisper. "They've seen me."

"We're right here." Malcolm nudges my right shoulder while Camille slips her hand around my left one.

"Let them eat their hearts out," she whispers.

A shadow looms over us, and I nearly jump out of my skin. But it's only Oscar, waiting for one of the cast moms to stand and let him into the row behind us.

"I thank you." He flashes her a friendly smile, and she sighs as she nods, no doubt taken by his vampiric muscles.

"Weapons. I don't smell any," he whispers between mine and Malcolm's ears when he sits. "Your majesty prefers me where?"

"Can you be backstage?" I ask him before Malcolm can respond. "He's back there."

"Guard the cask?"

"He's not my cask." I cringe. "He's more than that. And yes, because there's a Blackthorn in the cast. I have Malcolm and Camille."

Oscar seems uncertain whether he should and looks to Malcolm. "Your majesty?"

"Do as the prince wishes," he says. "Keep a distance so that no one reports a big, intimidating man hanging outside a teenager's dressing room."

With a nod of duty, Oscar stands and makes his way past the mom, who remains seated so that he has to climb over her. When he's gone, she sighs again.

Camille tenses. "Take my hand again, Casper."

"Why—" but then I see. Mr. Young has appeared in front of the orchestra pit, glaring at me. His face is beet red except for the dark circles under his eyes. His hair, usually so well-kempt, is a mess. Clearly he hasn't slept since Rowan ran away.

He stalks past the first row, heading toward us, but the lights dim before he can reach us. Mrs. Spencer makes her way down the aisle as a hush falls over the audience. When she reaches Mr. Young, she smiles and pats his arm. "Enjoy the show, headmaster. Your son is going to blow you away. If you'd take your seat . . ."

He glares at her. She keeps smiling, with an air that says, *I see what you're doing.*

With a final scowl, Mr. Young sits in the nearest seat, and as Mrs. Spencer ascends the steps to the stage, he has no choice but to look away from me.

Applause breaks out, and I roll my program in my hands, my heartbeat picking up.

"Good evening!" she announces, "Welcome everyone to Mockingbird Preparatory Academy's Production of *Pippin*!"

CHAPTER THIRTY-THREE
ROWAN

"Rowan!" Dakota runs toward me when the curtain is swept closed at the end of the first act and the cast is whooping and applauding for each other. I climb down from the scaffold with the throne, adjusting the crown slipping down my forehead.

My hands won't stop trembling. "Yeah?"

"Where has Rowan gone, *Pippin*? You're incredible," she says, grabbing my face, "You didn't sing "Corner of the Sky", you *lived* it."

"Thank you," I say, pulling back. I'm not even sure exactly what it is I'm doing out there. I'm too distracted by everything that could happen, counting down to the real show time. "I'll, uh, I'll keep it up."

Sophie bounds up and locks her arm through mine as she escorts me backstage to the makeup table. "I'm so, *so* proud of you. We didn't get to talk before the show started. How are you?"

"I'm fine," I say. "I'm here. And Casper's out there. We are fine."

"He's out there?" Dakota asks, loudly. "Why didn't you tell us? We've been so worried about him."

"It's been a whirlwind." I dart my eyes around for Quentin. "We're just lucky he's in the building."

Sophie's arm drops, and she purses her lips. "Yeah. Lucky."

"What have I done now?"

"He should be here with us doing the show, not sitting out there," Sophie says. "Everyone should know those videos were all lies and that you two are—"

"Listen." I take off the crown. "I know that you want us to shout from the rooftops that we're together and that everything's going to work out. But you have no idea how hard it was for either of us to even risk coming tonight. I know you've been in a secret relationship, too, but it's different, okay?"

Sophie looks like she's about to argue but stops to consider. She shrugs. "You're right. Everyone's experience is different. I still wish you'd use your voice, though."

I don't feel like I have much of a voice left to use. The important thing is that Casper and I are here. And, so far, safe.

That has to be enough. Right?

"I, uh . . ." I take a step back from Sophie and Dakota, offering them a weak smile. "I have to retouch my makeup."

Neither of them looks like they want to leave me, but Dakota finally nods and tugs Sophie along, retreating to the girls' dressing room.

I turn to the mirror, lifting a white cloth and dabbing the sweat on my forehead, taking in my reflection, framed by golden bulbs, and—there's Pippin, the heavy makeup and eyeliner making my eyes appear huge and wild. But there's a patch where it has started to rub off. I'm under there too.

I sit, reach for the makeup palette, and—

"Hey, Rowan."

My eyes shoot up to the mirror. Quentin stands behind me, appearing like a ghost in his Charlemagne makeup. "I have to hand it to you, you and that bloodsucker have some heavy balls to show your faces."

"Go away."

"Act two gets pretty intricate," he says, laying a hand on my shoulder. "You sure you can handle it, with everything? You know I'd be happy to go on for you, if you two just want to get out of here."

I flick his hand off me and stand to face him. "You need to back up about twenty feet—"

"I'll take it from here, Mr. Knoll."

My spine shivers as my father comes through the stage door. Oscar watches him from out in the hall, his fists at the ready.

With an eye roll, Quentin disappears into the wings.

Dad takes a step forward, clapping his hands. "Aren't you the impressive thespian," he says.

"Hi," I say, my voice shaking.

"Where have you been?"

"You know where."

"With Casper?" he asks, and I wince. "You want to leave me, like your mother did? Because you think you're gay?"

"You don't get it—"

"It's like I don't know you at all anymore."

"Maybe you never did, Dad."

He studies me, as though seeing me for the first time and trying to decide whether or not I really am his son. "Why didn't I get to the bottom of this sooner? I knew something had taken hold of you."

"You don't know him." I pound the makeup table, my chest shaking. "Leave us alone."

With a slight shake of his head, he saunters to the stage door. "We'll discuss what to do after the show. Enjoy it because you're not going to have much in the way of freedom for a while."

He swings open the door and slams it as he exits.

"Oh god," I whisper, sitting back down as tears ruin my makeup again. "Shit-shit-shit—"

The door cracks open, and Oscar's face appears. "Boy. Alright?"

"Yes!" I shout. "I'm fine! I'm safe. Go protect Casper."

"Orders. Protect the boy—"

"I don't care what he ordered!" I throw a makeup sponge on the table as hard as I can. "The Blackthorns are out there; go be his bodyguard. He can take it up with me later."

Without another word, Oscar leaves me alone, and I resume reapplying my makeup.

"Five till places!" Stella shouts across the stage.

"Thank you, five," I call back. Laying the makeup sponge on a paper towel, I plant my palms against the table and try to steady my breathing.

Dad's trying to scare me. Scare *us*. I can't let it happen. But . . . are we doing the right thing after all? Last night, it was all so clear: show them we aren't afraid. But at what cost? One or both of our lives? We could both be safe a hundred miles away by now.

No one out in that audience has any idea how difficult it is to even stand on that stage tonight. No one knows the truth about what's going on.

"What do *you* want, Rowan?" I whisper to my reflection, but I already know the answer. I've always known the answer.

CHAPTER THIRTY-FOUR
CASPER

The show is hurtling towards the climax, and I don't know if I'm ready. What if we were wrong? What if the Blackthorns *would* stake me and my family in front of everyone?

The cast swings into the finale, and here it is: the big moment. I tense up, waiting for the curtain call so we can rush out of here and plan our escape.

Rowan is high up on a platform; the ensemble is begging him to jump into flames made of orange fabric and lighting, where he'll burn to death. But just before Rowan starts his last song, where he sings about how it's okay to be average and in love with someone, something is . . . off.

He's not doing his blocking, at least not how it was before I got suspended. He starts singing, slowly, each syllable stretched and pained. He's not singing as Pippin—he's singing as himself.

He's supposed to sing to Dakota, but he's staring into the audience, making me shrink in my seat. He's staring at *me*.

"We should go," I whisper to my family. "This was a mistake."

Pushing myself from my seat, I step over Malcolm and dart up the aisle as he whispers, "Casper, where are—"

"Stop!" Rowan yells.

The band stops playing. Heads turn, trying to figure out what could be going on, unsure whether or not this is part of the show. The Blackthorns stand and make their way into the aisles. My family stands, too. Onstage, the cast is a herd of deer watching a semitruck barreling through the auditorium toward them.

Sophie tries to act as though nothing is wrong and moves on with her next piece of dialogue, but Rowan waves her off and marches center stage. "Some of you have seen what's been going around . . . a lot of things that aren't true. Things meant to victimize one of my classmates. Implying he's controlling me, like some sort of predator . . . all of this could have been avoided. No one could say I was being manipulated if . . . A lot of you have known me my whole life."

He keeps his eyes locked on me the whole time he speaks. "Actually, my whole life has always been on display. But I've kept some parts to myself.

"This past year," Rowan continues over the murmuring of the audience, "I've had to accept a few things. One being that . . . none of you really know me. Actually, there's only one person on this planet who I think knows everything about me."

I turn, walking faster down the aisle. Have to get out. Need to go. My heart is speeding so fast, I wonder for a second if I've suddenly become mortal. And I think I'm going to be sick. And—

"Don't let him leave!" Rowan shouts, pointing.

I resist a hiss and shield my eyes from the bright spotlight that is illuminating me for the entire audience to see.

"Everyone, this is Casper. I've been hiding him, and he's been hiding me. We thought that was the best idea. We thought it was the only way to be happy. But we were wrong. All we want is to be seen," Rowan says, stumbling over the last words as his chin trembles. His eyes lock into mine. "What *I* want," he says, "is for you, Casper, to come up here, and let everyone see you. Not what our classmates want to see. I want them to see *you*."

I'm cold. And ill. And my heart is beating so loud and fast I think it could give out.

"Casper," whispers Rowan. "Come up here . . . if you want to."

Do I want to? Am I going to get booed or killed right here in front of everyone? My eyes slide to my family, who are all watching with great interest. Victor stands frozen in the aisle, the whole fencing team behind him. They're locked in place, too.

Slowly, I inch toward the stage, inch around the Blackthorns, my eyes falling on several faces trying to understand what's happening.

Someone in the audience starts clapping when I near the steps, and before I know it, the entire audience has erupted in applause. For me. I take the stage, keeping my eyes on Rowan as I approach him.

"What are you doing?" I whisper.

"What I should've done a long time ago," he says, sliding his hand into mine, which cues a series of gasps. "Casper is my boyfriend. I'm gay. Some people didn't like us together and made it look like something terrible. But I refuse to keep it a secret anymore. Anyone who has an issue with Casper can take it up with me."

"HELL YES!" Sophie shouts, and the entire room erupts into another round of applause, some people leap to their feet, phones and hands waving. I can't believe it. No one is booing; no one is shooting at me. Rowan squeezes my hand tighter.

"No more hiding," he whispers.

I purse my lips, unable to react to anything. I'm so overwhelmed, I don't know whether I should kiss him or take a bow or even smile.

"Ladies and gentlemen," Sophie, back in character as the Leading Player, calls out, a new ending rewritten on the spot. "It may not have been what you expected, but I am certain that this was a finale you will remember for the rest of your lives!" Another round of applause breaks out as she rushes to the edge of the stage and mouths something to the pit, and the final reprise of the show kicks up, the cast performing it as though all of this was meant to happen.

At the end, Rowan joins hands with me and the rest of the cast, and Dakota slips next to me, taking my other hand as they pull me into the company bow.

"That's my son!" Camille shouts from the audience, and my vampire family whoops for me as we bow again and the curtain sweeps closed, separating us from the applauding public.

The cast is on us in an instant, gathering around, clapping Rowan and I on the back, a flurry of questions and reactions swirling around us.

"That was *historic!*" Sophie shrieks.

"You did that," I say, still processing. "You actually did that."

"And look"—Rowan grins—"we're still alive."

I pull him into a hug, burying my face in the crook of his neck as the cast *aww*s.

It doesn't occur to me how it appears, my mouth near his neck, until the lights flip off, plunging the stage into pitch blackness. The rest of cast screams as multiple sets of hands grab me and drag me through the dark.

CHAPTER THIRTY-FIVE
ROWAN

Screams. Hands. And—hissing.

Casper, somewhere feet ahead, is hissing.

"Get off!" I scream as what feels like two people hold me by the arms, and the world becomes darker as a bag is pulled over my head. This is it—this is what we've been dreading. Flashes of Scarlett's story burn through my mind. Flashes of people being staked. I can't breathe. My knees give out as I'm dragged from the auditorium.

I don't need to see to know that they're taking us to the restricted building, their meeting place, and I curse myself for not making sure Casper's family knew where to find us if this happened.

Once they've gotten me inside, tied to a high-backed chair, they slam it against something, and I hear a soft cry from Casper. They've got us both, back to back. His fingers find mine, and my heart breaks to feel that he's trembling. I need to get these ropes loose so I can help him, get him to safety. But I can't do anything.

The bag is pulled from my head, and I take in a deep breath as my eyes adjust to the candlelit room. We're surrounded by hoods and masks, a human gate between us and what had seemed like a happy ending only minutes ago.

"Let him go," Casper says, his voice steady and scarily quiet. "This isn't his fault."

"No, let *Casper* go." My grip on his fingers tightens. "Deal with me."

"Shut up!" one of the Blackthorns shouts beneath his mask. It's Victor, no longer bothering to warp his voice. "We thought we made ourselves clear. Why did you disobey us?"

"Because it isn't your business," Casper says.

The Second Son, his mask marked with a number two, lunges at me. My feet instinctively kick at him as I struggle against the ropes, but I'm held still as he pulls down the collar of my costume tunic so hard and fast that the seam rips. He pushes my head to the side so forcefully my neck cracks, and I wince.

"Just as we thought," the Second Son says. It's Ben's voice. "The demon has been feeding on him." The Blackthorn's murmurs become louder. "That must be how he got the Thirteenth Son under his control."

The murmuring becomes frenzied hysteria as two Blackthorns come at Casper. He kicks, bucking them away with his vampire strength, hissing so loud I press an ear against my shoulder to muffle it.

"Hold his feet!" Victor screams. "Bring me the holy water!"

"Back off!" I shout.

"We don't answer to you, Rowan," he spits back. "Not anymore."

Ben comes forward with a bottle of clear liquid. Popping off the top, he pours it all over Casper. This, of course, does nothing except create a soaked vampire.

"I haven't done anything to any of you!" he shouts, droplets raining around him from the furious shakes of his head. "Why can't you leave us alone?!"

"You can't even shed tears." Ben grabs a fistful of Casper's hair. "You're as soulless as a cow. A squirrel that won't get out of the road. A disgusting *thing*—"

"SHUT. THE FUCK. UP!" I scream, so loud that everyone takes a step back. "I have been watching you abuse my boyfriend *all year*. This isn't up to any of you! It's not about you!"

"For once, you're right," a voice echoes through the sanctuary, and we all look to the double doors where another robed figure stands, the First Son's mask practically glowing in the dark. "This is about right and wrong. Good and evil. It's clear as day and night."

My heart drops into my stomach. Goosebumps rise all over the back of my neck, and beads of sweat drench my forehead. I know that voice. I've known that voice my entire life. Please let me be wrong.

The First Son reaches up and pulls off his mask so that I'm staring at—

"Dad?" I say, my voice giving out.

He removes his robe, gesturing for the others to do the same. One by one, the Gregorian monsters are replaced with our classmates: Victor, Diego, Ben, Quentin, the rest of the fencing team.

"You," I say, and Casper's hand squeezes mine. "You knew about all of this."

"I wanted you to figure it out for yourself," Dad says, sauntering towards us. "You wouldn't believe unless you saw it, just like me when your grandfather told me. I knew by placing you in the room with him, you'd find out quickly enough."

"You were playing a game with me!" I shout. "With all of us!"

"No. This is our lineage. Our life and our duty."

"You're the reason," I snarl, hardly able to breathe. "You did this!"

"Not all of this," Dad says, peeling his eyes from me and glaring at the other boys. "I did *not* tell them to post those videos, and I will deal with that later. Do you see now why you need to tell me things when I ask what's wrong?"

I still can't process this. This is why Youngs have always been the headmaster. They've been keeping the order alive the whole time. And now all my old friends believe that Casper is . . . that I'm . . . how could he do this to me?

"Did Mom know? Is this the reason she left?"

Dad sighs, reaching for my shoulder. I try to lean away from him, but I'm tied in place. His thumb digs against my shoulder joint. "Elise never understood the necessity of this," he says. "Maybe now that this has happened to you, she'll figure it out and—"

"Why didn't she take me with her? If she knew, why did she leave me here with you?"

"Don't think she didn't try."

I can't think. Or feel. My heart's been stabbed out of my chest and my soul with it. "She . . . wanted me to go with her?"

"I wasn't about to lose you both," says Dad. "Now, this demon has control of you, and we need to expel it."

Casper peeks over his shoulder. "Don't listen to him—"

"Shut up, leech!" Dad screams at Casper.

"Leave him alone!"

Dad turns back to me. His expression is breaking, his cold, uncaring expression withering into one of deep concern. "You're not well," he says, his voice suddenly gentle. "This thing has you confused."

"No," I say. "This is me."

"I'm sorry, son," he says. "We'll make it right. We're going to reverse this."

"My family is here," says Casper. "They're going to be here any minute."

Dad laughs. "By that time, you'll be a pile of ashes—oh. Oh my lord, it's pretending to cry. You don't have tears; you can't. Are you hearing this, son? Are you hearing his pathetic sniffles?"

I hear them, but I know better. Casper *is* crying internally, in his way. I wish I could hold him, but it's useless. We're trapped and alone.

"It may look like a harmless human boy," Dad continues, "but it is a monster."

"*You're* the monster."

The back of his hand claps against my cheek, and I force myself to react as little as possible. I won't give him the satisfaction.

"You'll thank me once you see the truth," Dad says. "Victor, release my son."

Victor does so, a low, grunting laugh echoing from his chest. The ropes have left indentations in my skin, and I rub the burning lines. I don't try to fight or run—it'll only make it worse, and with Casper still tied down, I'm afraid of risking too much.

Dad grabs me and spins me so that I'm facing Casper, who's trembling, eyes boring into mine with glassy, cloudy tears he can't shed.

"Look, son," he says. "Look how pathetic and small it is. It's not human. Do you hear me? It's not real."

Blinking a tear of my own, I nod.

"Good. Victor, bring your stake here."

Mine and Casper's eyes widen. "Dad . . ."

"I know you're afraid, son. But this will fix it." He takes the stake from Victor and shoves it into my right hand. My knees shake. "Stake it through the heart."

They're not going to kill him while I watch. They're going to make *me* do it.

"No!"

His grip clenches, digging into my skin so deep that the deepest tissue in my body screams. I cry out. "This is our life, Rowan. This is what is right. I know it's hard, but you have to do the right thing. Kill. Him."

"Rowan," Casper says, his voice so low and shaky I can barely hear him. "Be safe."

I shake my head. He's telling me to do what I'm being told just to protect myself. He's forgetting how much I love him. "I'm not killing him."

Dad digs his fingers in deeper, and I cry harder. Heaving his breath, he grabs the stake out of my hand and tosses me to the ground. "Then I can't help you anymore." He peers at the other Blackthorns, who stand stiffly, their eyes bugged out. "Victor, you do the honors."

Victor blinks. "You . . . you want me to *kill* him?"

"You know we must!" Dad shouts, looking around at them all. "They're taking over our school! Our world! Are you going to let them overrun us and turn us all?"

"I can't, sir," Victor says. "I'm all for getting rid of him, but . . . I don't think I can *kill* someone."

"Fine," Dad shouts. "Ben, you're up!"

"My dad doesn't even like that I'm here," says Ben. "He said he'll cut me off if it goes that far."

"He's friends with my ex-girlfriend," Quentin explains. "If I do that, she'll ruin me."

Dad's eyes finally land on Diego. He winces as my father stalks toward him, holding out the stake. "Diego," Dad says evenly, "you're my son's best friend. Won't you protect him from this demon?"

Diego looks between him and me, until finally, he takes the stake.

A flood of expletives fills my mouth, but before I can release them, he says, "No, I . . . I think I've hurt your son enough." He throws the stake as hard as he can to the other end of the chapel. It lands with a hollow clatter on the marble floor. "This is too far. I'm sorry, Rowan."

Dad lets out the most ungodly shriek I've ever heard. "You pathetic, whiney little girls! I won't stand for this." His eyes are wild, searching the floor, until at last, he spots the stake. He lunges for it.

"Dad, no!" I yell, jumping to my feet and rushing at him. "No one wants this."

Dad blinks, stunned, before letting out a low, rumbling laugh. "You're not the parent. And you certainly aren't going to parent *me*."

He's on the stake in an instant.

"Rowan, look out!" Casper screams, just as Dad is standing back up and making to swing. I jump on his back, trying to reach for the stake as he writhes and struggles to knock me off.

"Rowan, stop!" he grunts, "you're . . . under . . . its . . . power!"

"This . . . is . . . me!" I yell, my hands prying the stake from him as I slip to the ground.

"He's just a vampire." Dad whirls around and clutches after the weapon. The stake is caught between our hands as we fight over it.

"I love him!" I yell in Dad's face, trying to mentally slam the words into his skull so he'll understand me once and for all.

Dad pauses, our stares meeting. His sudden hesitation loosens his grip, and the stake thrusts through my hands.

I gasp, my hand digging into his shoulder. A freezing chill envelopes my body.

"Rowan!" Casper cries out, struggling against his ties.

But I'm fine. My eyes slowly drift down Dad's torso as he stands trembling, holding onto me in a way he never has before.

"Dad . . ." I whisper. The stake is buried in his stomach. I look back up at him, barely able to speak, I'm shaking so badly. "Daddy?"

He falls onto me, sliding to his knees.

CHAPTER THIRTY-SIX
CASPER

The smell of iron. Salt. Sweat. Musk.

The sound of a guttural growl skidding across my vocal cords. The pounding of my feet stomping against the floor as I writhe beneath the ropes, my whole body convulsing, itching, *begging*.

Blood.

I heave, my nostrils flaring as heavy breath pulses in and out of them, my eyes zeroed in on the blood trickling from Mr. Young's abdomen. If that stake is pulled out, it'll gush everywhere.

Rowan stands, his costume smeared with red, gaping at his father, who has crumbled to the ground.

"Daddy?" he repeats, his voice a broken murmur. "Somebody get help!"

Just. One. Taste.

My veins are on fire; every cell in my brain is screaming for it. End him. Drain him. Suck his life force from him until he's a cold, still memory lying on the floor. He hurt me. He hurt Rowan. He's the problem.

Get. Free.

The ropes are tight against me, cutting into my flesh as my arms convulse, as all of my body seems to puff out. I feel as strong as Oscar—no, *stronger*. Stronger still, as my wrists fight against the fraying ropes. My vampiric strength, bolstered by the promise of so much blood, is no match for the Blackthorns' attempts to bind me. They come loose enough for me to pull off, at last freeing me.

"It's gotten free!" A Blackthorn screams somewhere in the chapel. But I'm staring only at the body of the man I could drain of blood.

Rowan, who's fallen to his knees over his father, looks up at me, wipes his tear-streaked face. "Casper, go!" he shouts as I snarl, drool sputtering down my chin. "Run and get away from here."

He stands to block me just as I take a single, striding step toward them. I levitate the rest of the way, knocking him aside.

Drain. Him.

"Casper!" Rowan shouts over the cries of the Blackthorns, "Get out!"

Is this how it ends? I suck the leader's blood, leave him bone dry as an example? I could. I could show them all why I was never the right one to let in. Then no one will ever dare hurt me again.

It would be easy enough. I need only to pull the stake from the wound. I kneel on the ground, taking a deep breath, filling myself with his scent. Below me, his body convulses, his eyes wild and frozen, watching and waiting for me to finish his life without a tremble. I wrap my fingers around the stake. He stares up at me with pleading eyes. I can almost hear him whispering, *Just do it.*

He wants me to kill him. Enough said. I inhale the scent of his blood, relish the failing of his heart as he lies dying, and every cell within me screams with joy because at last I'll get to feed. It doesn't matter if I do. He's going to die either way, and it's his own fault. And I need blood.

I'll do it, and then everyone will know that—*I'm a monster*—no, I'm not; they'll know I'm not to be messed with. Him and people like him are why we have to hide. With him dead, it'll prove that I'm—*dangerous*—no! It'll show that . . . that . . .

Kill him, a voice inside me barks, and my head snaps back to him, drool flying from my lips. It splashes against the wound. My face inches nearer and nearer, fangs ready to rip open the wound even further. I try to pull back, scrape my fingers against the ground to stop myself. No! No, I can't do it. Not like this.

I will—*drain him*—not let Rowan lose a father. I throw myself back.

I can't change how the Blackthorns—*deserve to die*—treated me. But I won't be the monster they expect.

They can't take it back.

But I can let it go.

With a quick jerk, I yank the stake out of the wound and raise it in the air.

"Casper, no!" Rowan screams as I bring it down—

Into the fleshy part of my right arm.

I scream, pulling it back out. I push my arm against Mr. Young's wound, watching my own blood as it streams and mixes with his. As it sets about saving his life.

The wound stings and throbs, and I feel lightheaded as more and more blood leaves my body. I don't have to forget in order to forgive. I don't have to get over it to let it go.

My eyes feel wet, and my vision blurs. My chest seems almost to open up as two tears tumble down my cheek. They can't be real. It's just the heat of the moment. I'm not—I can't—

I am. I'm crying. My wet, hideous, snotty face is dripping with tears.

A violent sob rips from my chest—over what, I'm unsure. Emotions from a past life, from other hurts. Tears I've wanted to shed all this time. They're finally free, but I'm not sure how or why now, why over Rowan's father.

The blood keeps pouring into him. The hurt and pain rushes from my body. I can't see past the tears. I'm flooded with memories of who I was before turning, and of the confusion and anger I felt from being kept in the panic room, and of feeling like I couldn't be me because I felt like the only me. Feeling that I was being erased.

It all floods through me and bursts whatever wall it is that keeps us vampires from weeping. Defying all reason and logic, these feelings and thoughts that have been bottled up inside me are finally washing out through these tears.

I can't breathe now. I'm hyperventilating, screaming through the pain, until finally, it all subsides. Until the sobs die down and the pain feels more like a hug around my soul.

The first thing I see, after I've lifted my arm and wiped the tears away, is flesh, bloodstained but healed.

CHAPTER THIRTY-SEVEN
ROWAN

I squirm in my folding chair. It's hard enough going to prom alone without having to watch happy couples and friends slow dance in front of a Styrofoam fairy-tale castle.

"They are kinda cute together," Sophie admits, nodding to Dakota and Reed, their hands stiffly locked around each other as they sway slowly.

"No, they're not," I say.

"No, they're not," Sophie agrees with a laugh. "Plus, we just got our friend group solid; they don't need to ruin it by trying stuff right before graduation."

I fiddle with a paper napkin, folding it into a terrible origami crane. It's been the four of us since opening night of Pippin. Since Casper saved Dad's life, and his parents decided to pull him out of school. I try to understand their reasons. They almost lost him and want him where they know he's always safe. There was no guarantee that there wouldn't be some sort of fallout from the Blackthorns or their parents. Also, they felt he'd been through enough.

I can accept that, and I can accept that Casper and I need to keep our interaction to just texting right now. That sneaking out alone might not be smart, because they have a point: someone could show up and hurt us. All the Blackthorns have fathers. There are other slayers. And I know it's temporary. But it doesn't make it easier.

Casper.

I stand up and straighten my tux jacket. "I need air."

"Do you want me to go with you?"

"I'm fine. Sitting with it for a minute will help."

Sophie doesn't seem convinced, but she nods.

Near the chaperone corner, Mr. Abadi performs a shuffling dance move while students chant "Go Amir, Go Amir, Go Amir." He flashes me a thumbs up when he spots me. Since Casper left school, I've spent a lot of my free time helping him put books back on the shelves. Sometimes he gets me to talk to them, which is honestly the most Casper-ish thing I've ever heard of. But it's helped.

Victor nods as I pass him. I return the nod. We'll never be friends, but least we're being civil.

Diego blocks my path, breaking from his dance partner. "Can I talk to you?" he asks.

"No," I say. "I know you're sorry. You keep telling me."

"I wasn't thinking right. I was wrong—"

"I know," I say. "I'm working on forgiving you. But not today."

I walk past him before he can continue. I will forgive him, someday. But I need time too.

Outside, a green leaf that's been blown off its branch skitters over the steps. A sob-chuckle escapes me because it makes me think of when I gave Casper the leaf bouquet on these same steps at homecoming.

Everything at this school is a reminder of him. The remainder of this year has felt like a pointless blur of tests and college admittance letters, as though they matter to me now. All I can think about is Casper and where we'll end up.

The music is still audible outside—another slow song, naturally. I sit on the steps and rest my chin in my hands. I only came because if I didn't, I'd have to spend the evening helping Dad get around the house, and I'm still working on getting along with him, too.

A rustle of the leaves stirs more memories. Casper in the woods. Casper on the steps. Casper storming off. Casper . . . on the steps.

Casper is on the steps.

I've been seeing him everywhere—flashes of him in the halls, him running over the grass field between the main stretch and dorms. But this isn't in my mind. He's really here—

Rushing around the side of the building the second I spot him. I run down the steps, chasing after him.

"Hey!" I call out. "Stop!"

Casper stops running and hangs his head before finally turning back to me.

"You're gonna leave without even saying bye?" I ask.

"You weren't supposed to see me," he says. "I shouldn't be here, but I wanted to see you in your prom outfit."

I pull the jacket open, showing off my green vest and bowtie. "This old thing?"

"You look incredible," Casper says.

"I can't believe you're here. Do your parents know?"

"No." Casper shakes his head. "I bribed Oscar to drive me. I can't stay, though. They'll notice I'm gone."

"Why can't you just stay?"

"You know why."

"Yeah, I know, I know." I scuff the ground with my foot. "Dammit, Casper, I miss you. If anyone was going to go out and stake you anyways, they'd have tried by now, don't you think?"

"My parents want to be certain," Casper says. "After what we've been through, I want to be certain too."

"I'm trying to understand," I say. "But you can't leave. Not until you've danced with me at least once."

Casper takes a step back. "Rowan, I can't—"

"One dance, Casper," I plead, reaching my hand for his. "It's prom. Please."

He looks around, and when he decides we're alone, he offers me a weak smile and takes my hand. My stomach grows warm feeling his touch again; I pull him closer to me. We step side to side to some lovelorn song drifting from the gym.

"How has school been?" Casper asks, settling his right hand on my tricep.

"Awful," I say honestly. "Dakota and Sophie miss you, you know. Reed also keeps saying how he wishes he could've known you better. We've all hung out a lot since . . ."

"I talk to them sometimes in texts. Dakota and Sophie, I mean. Not about much. But that's how it works. I can't tell them everything. Ever."

"How is your family?"

"Weird," Casper laughs. "How's your father?"

I shrug. "Fine. I guess. I don't really care."

"He's your father, Rowan—"

"He tried to kill you," I say. "And he lied to me my whole life."

I spin him under my arm, and he rolls his eyes before ultimately smiling. He does it to me, and soon, we're goofing off, being over the top about our one and only prom dance, until we're both laughing and spinning each other around and around. He rests his head on my shoulder.

"It's your relationship with him," Casper says. "But I do hope you forgive your dad. Take it from me, it feels a lot better than holding onto it forever."

"Let's not talk about him," I say, brushing my lips against the waves of his hair. "So, once we're certain everything is fine and once your parents realize you're safe and you're allowed out, we'll still be together, right?"

Casper lifts his head. "What?"

"We weren't going to be separated forever," I say, noting how Casper's eyebrows dip together. "Just while the year finishes and . . . Casper, I am going to see you again, aren't I?"

"Rowan, I . . ." he sighs, and in his eyes, I see the hint of tears, though they don't fall. "I'm leaving the country soon. I'm getting my tour."

I sigh. "Oh. Is that it? That's great! That's what you were working for. You're going to have a great . . . time . . ." I curse the feeling of my heart sinking into my stomach. "You don't want to come back to me, do you?"

"That's not what I'm saying at all," Casper says. "I'm going to be gone for quite a while, and—"

"So you're here to say goodbye." I nod. "You're just . . . you're just done."

Casper's hands squeeze me closer, but I push against him. "Please, just listen to me and let me explain. That's not what—"

"I can't believe this!" I stumble back, raking my fingers through my hair. "After the complete hell we went through to be together, you're just gonna fly off and leave me here."

"We both knew I would be leaving, Rowan," Casper says. "I'm not saying I don't want to be together. I'm saying that you deserve a life where you're not put at risk by a vampire."

"So do it." I thrust my wrist out to him and note him inhaling my scent on reflex. "Change me, and let's be together."

"That's a huge decision to make on impulse," Casper says. "Rowan, you only just now get to find out who the real you is. You're about to graduate high school. You deserve to go to college, and to keep finding out what you're going to be. You can't throw an unlived life away on me."

"I'm not throwing anything away," I shout. "You're throwing me away!"

The words land in silence, somewhere along the dewy grass between us. I wish I could take them back. But I can't. I can only stand here, my hands in fists, my heart racing. Casper isn't even looking at me anymore. I take a deep breath.

"You're right," I say. "I'm sorry. I . . . I don't understand. We love each other, but you don't want to make it work, and I . . . I don't want to lose you."

"I don't either," Casper says finally. "I'm not saying that I don't want to make it work. I'm not here to break your heart. What I'm trying to say is—"

"Rowan!" Sophie shouts from the steps, and I spin around to look at her.

"Hey, Sophie!" I call out. "Look who it is—"

But Casper is gone as quickly as he came. I spin around, searching for him. But no leaves stir in the hedges. Not so much as a breeze kicks up.

Casper is . . . gone.

"Who were you talking to?" Sophie asks.

I blink back the tears. "Myself. What is it?"

With a grin, Sophie takes my hand. "We have to go dance in front of the whole school."

"You're nuts." I force a laugh. "I'll be there in a second."

"No, you cheese ball." Sophie smacks my shoulder. "We have to *now*."

I stiffen. "You got prom queen, didn't you?"

"You know it!" Sophie jumps three feet in the air. "Come on, King. And don't get used to me calling you that. Told you they'd put you back on top."

I let Sophie pull me by the wrist back to the gym. With one last glance over my shoulder, I try to spot Casper. But he must be far from here by now. And I'll never see him again.

I can't take the graduation cap off my head quickly enough. I need to get out of here before the memories of my vampiric ex-boyfriend reduce me to a puddle.

Dad grunts when I help him get seated in the passenger seat, and when I'm behind the wheel, I pull through the gates of Mockingbird Prep. To my surprise, my heart flips and then drops into my stomach. This could be the last time I ever exit through these gates. I'm gone. From the school, the dining hall, the auditorium where I actually sang in front of a huge audience, from the old chapel and its secret societies, from wooden stakes and forgotten cemeteries. From the dorm. The dorm I wanted all to myself so badly, and then when it was . . .

I breathe deep through my nostrils and command myself not to cry in front of Dad.

"You did it," Dad says. "You really did it. With flying colors. I'm proud of you, son."

"Thanks," I say, my voice tight.

"I was worried, but you pulled through. That's the Young way."

The car falls silent, the only noise the tick of the turning signal at the fairway stop that will lead us to our big for-show house. Inside, I'll deposit him in his room and then go to mine, and we'll resume avoiding each other.

"Soon," Dad says, with caution, "we'll be packing you up to leave."

My tongue pushes against the back of my teeth. "Mhm."

"I . . . I guess I have to wonder . . . if you're leaving me for Cornell or . . ."

I roll my eyes. "You know damn well I can't go to the 'or'. You have the scar to prove that."

"Pull over, please."

"I'm behind the wheel," I say, "and I really don't want to talk about this with you anymore."

"Well, I do, dammit, so pull over!"

I swerve and park against the curb.

"Rowan, I could have died that night." Dad locks his gaze on me, and I fight the urge to shrink. "You might have ended the year by burying me."

"I know," I say, feeling the tears already flooding the back of my eyes. "I still have nightmares about it."

"But you didn't," he says.

"That doesn't change anything. You nearly killed yourself because you wouldn't listen. I'm glad you're alive, but we're not okay."

He sighs. "Rowan, please let me say this. It's not easy for me." I tilt my head, my hands tighter on the steering wheel. He takes a few deep breaths before looking at me again. His eyes are soft now, almost glistening. I don't think I've ever seen him look like this before. "I could have died. Yes, by my own hand. But I didn't. The reason I'm not dead is because that vampire stopped the bleeding. He could have drunk from me. He didn't. He could have run off and left me to bleed out. He didn't. I've thought a lot about that."

"Casper's not a demon," I say. "He has more empathy in his right hand than most mortals do in their whole being. I tried to tell you, but—"

"I wouldn't listen," Dad says. "I owe him my life. No more threats, no more watching. Not unless some rogue vampire comes at us first. I'll have all the books about vampires reinstated in the library. If another teenage vampire comes around, we'll be better prepared to accept them."

"So it's all rainbows and 'free to be you and me'?" I ask, trying to keep my face as emotionless as possible. "Because he chose not to let you die?"

"It made me think that maybe our ancestors were wrong about some things," he says. "I'm far from perfect, but I'm not a mustache-twirling villain."

"Just a masked cult leader." I roll my eyes. "But thank you. I'm glad you finally told me something right off. But I'm still not okay with you."

"Why?" he blinks, and the tears start falling. "I love you."

"You thought you could fix me," I say, my voice rising. "My entire life, I only ever wanted you to be proud of me. And when you found out I was gay, you took that pride back, like it was on loan. You thought I was confused or being preyed on by a vampire, and you made me feel so disgusting and scared."

"I'm sorry," he says. "I don't think you're confused. Not anymore. Rowan, I don't have a problem with you being gay. That wasn't it. It was the timing. I was afraid he'd—"

"Do not say it again!" I shout.

"I only knew what I was taught," he says. "I know I was wrong, about all of it. I'm trying and learning. I also fail. I'm not above that. But I'm trying."

Now I'm crying. "Even Mom couldn't deal with you."

"You were a child," Dad says. "It wasn't just about slayers and vampires. It was more complicated than that. You needed somewhere to put the blame, and I took it. Rowan, I am sorry. But I don't want to lose you, too."

"Then let me go." I wipe my cheek with the back of my hand.

Dad falls silent.

We sit staring out the windshield for what feels like an hour or more, the sound of our breaths rising and falling, always out of sync.

"Don't ever become a father," Dad says, his voice soft and light. "Even us professional fathers who've been at it for years can't bear the pain of it."

"I'm not trying to put you through pain. I just want to be."

"I know." He reaches for my hand, and I let him take it, too tired to fight him anymore. "It all takes time. But I still think you hung the stars, pal. Whoever you're with, whatever you do, keep stringing those suckers up. I'll catch you if you fall from the ladder."

Lake Mockingbird is as smooth as a windowpane as I walk onto the dock that stretches from the backyard of the lake house. I didn't think I'd ever come back here. But when I woke up this morning and the first thought I had was *Happy Eighteenth*, all I wanted was to do this. To start legal adulthood the only way I know how.

When the toes of my shoes reach the end of the dock, I reach into the sack and pull out my Thirteenth Son mask, the stake, and the pendent.

With one final look over them, I toss the mask like a frisbee over the water until it lands with a tiny splash and sinks beneath the surface. Then the stake, and the pendent. Just like that, the Thirteenth Son drifts out of sight, hopefully out of mind, and takes its rightful place at the bottom of the lake.

It's like saying goodbye to another life. Goodbye to high school. Goodbye to the Rowan I started this year as, and to the Rowan I would have become if Casper hadn't come along. Goodbye to what might have been if Casper hadn't left.

Dammit, Casper.

I wipe my right cheek with the back of my hand. I'm not going to cry over him again. It wouldn't bring him back into my life. All I can do is let it all become memories and move on.

Finally, I make myself leave the dock and head back up to the lake house. When I reach the edge of the house, I notice a car has pulled up the gravel drive. A long black one.

Scarlett Belamy strides towards me in round sunglasses, carrying a manila folder. I race down the hill, meeting her halfway.

"Hi," I say, my heart leaping into my chest.

"Your father said you were here," she says, her tone all business. "How have you been? Since . . ."

"Okay." I shake my head. "How's Casper? Did he come with you?"

"He doesn't know I'm here," she says, and my heart deflates. "I hope you know that this is very hard for him. Being without you. The way he carries on, you'd think he lost an arm."

He did lose an arm. So did I.

"You need to understand that it isn't easy being a vampire," she continues, lowering her sunglasses. "When you let a mortal in, there comes a point where your presence in their life is a hazard. Casper doesn't want to be a hazard. He wants you to be safe."

"I'm safe." I force myself to keep from shouting. "I couldn't be any more safe. Where is he?"

Her tongue flicks over her upper lip as she considers the question, her business-like expression changing into one of conspiracy. She eyes me before saying, "I don't think we had the best first impression of one another. I can't imagine what you must have thought of me, breaking into this house and commanding Casper to kill you." She pauses for a response, but I honestly don't have one. "I didn't understand at first. My concern is first and foremost his safety. I know our family isn't exactly nuclear, but to me, he is my nephew. And my nephew deserves someone who is going to make him happy, and keep him safe in turn, and fight for him. Is that you?"

I look up at her, sheepish and exposed. What can I say to make her believe me when I say that yes, I would do all of those things? I say the first thing that comes to mind.

"You said you knew all about my lineage. So you know it's not exactly in my genes to just give up. I might not agree with what they so steadfastly believed and went after, but I'm just as stubborn and pig-headed as they were. I'm not giving up on Casper."

Scarlett keeps staring, waiting for some sort of crack or a sign that I'm just saying what she wants to hear. Finally, she raises her eyebrows. "No," she says. "I don't think you will."

She thrusts the manila envelope at me. I take it without thinking. It could be filled with anthrax and I'd still take it if it meant there was some sort of chance I'll see Casper again.

"Malcolm said you can be ours if you want to be," she says. "I know you have a lot to figure out, but if you think you might want to be ours someday, then consider what's in there. If not, well, that's alright, too."

I keep staring at the envelope, wondering what could possibly be in here.

Scarlett slips a gloved finger beneath my chin and raises it so that I have to look at her. "Either way, keep strong. Alright?"

I nod, and she lets go, returning to the car without another word. I wait until she's speeding out of sight before tearing open the envelope.

CHAPTER THIRTY-EIGHT
CASPER

"This is ridiculous!" I adjust the black hat with Mickey Mouse ears attached to it on my head while Scarlett snaps a picture of me with Camille and Malcolm. "I'm not going to Disney World."

"If a slayer decides to go rogue, we need them to think you're elsewhere," says Scarlett. "If I post you with anything from your itinerary, I may as well hand them your room key."

"Listen to your aunt," Malcolm says.

Camille tightens her grip around my shoulder. "I didn't believe this day would really come," she says. "It's one thing going to school across town, but going across the sea . . . I can't bear this."

"There, there, my queen," Malcolm says. "Fish gotta swim, birds gotta fly, and royal vampires have to be diplomats."

"My young man." Camille clamps her face against my cheek. "I'm going to miss you so much."

I roll my eyes. "It'll just be a blink in eternity."

"A blink you'll remember until the end of time," Camille retorts. "This step is even more important than proving you can be around mortals."

They continue on, debating if I'm old enough, how they'll miss me, if Oscar is really enough protection while I tour crumbling castles and navigate foreign vampire courts, but I keep looking up at the blinking clock over the terminal, over the crowd of people waiting in chairs and leaning against columns, wolfing down sandwiches or buying last-minute gifts, people taking things home from their American trip, others excitedly ready to go on their European excursions.

I don't see the sandy hair and green eyes I wish I could. Not that I have a right to feel upset over it. I'm the one who left Rowan on prom night without explaining. I was too afraid Sophie would see me. Then I was too afraid to contact him later.

But all I can think about is the Blackthorns kidnapping him and trying to make him stake me. There's danger at every turn with me, and he doesn't deserve that. He deserves to live a normal life. He can't paint fences white if he's always drenched in blood. I can't be the reason he misses out.

Scarlett squeezes my hand as she removes the Mickey Mouse ears from my head, "Hey, you copacetic?"

I shrug. "I'm only reminding myself that it's better this way."

"What is it?" Malcolm has overheard the last bit of my sentence.

"Nothing," I say. "I'm really happy."

Malcolm doesn't look convinced and waves me over to him. I obey, and he wraps his arm around my shoulder. We walk toward the wide airport windows. A landscape of asphalt and planes glinting in the sun lies before us.

"You worked hard to get to where you are," he says when we're out of earshot. "I know your heart is broken. But I don't want that to take away from your tour."

"I don't even deserve to go," I say. "I failed at everything. I was discovered. I drank from a mortal. I almost started another war with slayers."

"Yes, but you also saved a man's life," he says, squeezing my shoulder. "A man who demonized you and tried to kill you. Many vampires of a higher rank than you, vampires who are much older, might not have done the same. You proved you deserve this."

"But it was my fault," I point out. "I'd have never even had to make that choice if not for failing at all the other things."

"If that hadn't happened, those boys would still have the wrong idea about us," he counters. "He could've gone after another vampire, one who wouldn't have saved his life. 'Coulda, shoulda', as they say. What you did could change a whole world."

"Either way, it could all just be a pause. They say they'll stop, what if they don't? Everything could easily revert to how it was, and I won't be here if they come for you—"

"Casper, I've survived centuries; don't you think I can take care of myself?" When I force a soft laugh, he adds, "You're not going to mope. Good?"

"Good," I say. "But there's something I still don't understand. When I was healing him, I started crying. Not just a few tears, either. But . . ."

"Thousands of them?" Malcolm asks, his eyebrows knitting together. "As though they'd been in there for years just waiting to come out?"

I nod. "Yeah. But I thought vampires can't."

He squeezes my shoulder. "It's simpler than it seems. You're right that vampires don't cry. Not forever. But some of us don't lose those mortals tears when they turn. They hold everything inside of them until they're finally ready to let go. That night, you got rid of them once and for all. We call it a final cry. Perhaps it was the extreme emotion of the moment, or the pain from the stake. Maybe it was as simple as forgiving that man. Something allowed them out. And now they're gone, along with the weight of them. Does that make sense?"

"Not entirely," I admit. "I wish I knew exactly what made it happen. But yes, I think overall I understand."

"Are you ready now?"

I check the clock again and nod as we head back to the others. Three more minutes is not enough for a miracle. Or even FaceTime.

Who knows what Rowan's gotten up to since prom? He could have decided to hate me, never wanting to hear from me again for putting him through all of that and then leaving him. I caused so much trouble for him. The best solution is for me to become nothing but a memory to him. A bullet that he knows he dodged when he curls up with his mortal future husband each night.

"Time. It's near," Oscar says, giving a half-bow. "The queue. You might consider it."

My lip quivers, but I have no tears. Nor do I wish to shed any. Malcolm is right—them and their weight are gone. Final cry makes it sound like I'll never feel sadness again. I don't think that will be true. But I think I'll be better able to handle those emotions.

"Alright," I say.

Oscar nods and picks up my carry-on. I reach into the pocket of my satin black jacket and put on my coke bottle sunglasses, preparing for the sun's rays shooting through the plane windows. Up there will be the closest I've ever been to the thing I most need to avoid.

I glance at the clock. One minute until they begin boarding, and the announcements are starting. I look down the length of the terminal at the other queues, toward the duty-free shops and the drink stands and bars, but he's not there. Of course he wouldn't be.

Swallowing, I push my shoulders back and lift my head, becoming the vampire prince that I am. There's an entire world waiting, and I can't be late.

I didn't get the guy, but I got what I came for. That will have to be enough . . .

It's enough. It's enough. It's enough.

"Wait!" a voice calls from behind, and I spin around.

The cutest, most irritating golden retriever I've ever seen is bolting toward me, a hand raised. His face is red, and he's panting.

"Rowan," I half-whisper. Then louder, "What are you doing here?"

"Getting what I want, like I always do," he says as he arrives. He pulls me in, his lips pushing against mine. My knees threaten to buckle, and I hear the faint applause of onlookers as blood pounds through my ears, my heart suddenly the rocketing rate of a mortal's.

When I pull away and take in the sight of him, I can tell he's been running for some time. "How did you even—"

"I'd have been here sooner," he says, "but Reed got a flat tire on the way, and it was a mess."

"You shouldn't be here," I say. "What about the Blackthorns? And college? And—how is your father?"

"Dad is a lot better," he says, and then he smiles. "He's a lot better, Casper."

"Better?"

"Casper," Camille says, approaching. "I'm sorry; I wish you two had all the time in eternity, but you're boarding."

"Right," I say, sighing. "I'm sorry I didn't explain, Rowan. I wanted to, but I know disappearing on prom night likely hurt you and—please understand. It's better this way. I put you in so much danger. And you deserve so much—so much better than that. You deserve to be happy and to find someone who can promise you won't be harmed. Someone you don't have to worry will bump into a slayer someday."

He considers my words with pursed lips and a subtle nod. But after a moment, he shrugs and says, "You make some valid points, but you forgot that I don't give a shit about that."

I gape. "Rowan! You can't be serious. What are you going to do, just piddle and plot until I get back?"

"Casper, remember what I said in the bunker? I promised once all was said and done that we'd be leaving together." He gestures to the terminal. "Won't you let me finally make good on that?"

I stare at him, unbelieving. We're leaving together . . . I can't process the words or discern their meaning.

"I didn't want you to know," Scarlett says, stepping forward, "if he didn't show . . . I didn't want you to know that when I booked the trip, I may have booked an extra person."

I scowl at her because I'm overwhelmed and not comprehending. "You what?"

"I booked him on the tour, Casper," she says. "I invited him. I was wrong about what I told you both, and I feel terrible. Just accept it."

My eyes zoom back to Rowan, who shrugs, and my heart picks up even more speed. I can barely hear myself for the pounding as I grin and ask, "Really?"

"If you want me to," he says.

"Are you sure?" I take his hands. This can't be real. We can't be flying away together into the sunset. This is too good. I was staked in my sleep and I'm in a weird vampire heaven. "I don't expect you to just up and fly off to another continent. Is that what you really want?"

"More than anything."

"But your life, Rowan," I say. "This is such a big risk. It could be a huge mistake—"

He takes my hands in his and kisses my knuckles. "We don't know anything about the future yet. Anything could be a mistake, or it could be the best choice ever. Whatever comes next, I want it to be with you."

I'm so happy I can't say a single word.

"You have to get on the plane now," Malcolm says.

"I love you." Camille kisses my forehead. She looks to Rowan. "And I love you, too. Keep him safe for me."

"I will," Rowan promises.

A few minutes later, we're scanning our tickets and making our way down the ramp toward the open door of the plane, our hands finding each other's.

He's here. We're here. And no Blackthorn, no banned vampire books, no classroom snickering will come between us. We made it.

When we get to the door, I pause at the flight attendant helping to direct passengers and show her my ticket.

"To your left." She smiles, revealing her fangs, just for a moment. "It is an honor to have you aboard, your highness."

I shoot Rowan a pursed-lipped smile.

We make our way to the first-class cabin, and I can't help but notice all the passengers with brightly colored eyes. The glowing skin and ethereal beauty. There are so many of us around when you take a moment to notice. None of us are ever the only one. Not really.

Before I know it, we're in our seats and the plane is moving, making its way toward the runway. We stare into each other's eyes as the plane picks up speed and lifts off.

My infuriating boy. We. Us. Maybe for the next few months. Maybe for a single lifetime. And maybe, just maybe, for eternity. For however long, we've got each other.

"We get to share the room over there," says Rowan. "Right?"

"We really have come a long way, haven't we?" I laugh. "Yes, we'd better share a room."

He rakes his fingers through my hair as I brush my lips against the crook of his neck.

ACKNOWLEDGEMENTS

Writing *Keep it in the Dark* was a journey, to say the least. Had I been alone with it, I hate to wonder if it would've seen the light of day at all. Thankfully, I had several good people to ensure that it did.

The book would not exist as it is, or at all, without my editor, Josh Perry. He was the first to be involved in the story's development and was instrumental in both helping me bring it from skeletal outline to finished novel and in shaping the story into its final form. I'd be remiss if I didn't credit the fact that Casper's ability to heal the wounded was his idea (which I foolishly almost vetoed). The character of Sophie also would not have appeared if he hadn't requested another friend for Casper. It's wild to think that two years ago, I was some random person slipping a campy witch story into his inbox, and now here we are with a second book to our credit. Sophie, "the Boys", and I can never thank him enough.

The first eyes to ever fall on the town of Mockingbird belong to Lou Wilham, a good friend and author of her own queer vampire books. When I was pitching it to Tiny Ghost, Lou was happy to play test subject to my mad scientist and read the sample chapters. Her enthusiasm for the project got me through the first, second, and third draft, and I will always be grateful for that.

Writing this book was a unique experience in that I was fortunate to see my protagonists before I was even finished with the first working draft. That's owed to this book's phenomenal cover artist, Jamie Flack. Whenever I got stuck with the characters, all I had to do was look at Rowan and Casper to get unstuck. Not only did he seamlessly pull them from my head to the cover, but he performed a really cool trick. Now that you've read the book, how many giveaways to the plot can you see in the boys' dorm room? Thank you, Jamie!

I'm fortunate to be an author at the best publishing house I could have wanted. Of course, it is only as good as its team, and the team at Tiny Ghost Press is so, so, *so* good. Without them, I'd just be a dorky mess with papers scattered everywhere. Beyond Josh, that team is Reuben Davies-Hoarse, who handles sales and ensures all of us authors are taken care of; editorial assistants Jeremy Gibson and Thomas Shah, as well as copy editor Melody Jaikes, who ensures me and Josh haven't left a mess in the creative frenzy; and of course, Kylie Koews in PR and Lewis Hughes in Social Media. They're the biggest reason you've even heard of this book, much less read it, and I bow to them all.

As I mentioned at the beginning, *Keep it in the Dark* was a journey. I didn't know when I sold this book that life would imitate art and vice versa. Luckily, I had many friends and colleagues who worked through it with me. Special thank yous to Willie Lock, Ricki Rose, Erin Aiken, The Ullerys, Julie Foreman, Jessica Mattingly, Laura Boyle, the whole "corner of the bar", fellow author Elizabeth Kilcoyne, the staff and board of the Paris-Bourbon County Library, and Lina Rodriguez (and your big idea to ink my wrist). And another thanks to them for believing me.

ABOUT THE AUTHOR

Justin Arnold is the author of gay fiction including *Wicked Little Things, The Prince and The Puppet Thief: A Gay Fairytale,* and *Keep It In The Dark.* He is also the twisted mind behind The NoSleep Podcast season 18 feature episode *Haunter's Game.* Before fiction, Justin reimagined numerous classics such as *Anne of Green Gables, Cinderella,* and *The Snow Queen* for stage, and his plays are performed by schools and community organizations internationally each year. When not writing, he is serving as CEO and co-founder of Triple Crown Theater Group, the first community theater of its kind in his hometown. He lives in the bluegrass region of Kentucky with a cat named Evie and Huckleberry, a wild raccoon who Justin foolishly feeds.

ALSO FROM AUTHOR JUSTIN ARNOLD

JOIN A COVEN, CATCH A KILLER

AVAILABLE NOW WHEREVER BOOKS ARE SOLD

FOR MORE SPOOKY QUEER STORIES SIGN UP FOR OUR NEWSLETTER AND FOLLOW US ON SOCIAL MEDIA

WWW.TINYGHOSTPRESS.COM
@TINYGHOSTPRESS

A ROMANCE TO HOWL HOME ABOUT

BOOKS ONE AND TWO IN THE BESTSELLING THE ALPHA'S SON SERIES ARE NOW AVAILABLE!

AVAILABLE IN PRINT, EBOOK, & AUDIOBOOK

WWW.TINYGHOSTPRESS.COM
@TINYGHOSTPRESS

9 781915 585219